PRAISE FOR TREASURE (

"*Treasure of the Blue Whale* is a tale spun into magic. We sense from the first page that we are in the hands of a master storyteller. Mayfield doesn't just tell a story; he spins a tale that is humorous, entertaining, delightful, and deeply satisfying. This is the kind of book we remember. This pleasure is why we read in the first place. We step into this world and when, we come back, we are changed."

- Mary Rakow, author of *The Memory Room* and *This is Why I Came*

"With *Treasure of the Blue Whale*, Steven Mayfield has written a fable for our time, a novel we need now more than ever. From the moment Connor O'Halloran and Angus McCallum find a treasure with all its promises, readers are swept up in a journey filled with plot twists and rich characters who continually surprise us with their humanity and ability to find hope."

Chris Dempsey, author of *Winter Horses* and former artist-in-residence, Idaho Commission on the Arts

"Steven Mayfield's *Treasure of the Blue Whale* is a fascinating and wildly inventive narrative that artfully weaves the timeless themes of greed, survival, and love into an epic American tale that grips the reader from start to finish. This story is told through the lens of a talented and empathetic writer whom I've long admired for his ability to observe and to make sense of our complicated world and the individuals who make a community. This is the novel I've been waiting for, and it does not disappoint."

- Thanh Tan, Two-time Emmy Award-winning journalist and multi-media storyteller.

"There are many splendid surprises afoot in *Treasure of the Blue Whale*, the first of which begins in the churning belly of a middle-age whale. Author Steven Mayfield launches his moral balancing act of a story with the greasy glob of maritime discharge that delightfully changes form throughout the novel, morphing from a town's hope for salvation to that thing which undermines its core.

Treasure of the Blue Whale is a mystifying tale capable of accomplishing what the great American novels often do. It fosters conversation and debate about who we are as people and what makes us tick, while entertaining to the very last page."

- Erick Mertz, author of *The Book of Witness* and *The Lies & Truth of Doctor Desmond Brice*

"Mayfield's storytelling combines whimsy and mystery in a clear and compelling writing style. *Treasure of the Blue Whale* hooks the reader to discover what wonders and foibles the Whale's ambergris will bring."

-Jennifer Bowen Neergaard, Founder of BookHive Corporation

"Mayfield writes with the confident voice of a true storyteller, entertaining with clean, fast-moving prose that's nonetheless rich with vivid imagery and cultural touchstones."

- Anna Webb, Communications Specialist, Boise State University, former columnist The Idaho Statesman.

TREASURE OF THE BLUE WHALE

Steven Mayfield

Regal House Publishing

Published by
Regal House Publishing, LLC
Raleigh, NC 27612
All rights reserved

ISBN -13 (paperback): 9781646030040
ISBN -13 (epub): 9781646030316
Library of Congress Control Number: 2019941553

All efforts were made to determine the copyright holders and obtain their
permissions in any circumstance where copyrighted material was used. The
publisher apologizes if any errors were made during this process, or if any
omissions occurred. If noted, please contact the publisher and all efforts
will be made to incorporate permissions in future editions.

Interior and cover design by Lafayette & Greene
lafayetteandgreene.com
Cover illustrations © by C. B. Royal
Author photograph by Rebecca Hunnicutt Farren

Regal House Publishing, LLC
https://regalhousepublishing.com

Printed in the United States of America

For Pam

Also by Steven Mayfield

Howling at the Moon

Ambergris: 'amber .gris, - .gre(s)\noun: a waxy substance found floating in or on the shores of tropical waters, believed to originate in the intestines of the sperm whale and used in perfumery as a fixative

- Merriam-Webster Dictionary.

"Who would think, then, that such fine ladies and gentlemen should regale themselves with an essence found in the inglorious bowels of a sick whale!"

- Herman Melville: *Moby Dick*

CHAPTER ONE

The *Baleia Azul*

The Whale was middle-aged—a great, block-headed beast nearly forty years old—and he bore numerous scars, the bushy spray from his blowhole yet to be quieted by a whaler's harpoon. Sixty-five feet long and father to many, he had lived a solitary life when not breeding. This is the way of the male sperm whale, the saddle tramps of the sea, their impressive fertility unaccompanied by paternal instincts. He knew the ocean from the Bering Straits to the Antarctic Ocean, from the coast of Japan to the waters around the Hawaiian Islands. Capable of diving more than 7000 feet and remaining immersed for up to ninety minutes, the Whale was indomitable and no non-human predators, including the feared orcas, dared challenge him.

In the spring of 1918 the Whale was off the coast of Japan. It was a dangerous place, heavily prowled by whalers, yet he was unconcerned. Despite a gigantic brain nearly five times the relative size of its human counterpart, he was entirely a creature of instinct with no ability to discern danger much beyond the tip of his great snout. The Whale was experiencing discomfort that day, the sort a fellow might treat with a little bicarbonate of soda. It was dyspepsia a long time in the making, undigested squid beaks in his stomach not only plugging its outlet but discouraging dives to the deepest part of the ocean where the water pressure on his rib cage squeezed the sharp points into his stomach lining. He cruised near the surface of the water, rolling and twisting and occasionally letting loose a great geyser

1

of spray from his blowhole. This caught the attention of a Japanese whaling ship around the same time the Whale's stomach contents began to roil and churn.

The underwater echo-locating clicks of a sperm whale can be as loud as the on-land backfire from a truck, but the sound the Whale made that morning as the Japanese attack dinghy approached was even louder. Curling very slightly, the Whale made a great retching noise accompanied by a high-pitched squeak, the latter recalling for one of the Japanese whalers the deafening scrape made by a steel-sided vessel as it slid down the launch ramp of the Fujinagata shipyard at Osaka. At the same time the whaler, a harpoon in hand, drove his spear deep into the Whale's back. The huge creature squealed and retched again. This time a black-gray, viscous mass the size of a boulder erupted from his underslung maw. He writhed about as if trying to escape the thing, as if it were a changeling sent to sting him. Then, he dove.

Down and down the Whale went, the whalers staying clear of the rope attached to the harpoon as it uncoiled and exited their boat in ferocious, swirling loops. The end of the rope was tied to a cleat, and when its full length was played out, the boat violently jerked. Two whalers tumbled off the gunwale, the rest clinging to the rails and oarlocks to stay aboard. The Whale then dragged the dinghy across the ocean for nearly a quarter mile before pulling it down, the remaining crewmen frantically leaping into the water, helplessly staring at the small maelstrom where their boat was last seen. They were now at least a half-mile from the mother ship and cried out for God to rescue them, terrified the Whale might return to exact revenge. Four lived—four others claimed that day by the sea. The Whale was never again seen. And the black-gray viscous mass? It sank about fifteen feet until its fat-marbled composition allowed it to achieve buoyancy. The huge mass then floated about the ocean for fifteen years.

In 1933 an earthquake measuring 8.4 on the Richter scale hit the Sanriku coast in Japan with its epicenter about 180 miles east of the city of Kamaishi, Iwate. The subsequent tsunami killed more than 1500 people, injuring over 12,000. The Whale's effluent, once a great mass broad as a Sequoia and tall as a boy of ten, was on the easternmost margin of the periphery. Black-gray and viscous when it exited the Whale, the mass had first turned brown, waxy, and shrunken as it floated about the Pacific. It was now hard and whitish and quite small—about the size of a football—and resembled how one might imagine a dinosaur egg would look were it found bobbing in the ocean. The massive undertow created by the earthquake emptied beaches along Sanriku. As it receded the Whale's dinosaur egg was rippled eastward. A year later it was less than two miles off the coast of California.

It was late in May of 1934 when Armando Souza was called to the bridge of the *Baleia Azul*—the Blue Whale—a Portuguese freighter operating out of the Philippines. The horrible odor was getting worse, drifting like smoke through every crack and crevice of the ship. Souza was the cook of the *Baleia Azul* and the crewman called upon to fulfill duties otherwise unassigned.

"I can still smell it, Souza. What is responsible for the delay?" the captain demanded.

"I'm sorry, sir, but what can I do?" Souza complained. "It's very large and I must take it up a shovelful at a time. No one will help."

The captain stroked his chin. His crew was a decent one and generally quicker than most to lend a hand. But he couldn't blame them for leaving Souza to his own devices. The gigantic blob in the bowels of his ship carried a sickening stench. Five days earlier a perfect storm of mishaps had created the thing— the sewage tank ruptured at the same time ten barrels of lard bound for Los Angeles came loose in the hold and broke open beneath the tank. The engineer had called the first mate. The first mate then called the captain who was already well aware, the odor preceding his petty officer's report. He pinched his nostrils shut and ordered Souza to clean up the mess.

Souza had no idea how to contain or dispose of it and began by adding his own stomach contents, followed by several bags of the sawdust kept onboard in the event of oil spills. This worsened matters, creating a pasty goo that Souza shoveled into a blob. By then the smell of oil and feces and lard had permeated every compartment of the *Baleia Azul*, sending most of the crew, including the captain, to the ship's rails where they shared their breakfasts with the sea.

"I have asked the cargo officer to give me enough canvas to wrap it. Then we could use the hoist to lift it out in one piece," Souza reported to the captain, "but he refuses. He does not want his netting to stink for the rest of the voyage."

"We'll pick up replacement netting at the Port of Oakland," the captain said. "Tell the cargo officer to haul the damned thing up and throw it overboard with the netting attached. We can't have it down there another day."

And so the horribly malodorous mass was wrapped in canvas, hauled up in the cargo net, and tossed overboard. It didn't sink; rather it floated like the great piece of shit that it was, for a time following the *Baleia Azul* like a whale calf trailing its mother. Time passed and the netting slipped off, followed by the canvas. A few more hours elapsed and the floating mass struck what looked to be a dinosaur egg, the egg embedding itself beneath the black-gray, viscous coating and through the sawdust-laden, brown waxy layer. A week later on the first day of summer vacation in Tesoro, California, the whole thing—lard, oil, sawdust, shit, and dinosaur egg—washed up on the beach below Angus MacCallum's lighthouse.

was the first day of my summer vacation from school, and I had a good deal of nothing planned for the next three months with no desire to replace even a minute of it cleaning up the enormous blob on the beach just because Angus MacCallum was too old to beat me to it.

"I don't want it, Angus," I repeated.

"Gimme a minute, laddie," the old man muttered. "I'll show ye wha' I mean."

He picked up a large shell fragment and began to scrape away the crust. The mass was large—as broad as the base of a giant redwood tree and nearly as tall as me. It smelled of manure and barnacles and was certainly the most disgusting object I had ever encountered. He continued to use the shell to claw off the outer coating. Slowly, the black gelatinous layer gave way to one that was brown and waxy. When more scraping revealed a hard, whitish core, Angus tossed the shell aside and used his pocketknife to shave off a few slivers, balancing them on the blade. He held the knife to his nose and sniffed, then extended the blade toward me.

"Smell it," he commanded and I did. Unlike the disgusting crust, the core of the thing had a unique scent, at once both animal and marine, yet oddly sweet with just a hint of rubbing alcohol. Angus pulled back the blade and again sniffed, then carefully returned the slivers to the white core, pushing against them with his thumb until they stuck.

"What is it, Angus?" I asked.

The old lighthouse keeper pointed his face at me, a pair of folds widening to reveal eyes bright with wonder and anticipation.

"Ah, laddie," he said, upturned lips separating themselves from his wrinkles. He took me by the shoulders, grinning. "Cannae ye understand? It's treasure, a bloody treasure. It's ambergris, laddie…Ambergris. It's a ton of bloody ambergris."

CHAPTER THREE

We become rich

It was eight o'clock in the morning when Angus and I discovered the ambergris. By 8:45 the news had made a couple of passes through our small town and a sizeable group was gathered on the beach to offer advice, roiling the air with intentions, good and bad. No one, including me, knew what the stuff was worth, merely that the word "treasure," and hence unimaginable wealth, had been attached to it by Angus MacCallum, a fellow who had been around the world as a merchant seaman a couple of times and likely knew a treasure when he saw one. A good many of those in the crowd had never lived anywhere but Tesoro and thought I ought to sell my claim, buy a fancy car, and then load up Ma and Alex, putting our little village in the rearview mirror. Others felt the treasure was under the jurisdiction of maritime law and belonged to the government—the government comprised of the people, and the people, coincidentally, comprised of them.

"Where does it come from?" someone asked.

"Whale's blowhole," another answered.

"It dinnae come froom no blowhole," Angus growled. "Whales chunder it up and it floats aboot the ocean fer years 'til it turn into ambergris."

More questions followed, all directed at Miss Lizzie Fryberg, who was rightfully seen as the town know-it-all because she more often than not seemed to actually know everything.

"Perfumers prize ambergris as a fixative…something to

help a fragrance last longer," Miss Lizzie told the group on the beach. "They're willing to pay top dollar for it…although who knows if any of them are prepared to buy a quantity of this size. No one disputed her as Miss Lizzie was almost six feet tall and fifty-one years old, her physical stature joined to a comfortable age when a woman can be smarter than a man while not giving a damn if he knows it.

"It will probably have to be broken up and sold to multiple vendors," she added.

"How much is it worth?" someone asked.

"Millions," Angus MacCallum offered, evoking a chorus of gasps that rivaled the slapping sound of morning waves against the sandy beach.

"Maybe," Miss Lizzie said. "I've heard pure ambergris can go for almost eighteen hundred dollars per ounce. A specimen this large…perhaps a ton." Miss Lizzie hesitated, her lips moving silently until a figure came into her head that lifted her perfectly highlighted eyebrows. "My goodness," she exclaimed, "Angus is right. This could be worth millions…maybe fifty million dollars or more."

She gripped my arm.

"We need to tell your mother, Connor," she said.

We left Angus to guard the ambergris and headed for the little cottage where I'd been born, amassing a parade of folks along the way. Now, my Tesoro neighbors in 1934 were reasonably industrious people. However, it had been a blustery spring with cooler temperatures than usual, and on perhaps the first pleasant morning of summer in early June, it didn't take much encouragement to make them to put aside what they should be doing in favor of just about anything else. Thus, the trailing crowd grew as we made our way off the beach and then hiked up the main road to the village. Before long we were enveloped in a festive buzz that was equal parts carnival and proclamation. Doors opened, heads popped out. "What's going on?" people asked. "Connor O'Halloran's discovered himself a treasure," was the answer. By the time we reached the cottage I shared with Ma and Alex, it seemed that at least one member of every household in town, other than Cyrus Dinkle's, had turned out. Of course, Dinkle was not part of it. He was the richest fellow in our seaside village and didn't mingle with us, spending most of his time inside the walls of his estate on the Pacific Ocean. At the time, I didn't give much thought to his absence, figuring our treasure was unlikely to tempt him since he had plenty of treasure already, most of it reputedly acquired by nefarious means. I was wrong, as you will learn, with money proving most alluring, as it usually does, to those who need it least.

The little home where I was born and raised was a tidy, shingle-sided affair with a cheerful red tin roof. Only the flowerboxes hanging from windows on either side of the door disputed the house's storybook affect, one of them filled with brightly colored blossoms, while the other contained dead ones. Miss Lizzie and I went inside, while the rest of the crowd milled about outside, crowding into the shade of the single tree in our front yard where they gossiped and speculated about the ambergris on the beach. Eventually, of course, the heat of the day shifted the talk into the usual topics: How kids didn't appreciate things like their parents did when they were growing up, and which of the crooks back in Washington D Almighty C deserved to get strung up first for plunging the nation into the Great Depression.

Inside the cottage, Miss Lizzie and I found my little brother at the kitchen table, examining a picture of baseballer Lou Gehrig on the front of a box of Wheaties. His eyes brightened slightly at the sight of Miss Lizzie, but he didn't speak. This was his way. Four years younger than me, Alex had an impressively wide, serious streak for a six-year-old boy, and on those rare occasions when he shared his thoughts, it came after he'd observed a thing long enough to figure out how it was put together. Once he did speak, his remarks could be uncomfortably insightful and blunt. Such unfiltered honesty is rare and more than a few folks around town found it unnerving. They avoided crossing paths with Alex, averting their eyes when he approached as if doing so would keep hidden whatever dark secrets or inhospitable feelings they didn't want their friends and neighbors to know about.

"Where's Ma?" I asked.

"Out back," Alex said.

I was glad to hear that Ma was out of bed. She had still been there when I left the cottage around dawn to deliver the *Chronicle*—indeed, had been abed for several days, recognizable only as a mound of bedcovers as she battled through one of her low spots. We found her in the back yard—a tiny space with more sand than grass—having a conversation with a loud mockingbird perched on the edge of the roof. I believed Ma could be the prettiest of all the mothers when she chose to fix herself up. But that morning she was a bit of a mess—her hair tangled, an attempt to apply lipstick having gone so awry it appeared as if one corner of her lower lip had made a detour south before wending its way back to where it belonged. She was chatty, as was always the case after emerging from whatever shadow had held her.

Doctors now have a name for the mood swings that gripped my mother, Mary Rose MacKenna O'Halloran. Folks in Tesoro preferred the simplicity of a metaphor, describing her as "a trifle cuckoo." *Trifle* was a kindness. Ma looped back and forth between swirling giddiness and profound melancholy with occasional, brief stops at normal. In that way she was like the flowerboxes beneath our windows—bright colors on one extreme, dry and brown ones on the other. It wasn't her fault. She had a gentle heart and did her best to be a good person. I loved her.

"Connor, you're back," Ma giggled. "And Miss Lizzie. How

delightful. Welcome. Let's go inside. I just put on a pot for tea. Would you like a cup? I don't have scones, but scones would be nice. Connor, run to the mercantile and get scones. Use your paper route money. I'll pay you back this time. I promise. Every cent. And get peaches. Scones and peaches...Perfect."

She went on like this for a while, the pitch of her voice scaling up and down like a cat on a piano, hands fluttering in the air, words racing to escape her mouth.

"Mary Rose, stop talking and listen. We've something to tell you," Miss Lizzie said. Ma immediately fell silent, as our town medical officer had a way of tethering my mother close enough to reality to carry on a conversation; indeed, Miss Lizzie tethered most people to reality whether or not they liked it. Don't get me wrong. Miss Lizzie was not overbearing. She had simply stopped bottling up what she thought. She was more intelligent and better educated than everyone in Tesoro and we all knew it, making any effort to keep it under wraps something she considered both disingenuous and inefficient. There can be a thin line separating that sort of indisputable reason from unwelcome judgment, and some around town mistook her no-nonsense demeanor for severity. I knew better. Miss Lizzie had a huge heart, a stiff backbone, and a wicked sense of humor. She was as well-read as an Oxford don; honest as her hero, Abe Lincoln; able to debate anyone, man or woman, into submission; as unafraid of opinions as the scandalous Isadora Duncan; and as fashionable as Coco Chanel.

Miss Lizzie apprised Ma of my discovery on the beach and its potential value. Ma listened without really listening, fingers tapping impatiently on one cheek, her eyes flitting about the room as if unable to find a place to alight. This sort of fidgetiness was typical of her up times, occasions where she mostly searched for chinks in one's conversational armor, hoping to jam in five or six sentences before an opposing talker could get so much as a prepositional phrase shoved in. This made actual understanding of what was being said an inconvenience and Ma failed to grasp much of what Miss Lizzie told her about the ambergris on the beach.

"Isn't that nice?" she hummed when told I might well be a millionaire. "I once found a button on that part of the beach. I am quite certain it was left there by Fannie Brice. Of course, no one believes me, but the button had the letters FB on it so who else could have lost it? There are no FBs in Tesoro and Miss Brice had recently performed in San Francisco. I still have it. I keep it in a cigar box next to my bed. Connor, be a good boy and get my box."

I did as she asked, and upon my return, Miss Lizzie seemed to have made some headway, as Ma now understood that we were about to become rich.

"My goodness, Connor, what will we do with all that money?" Ma fretted, wringing her hands. "What can anyone do with so much money?"

I didn't answer, although I had a pretty good idea of what one might do with a lot of money, most of it involving a big house, a diamond necklace and mink stole for Ma, a pair of sneakers for Alex that weren't handed down from me, and a real radio inside a polished wood cabinet to replace the crystal set on which I listened to faint, static-laced episodes of *Jack Armstrong, the All-American Boy* and *The Lone Ranger*. I suspect such unabashed materialism may seem selfish, but in my defense, I'd had damned few temptations in life and was understandably susceptible to a treasure some whale with an upset stomach had dangled in front of me. Moreover, my little family relied on a small inheritance from Ma's late parents, my paper route money, and the benevolence of our neighbors. It was a fragile subsistence at best, and I'd thought myself the man of our house long enough to feel man-of-the-house pressures, particularly in the midst of the Great Depression; a time when fellows back in New York City with far fatter bank accounts than ours were jumping out the windows of skyscrapers—well-heeled tycoons one day and flat broke corpses the next.

"Dinkle's rich," Alex said. He had quietly come outside and now stood behind us. We turned to his voice. "Hasn't done him much good," he went on. "Everyone hates him."

I studied my little brother. His eyes were leveled on me, dark brown caramels that seemed capable of reading my mind.

"We should share it," Alex added.

I scowled at my brother, partly because it was my treasure and not his. I didn't appreciate it being offered up without discussion. However, my ill-temper was mostly because I knew that he was right, and I would do well to take his advice, given that riches hadn't prevented Cyrus Dinkle from turning into a sour old bastard with no family who would have him and no friends who weren't contractually obligated in some way. What I'd seen of Dinkle suggested that he didn't mind being despised, but I was not so sanguine. Even at ten years old I wanted to be well-thought of, if thought of at all, and the burden of prosperity that confronted me when Miss Lizzie put a figure on our ambergris suddenly seemed less a yacht than a sinking ship. Besides, I knew it was only fair. Alex and I were fatherless children with a mother on an emotional seesaw. We'd reached the ages of six and ten with the help and kindness of our friends and neighbors in Tesoro, and our little family owed a lot to the town. Now, with my discovery of the ambergris on the beach, good luck had come our way and I had to agree with my brother. It was reasonable that those same friends and neighbors would get a piece of it as well.

"Don't worry," I told Ma as if the idea had been mine. "We'll share the treasure. Everyone in town will be rich. Not just us."

Ma was puzzled, eyes darting back and forth between me and the mockingbird on the roof, while Miss Lizzie offered her approval with the whisper of a smile. Alex remained impassive even though my startling display of generosity belonged more to him than me.

16

"Do you understand, Ma? We'll share it," I reiterated. "All the money. We'll divvy it up...share it equally."

The mockingbird suddenly flew off, and with no rival for her consideration, I was able to help Ma understand what I'd proposed. She was genuinely delighted, giving me a big hug and then aiming a sloppy kiss at my cheek that I managed to mostly dodge. Afterward, we walked back through the cottage and went out front to meet with the crowd still waiting there. No one had left; indeed, the congregation appeared to have recruited a few new members, a low hum of anticipation greeting us that quickly gave way to a good many questions and a few jokes: *What you gonna do with all that money, Connor? You richer than Dinkle now? You gonna build yourself a mansion? You staying in Tesoro? Hey, Rockefeller, how about a loan?* Miss Lizzie deflected the questions with a raised hand and the comedians with a pinch-nosed expression. Once the commotion had been replaced by the sound of the morning breeze, she made the announcement that would tangle the town's mainsail lines for the next several months.

"It's worth millions and Connor O'Halloran wants to share it equally with you all," she revealed.

A wide array of behaviors followed Miss Lizzie's proclamation: gasps of disbelief, laughing, crying, silly dances, expressions of gratitude to God, and at least one fake swoon capably performed by Coach Wally Buford's wife, Judy. Coach Wally, a walking bag of bombast, was torn between his wife's swoon and a self-anointed mandate to boss people around. It briefly paralyzed him, but after Judy sat up on her own he leapt into action, blowing on the omnipresent whistle that dangled from a shoestring around his neck, at the same time inexplicably attempting to organize people into rows. Miss Lizzie had made a career of thwarting Coach Wally's efforts to be important. She put a stop to it.

"We need to move Connor's ambergris off the beach and weigh it, then have a town meeting," she said.

This idea was well-received by all and Fiona Littleleaf—who operated both the mercantile and the Kittiwake Inn along with her aunts, Rosie and Roxy—drove her flatbed truck onto the beach where the mass was eased onto a tarp and then hoisted onto the flatbed. She then transported it to the port scale where half our fortune evaporated when the thing turned out to weigh not a ton, as Angus had estimated, but just over 1000 pounds. A few groans abused the morning air when the needle on the scale settled on the half-ton mark, but the general disappointment was short-lived. In 1934 a half-ton of ambergris had an estimated value of $28,616,000 or about $146,000 for each of the 196 households in Tesoro, the 197th—home to Cyrus Dinkle—to receive nothing as a lesson from me to him for being miserly, cantankerous, and allegedly felonious. One hundred forty-six thousand dollars may not seem like much, but consider this: If I went to a grocery store today, a quart of milk would cost a dollar and thirty-nine cents. In 1934 that same quart of milk cost eleven cents. Thus, to match the $146,000 I offered to the citizens of Tesoro as a ten-year-old, I would need over 1.8 million dollars per household today.

I'll bet you're paying attention now.

CHAPTER FOUR

The first town meeting

The city charter required four days' notice before a town meeting, but the prerequisite was waived because everyone other than Cyrus Dinkle knew about my ambergris by mid-morning. C. Herbert Judson the Lawyer was dispatched to inform Dinkle even though the old scoundrel routinely kept himself distant from community affairs. "If we notify him, he'll ignore us. If we don't, he'll sue," Mr. Judson explained to Miss Lizzie and Roger Johns the Banker. The remaining citizens of Tesoro headed for the town hall, a wood-frame building that also served as a church for both the Methodists and the Catholics, the only denominations with a foothold in our little village.

Across the street from the hall was Fremont Park. It boasted a gazebo donated by the Tesoro High Class of 1916 along with a smattering of benches and picnic tables, some playground equipment, a water fountain, and a rusting Spanish-American War-era cannon, its barrel opening covered with chicken wire to prevent birds from nesting inside. There wasn't much else in town—a branch of the Sonoma State Bank, Fiona Littleleaf's mercantile and adjacent Kittiwake Inn, a car lot, the Tesoro public school, a Sinclair gas station, a few shops catering to tourists, the Last Resort Bar & Grill, a cemetery. Miss Lizzie Fryberg, a pharmacist by trade, served as general medical officer as well as midwife and mortician, thus tending to the beginning, middle, and end of the life cycle. We had a lighthouse manned by Angus MacCallum and a somewhat ramshackle port where an occasional small cargo ship or fishing vessel still harbored. There was a marina, the slips occupied by dinghies, sunfish sailboats, and C. Herbert Judson's sloop, the *C. Breeze*. One road accessed the town, leading both in and out, the western city limit demarcated by Cyrus Dinkle's estate on the Pacific Ocean.

As the town hall began to fill up and the day grew warmer, there was talk of shifting the meeting to Fremont Park. However, Roger Johns the Banker, our usual moderator, liked to hear his deep voice resonating off the slightly curved aspect of the assembly room's ceiling. "I believe our discussion will benefit from the dome's acoustical enhancement," he explained, and because he was habitually congenial and most didn't know what he meant by "acoustical enhancement," we all crammed ourselves into the hall's central chamber with Mr. Johns, Miss Lizzie Fryberg, Fiona Littleleaf, Last Resort Bar & Grill proprietor James Throckmorton, Coach Wally Buford, and C. Herbert Judson taking low seats on the stage at the front.

Except for Coach Wally, who routinely jammed himself into town leadership positions as if vying for the last seat on a lifeboat, there was neither hubris nor expectation attached to the seating arrangements. Tesoro was unincorporated. We had no formal government and convened town meetings when an issue or dispute arose. We didn't have many of either—most agenda items involving street repairs, beach cleanup, repeal or re-enactment of Blue Sundays, harbor regulation, and an occasional disagreement about whose fence was on whose property line. Our way of resolving things was pure democracy and surprisingly efficient. The six folks at the front of the room functioned as an unofficial town council—a practical arrangement as people in Tesoro routinely sought opinions from five of the six when a serious matter was before them and had long ago learned that it was impossible to escape Coach Wally Buford's views, which he spat about town like tobacco juice.

When I entered the assembly room, Miss Lizzie motioned

for me to take a seat on the stage, a vantage point I found exhilarating as it allowed me to touch beautiful Fiona Little-leaf's elbow and catch the scent of her soap and the warmth of her breath. She wore high-waisted pants and her blouse was sleeveless, an outfit some considered scandalous at the time—a woman with her legs covered by slacks and her arms mostly not covered at all inexplicably salacious to some book-of-etiquette long-nose who likely possessed arms and legs no one had much interest in viewing, anyway. Her honey-colored hair was pulled back, her face free of makeup save a hint of lipstick. I thought her the most beautiful creature ever put on Earth.

"Hi, Connor," she whispered, and I gave her the sort of goofy grin a fellow in love pastes on when the girl he worships is around. Some folks believe ten-year-old boys don't have such feelings, but they do and I did.

Mr. Johns called the meeting to order, followed by a bit of disorder when Coach Wally Buford mounted his usual effort to shanghai the moderator's gavel. Our village's charter required that each town meeting begin with the election of a new moderator. Mr. Johns always won the election, despite Coach Buford's indefatigable candidacies.

"I think we can all agree that Roger Johns has been a disaster as moderator," the coach announced, his demeanor a cross between a bulldog ripping a hat to shreds and a bulldog that wants to rip a hat to shreds. "I'd like to offer myself as an alternative," he went on. "I'll do a tremendous job."

The coach—forty years removed from his heyday as a star athlete for the junior college in Sonoma—taught industrial arts at Tesoro High, a consolidated institution drawing from our town and the surrounding area. He also coached the school's football team, a forlorn program last victorious eight years earlier. Coach Wally was a fire hydrant of a man—a stubby, chronically red-faced fellow full of belly and opinions but lean on tact and self-awareness. These were ingredients for a recipe

21

that would likely elect him to Congress in today's world. However, in the Tesoro of 1934 he was rightfully considered to be both a dimwit and a loudmouth, his excessive fondness for fiery post-game speeches driving more than one player off the gridiron and into the less noisy folds of the marching band. Accordingly, no one at the meeting had any interest in handing him a gavel, especially when our regular moderator, Mr. Johns, was a waxily handsome sort who had been president of his college fraternity and was quite simply as inoffensive as a person can be.

"I nominate Roger Johns to be moderator," Miss Lizzie called out.

"Second," Mr. Judson added.

Coach Wally nominated himself, but as there was no second, his name was left off the ballot and Mr. Johns was elected by acclaim. Afterward, the coach huffed and snorted and conspiracy-theoried a bit, and because the day was growing hotter and the quarters of the packed room closer, some huffing and snorting and conspiracy-theorying arose from the congregation in response. Eventually, Mr. Johns settled everyone with a few knocks of his gavel on the podium and the meeting proceeded.

"We must begin by offering our thanks to the person responsible for our good luck," Mr. Johns said.

He nodded for me to stand and I did.

"Let's have three cheers for Connor O'Halloran! Hip hip…"

"Hooray!"

"Hip hip…"

"Hooray!"

"Hip hip…"

"Hooray!"

With the hip hip hoorays out of the way, Mr. Johns then asked for a motion to divvy up the ambergris by household rather than person. A couple of Methodists were quick to offer the motion and its second, but in the discussion that followed,

the Catholics were in a huff as their papal directive to prop-
agate the human species like rabbits offered them an obvious
advantage in a per person allotment. Mr. Johns gaveled them
down and the vote carried as the Methodists in our town far
outnumbered the Papists. Mr. Johns next asked Miss Lizzie
to give a breakdown of the particulars. When the figure of
$146,000 per household was given, a low hum rose up and
hovered atop the congregation like fog over the beach at dawn.

"How you gonna break it up and make sure it's even?" one
man asked. "If Miss Lizzie is right, an ounce here or there will
be a pretty big deal."

Everyone thought this an excellent question and much discussion ensued, until it was decided to leave the ambergris in
one piece with each household receiving a certificate allotting
them just over five pounds of the precious stuff. Mr. Johns
then successfully orchestrated a pooling of the ambergris
shares in order to more effectively bargain with the perfumers.

"Wait a damned minute," Milton Garwood the Misanthrope
griped from the back of the room after the motion to pool the
shares carried. "Nobody's telling me what to do with my end."

Milton, the town blacksmith and welder, was a whip-thin,
leathery fellow with a thumb he'd hammered flat years before
and permanent grime in the creases of his hands that made
them nearly as black as his typical mood. Everyone in Tesoro
was well aware that no one could tell him what to do, primarily
because Milton was quick to remind us of it as often as possible.

"You all wanna trust your fortunes to one person," he continued, flinging his words at the assembly like darts, "but who's
gonna be doing the bargaining? You, Roger? Ain't you got
enough of your damned fingerprints on our money already?"

"Now Milton," Roger Johns began. He was a nice fellow
who always seemed freshly shaved and showered to me, his
fair hair and smooth face like polish on a shoe. Mr. Johns had a

way of disarming people, a nice skill to have if one was in the business of reassuring depositors during the Great Depression. However, he was no match for a vinegary, old strip of hardtack like Milton Garwood, who had made a science out of being contrary, and the town blacksmith with the flat thumb easily interrupted Mr. Johns into submission, sputtering and complaining and accusing until Miss Lizzie invited Milton to shut up.

A number of names were subsequently forwarded as potential agents to broker a deal with the perfume companies, including car dealer Skitch Peterson the Hornswoggler, C. Herbert Judson the Lawyer, and Coach Wally Buford, who nominated himself. Buford was quickly dismissed as a nincompoop and Peterson's choice of occupations was determined to render him irretrievably shady. That left Mr. Judson and Miss Lizzie Fryberg, whom many considered to be the ideal candidate as she was an expert on makeup and perfumes; indeed, she was always made up to the nines, even when delivering a baby. "Miss Lizzie has an entire room devoted to nothing but face creams and blushes and lipsticks and eye shadows, with another filled from floor to ceiling with perfumes from across the world," folks around town often claimed. Even though I'd been in Miss Lizzie's home many times and never seen such a room, I didn't doubt its existence. Her eyebrows were always fastidiously plucked and penciled, her lips perfectly highlighted, the subtle fragrances she radiated rarely repeated.

"So, you wanna hitch your wagons to a damned lawyer or a woman? That's what you want?" Milton Garwood snarled, randomly finger-pointing as he spoke. "I ain't gonna be told what to do by them or anybody else. I'm taking my shares and leaving."

"You can't do that, Milton," Roger Johns interjected. "There was a vote. We agreed to abide by it. You, too."

"Oh yeah? Well, nobody tells me what to do. I can withdraw my vote if I want, and I'm withdrawing it as of right now."

With that, Milton stomped out of the town hall and went across the street where he took a leak behind the gazebo before returning. By then, a little fresh air and an empty bladder had apparently softened his stance and he kept quiet when the vote went in favor of a team of negotiators to include C. Herbert Judson the Lawyer, Miss Lizzie Fryberg, and Roger Johns the Banker.

CHAPTER FIVE

Ma

After the meeting, Ma and I retrieved Alex from Fremont Park and headed home.

"Tuck Garwood's grandpa thinks we're crazy," Alex announced. He needed a trim and auburn hair fell across one eye, partially covering a face that would serve him well as a man. "Tuck says only crazy people would give away all that money," he added.

Tuck—older brother to my best friend Webb Garwood and one of a herd of grandchildren tracing their origins to Milton Garwood the Misanthrope—was two years older than me but already well on his way to living down to his grandfather's legacy as a fellow who saw dog excrement on the bottom of every boot.

"Tell Tuck Garwood his grandpa doesn't have to keep his share," I said.

"Okay," Alex replied, and I knew he would do exactly that, likely earning himself a sock on the arm or a pinch. I've alleged that my little brother had no filters and this is no exaggeration. He typically said what he figured needed saying, regardless of whose pillows got knocked off the bed. He wasn't being mean—guileless, no doubt, but never mean.

"I'm only kidding, Alex," I said. "Don't say anything to Tuck. It'll just cause trouble."

"Okay," Alex said.

"I don't think sharing the money is crazy at all, Connor," Ma

26

offered. She was remarkably composed, her hair brushed, the errant lipstick wiped off. Her illness was like that—periods of calm dotting a sea dark and bottomless in places while filled with capricious eddies in others. "I think what you're doing is quite wonderful," she added. "I'm very proud of you."

Her approval warmed me, even though our roles as caretaker and charge had been more or less reversed since Alex's birth and my father's subsequent departure. By the time my brother was two years old, Ma's mental inclemency had functionally invalided her, with Alex and I relying on townsfolk such as Roger Johns, who made sure Ma's inheritance from her parents was frugally managed; and Fiona Littleleaf, who provided discounted or free food and clothes from her mercantile; and Miss Lizzie Fryberg, who unfailingly brought sweets and gifts at Christmas and on our birthdays. Indeed, Alex and I spent many nights with Miss Lizzie or Fiona, both women opening their doors when Ma was not up to handling a pair of loud, constantly hungry boys. I loved staying with them. It was a holiday, although I never slept in; instead, I returned to our cottage early the next morning to make sure Ma didn't wake up and immediately stick her head in the oven or go for an ocean swim after a stroll through town buck-naked.

I also had to make her take whatever new medicine Miss Lizzie had formulated. Our town medical officer well remembered young Mary Rose MacKenna, the pretty and inquisitive girl who had fallen under the spell of a young second-generation Irishman named Seamus O'Halloran. She was determined to find a cure for the paralyzing mood swings that imprisoned my mother shortly after my father skipped out on us. A good many attempts at a cure had failed, but Miss Lizzie had high hopes that summer for her latest remedy—a thick, bile-hued liquid with the color, consistency, and appeal of vomit.

What I've told you about Ma and Alex and me may seem the stuff of Dickens—a pair of orphans, or nearly so, a frail mother, and my family's reliance upon neighbors who mostly had a hard time finding two nickels to rub together for themselves. It was, however, nothing of the sort. Alex and I were lucky. Our mother, despite her mental infirmity, loved us. Moreover, the citizens of Tesoro—save Cyrus Dinkle—embraced us, providing not one or two parents but nearly four hundred, all of whom made certain our bellies were full, our shoes sturdy, our homework completed before bedtime, and an occasional orange or piece of candy was discovered in our lunch pails. Folks were not shy to remind us about *please* and *thank you*; we were routinely subjected to unscheduled ear, teeth, and fingernail inspections; and when I wanted a little extra spending money, Fiona stopped selling the *San Francisco Chronicle* at her mercantile, forcing people in town to have me deliver it to their doorsteps each morning or risk falling hopelessly out of touch with the antics of *Little Orphan Annie* and the politicians in Washington D Almighty C. Most important, Alex and I were given moral compasses that allowed us to discern philosophical north from south. Miss Lizzie and Fiona Littleleaf—both ecclesiastical skeptics—were our primary guides in these affairs, although Ma did drag Alex and me to Methodist Sunday services when she felt up to it. This planted the stubborn idea of God in my head, a notion I have doubted during my lifetime and yet have never entirely escaped.

"What *will* we do with all that money?" Ma asked as we walked home. The day had gone from warm to hot with little breeze to cool us as we zigzagged back and forth to take advantage of shade provided by the broad-leafed sycamores haphazardly lining the road. Her question was a good one. Tesoro was a lovely place, but there weren't many ways to unload one's cash unless you fancied the doodads Angus carved for tourists or were old enough to throw back a few drinks at the Last Resort.

"Maybe we'll live like people in the movies," I said. I had seen my share of moving picture shows, the last one a feature in San

Rafael that Alex and I had attended with Miss Lizzie. The folks in *King Kong* had been rich enough to fund a giant ape-hunting expedition to Indonesia and still have enough left over for a return cruise to New York City where they wore tuxedos and evening gowns and drank champagne, their tuxedoing and evening-gowning and champagne-drinking so aggravating the big gorilla that he decided to snap his chains and make off with the prettiest girl at the party. "Maybe I'll go find another King Kong," I joked.

"Hmmm," Ma said.

"King Kong isn't real," Alex said.

Later that night, as Alex and I lay awake in the dark of the room we shared, my brother whispered what we both wanted.

"We'll find a doctor to fix Ma," he said.

CHAPTER SIX

Cyrus Dinkle

There is a limited repertoire of human behaviors, particularly for a mostly one-dimensional rascal like Cyrus Dinkle. A fellow my age has observed pretty much all those behaviors and it is not difficult to predict what a scoundrel might think or do in a given situation. For example, I never underestimate how low a villain might stoop to get what he wants or how shamelessly bold he can be in his deceit. I lacked such prescience at ten years of age, and thus, had little idea in the summer of 1934 what Dinkle might think or do ahead of an actual declaration of what he thought or the act of doing something to show it. I only knew that I was scared of him. However, having now survived more than nine decades, it is not a boast to say that I can predict with the precision of the most amazing clairvoyant the behavior of the Dinkles of the world. Nor is it a boast to claim that such men no longer frighten me.

Angus MacCallum—an old man then like I am now—wasn't afraid of Cyrus Dinkle either. He'd several times fought off the old man's efforts to buy the lighthouse and beach below it. "Dinkle claims we dinnae need no lighthouse, but wha' really pats 'im aff his heed is tha' I might train me spyglass on his place," Angus believed. "I dinnae ken why he think I care aboot wha' he might do o'er there. I dinnae have no interest in 'im."

Angus had thus far managed to thwart Dinkle, citing a container ship that ran aground in 1927 after a storm temporarily knocked out power to the revolving searchlight and three times convincing old friends still active as ship's captains to register concerns about the Tesoro coastline with the Bureau of Lighthouses. After years of effort Dinkle had stopped trying, apparently willing to see which of them would die first, but the dispute still rankled both men enough to make them hate each other. "He ain't noothin' but loocky sperm," Angus often opined, making clear how little he thought of those whose affluence was a result of their fathers' perspiration.

Angus had a right to speak his mind on such things. He had been fending for himself since the age of fifteen after he went to sea to escape the fire-and-brimstone disapproval of his father, an elder in the Presbyterian church of Inverness, Scotland. "I figgered there was nae chance for me to be one of the Elect and get to Heaven and so I set sail to raise some hell," Angus claimed. He'd appeared in Tesoro around twenty-five years earlier, his face pickled into dusky wrinkles by years of sea spray. He was small, sinewy, weather-beaten, and profane with a badly twisted leg—his foot pointed west when Angus was headed north—the result of a losing tussle with a cargo net in the port of Manila in 1905. Angus wanted to believe Dinkle had been handed his fortune, but Miss Lizzie knew otherwise. She'd known the old man for years and was one of the few in town who called him by his first name.

"Cyrus wasn't always walled up at his estate," she told folks. "He was married when he first arrived. His wife and my mother were friends and the Dinkles were at our house for dinner more than a few times. He didn't inherit a dime. He was a trader in the Indian Territories and made his money in the black market. Gun-running, too. My father knew all about it. Papa said Cyrus had already made a fortune by the time he arrived in town. He owns land all over…California, Idaho, Montana, Wyoming. Probably other places, too."

Miss Lizzie had been merely a child when the former Indian Territories trader arrived, but well remembered a fellow who looked nothing like the mostly bald, paunchy Dinkle I knew, his lips dusky, his hands liver-spotted, a slight, fixed curl to his back giving him both the personality and body habitus of a vulture. "He was a young, fit man with lots of dark hair and a moustache," Miss Lizzie recalled. "Mrs. Dinkle was very pretty. She was obviously afraid of her husband…Only lasted about two years in Tesoro. After she ran off, Cyrus hired his man."

No one knew why Dinkle settled in Tesoro. The sea, maybe. He didn't sail, but C. Herbert Judson described the old man as a fixture at the bay window of his study during their rare appointments. "He stares at the horizon as if waiting for a ship to appear," Mr. Judson once told Miss Lizzie when I was close enough to hear. Upon arrival in our little village, Dinkle had rented what was the largest house in town at the time; then he acquired one hundred acres bordering the ocean and immediately began construction on a compound. "Papa was an architect and worked on all the buildings," Miss Lizzie claimed, the Dinkle estate eventually including four edifices: the main house, a guesthouse, a servants' barracks, and a stable that now served as a garage. Except for the main house and the garage, the buildings had long been empty. The garage included an upstairs apartment, occupied by Dinkle's man, and housed one car—a long, elegant Duesenberg that was fired up every week or so when Dinkle needed to make a trip to San Francisco.

Dinkle had three maids to keep the empty house spotless, a small army of gardeners to manicure the deserted grounds, and a cook to prepare meals. Despite the spacious servant's quarters, none were in residence, leaving Dinkle's man—a tall, cadaverous fellow with an accent—as the only live-in staff member. Rumors surrounded the mysterious manservant who simultaneously occupied the roles of butler, valet, and chauffeur. "He was a duke or some such in one of them European principalities," some folks said. "He was a gangster in Chicago. He worked for Al Capone," others claimed. A spooky creature about thirty years younger than his nearly eighty-year-old employer, Dinkle's man had a habit of popping up at Fiona Littleleaf's mercantile as if materializing from thin air, a phantasmagorical event unnerving more than one tourist about to shell out a nickel for a Coca-Cola or a box of Milk Duds. "Mister Dinkle's mail, please," he'd request in an eerie drone. Afterward, he'd offer an equally sonorous, "Thank you," before departing without another word. Most kids in town were terrified of him, quite certain he was exactly the sort of ghoul his appearance suggested. I wasn't. I had once seen him steam the glass on the window of Fiona's mercantile with his breath, afterward drawing a heart in the condensation. Only a man with a soul would do such a thing.

After our first town meeting, C. Herbert Judson lost a coin flip with Miss Lizzie and was given the job of informing Dinkle about his exclusion from the town ambergris collective. Mr. Judson had been on the estate more than once as he occasionally prepared a legal document for the old man. Still, he didn't relish the task, later telling us that Dinkle had initially offered no response when apprised of the news, instead moving to the liquor cabinet in his study where he poured exactly one finger of scotch into each of a pair of tumblers.

"One finger before lunch can lead to inspiration. Two is recreational," he'd said, offering one of the tumblers to Mr. Judson. "Three is usually celebratory for me…and commiserative for my competitors."

According to Mr. Judson, Dinkle next went to his study's huge bay window where his gaze drifted out to distant whitecaps—innocuous forerunners to the tall, fierce waves crashing onto the beach at high tide. Judson's news wasn't a surprise to the old gunrunner. The estate's servants were incorrigible tongue-waggers and Dinkle routinely eavesdropped when they took their lunch in the kitchen in order to keep abreast of the goings-on in the village. Their account of my discovery and its worth had provoked skepticism at first, but after retiring to his study to read about ambergris in one of the thick volumes of his *Encyclopedia Britannica*, it seemed to the former Indian Territories trader that there may, indeed, be a fortune tantalizingly within reach if a man were well-experienced in the art of slipping his hand into someone else's pocket. This explains why Mr. Judson's uneasily offered disclosure that Dinkle would not share in the town's new wealth did not anger the old man as our town lawyer had expected; rather, it provided welcome corroboration that booty was within reach, causing Dinkle to luxuriate in a larcenous tingle that was both familiar and comforting.

Years in the Indian Territories had taught Dinkle to snatch up an opportunity as ruthlessly as a coyote makes off with a stray cat. A decision like mine—to simply toss away most of a rightfully acquired fortune—was a concept as foreign to him as his man's mysterious heritage. "This O'Halloran boy...you say he came up with the idea to give it away on his own?" he posed to Mr. Judson.

"He's that kind of boy," Mr. Judson said.

"Maybe," Dinkle replied. "In my experience, no one is that generous."

After Mr. Judson left, Dinkle remained at the window, sipping his scotch as waves coursed onto the beach and then just as quickly receded. As always, the distant, flat horizon recalled his years in the Indian Territories where a man could ride for days without seeing a drop of water. He had promised his wife that water would be visible on a whim when they moved to California—a vow he'd kept—and yet she'd left him anyway, no amount of either water or money enough to keep her in his bed for even one more night. He didn't miss her. The woman was beautiful but complained incessantly. Dinkle had once owned a couple of Indian squaws in the Territories and sometimes wished he'd kept one. "They do what they're told and keep their mouths shut," he occasionally professed to his man, the tall valet-chauffeur invariably offering no response as he well knew that no response was exactly what his employer required of him.

Dinkle moved from the window to the liquor cabinet. He poured a second finger of scotch and then sat at his massive desk where he pondered for a time, one finger tapping the tip of his nose like the pendulum of a metronome. When he was done thinking, a broad smile had replaced his customary scowl and he allowed himself another finger of scotch.

CHAPTER SEVEN

The second town meeting

A week after I discovered the ambergris on the beach a notice was posted to the announcement board of the town hall, on the public kiosk in Fremont Park, and inside the front window of Fiona Littleleaf's mercantile.

CITIZENS OF TESORO
A MEETING WILL BE HELD AT THE TOWN HALL
ON THE EVENING OF JUNE 9 AT 7:00 P.M.
PLEASE BE ON TIME.
AGENDA
I. ELECTION OF MODERATOR
II. APPROVAL OF MINUTES
III. AN OFFER FROM MR. CYRUS DINKLE

Item III provoked a torrent of gossip as Dinkle and "offer" had rigorously kept separate houses in the past.

"What do you suppose he's up to?" I asked Fiona. I was at her mercantile where I often hung out, hoping she might stop stocking shelves or sorting mail or scribbling in her account book long enough give me a sign that we would one day become husband and wife. Fiona Littleleaf was the prettiest woman in Tesoro—the prettiest in California in my estimation—a wheat-haired beauty with coltish eyes. I thought her perfect—as clever as she was beautiful, unafraid to argue with the devil, and able to pound a nail straighter than a master carpenter. We shared a history of sorts, both of us fatherless, our mothers infirm. Fiona's father had been killed in the Great War, her mother lost to the flu pandemic of 1918. After her parents died, the six-year-old little girl had been adopted by spinsters Rosie and Roxy Littleleaf, a pair she called aunts even though they were actually cousins.

Precociously capable, the little girl had a flair for business and was running the mercantile and postal exchange by the time she was fifteen, something her aunts welcomed. The general store was part of their inheritance from their father and they had already come close to sinking it several times before their niece took over. "I love them dearly, but they're better at yarn selection than balance sheets," Fiona once told me. Rosie and Roxy made Fiona a full partner shortly after the young woman graduated from high school and the new co-owner immediately added the Kittiwake Inn next door to their little empire. It, too, was profitable and Fiona Littleleaf and her adoptive aunts were well on their way to moving into the sparse, upper financial echelon of Tesoro's families when the stock market crashed. Tourism dried up for a time, but Fiona had already set aside enough money to keep them afloat, and now after almost five years, the tourists were trickling back into town.

In 1934, Fiona Littleleaf was twelve years my senior and undoubtedly loved me in the same way an aunt loves a nephew. I had loftier intentions as I was merely ten and believed I would eventually get women figured out. I'm ninety-one now and still haven't, although I've learned that baffling men is part of a woman's charm. We baffle them, too, although I suspect they are more often annoyed than baffled.

Fiona was reorganizing bolts of fabric when I asked her to speculate on Dinkle's intentions. Of course, I already knew her answer. An offer of any sort from Cyrus Dinkle was uncharacteristically magnanimous, given that he was a man legendarily indisposed to magnanimity.

"I don't know what he has in mind, Connor," Fiona said, "but there will be fine print on it, that much I'll guarantee." She moved a bolt of thin cotton material boasting a gaudy floral pattern from one open compartment to another. The first cubicle had seemed adequate to me, the entire transaction pointless. However, Fiona accomplished it with such grace, indeed, was so assured that I found myself utterly captivated. She had a way of moving that seemed at once purposeful and unpretentious—a woman who both knew the effect she had on men and yet seemed not to know it at all. Once I was far enough clear of adolescence to think straight, I learned to attribute such an affect to confidence. As a boy, however, it was simply hypnotic. She looked at me and fashioned a quizzical expression.

"That's quite a face. Penny for your thoughts?" she asked.

About a year earlier I had seen a moving picture in San Rafael starring Frenchman Maurice Chevalier. It depicted a fellow in love who burst into song or spouted poetry whenever confronted by the woman he loved. Ma and Miss Lizzie took my brother and me to see it and thought Chevalier's reaction not only entertaining but entirely plausible. Alex and I thought the whole premise silly. We giggled throughout the picture with Miss Lizzie occasionally aiming a narrow eye our way to shush us. However, in the mercantile that morning I was a year older. With Fiona waiting for an answer to her question—her perfect face offering an inquiring expression, a strand of honeyed hair falling over one eye—I felt suddenly and inexplicably musical. Unfortunately, I lacked Chevalier's talent for verse or staying on key.

"Just thinking about the meeting tonight," I answered, disappointed to provide nothing more than a one-note response with no rhyme. Nevertheless, this seemed to satisfy her as well it should have. Merely a week had passed since the first town meeting to discuss the ambergris. A second gathering so soon was unprecedented and lent the sort of stature to the get-together typically reserved for holidays like the Fourth of July. The twilight start time added to the excitement; indeed, a meeting convened in the evening was a festive affair, often preceded by a picnic in Fremont Park—the cuisine leaning toward fried sand dabs, potato salad, and corn on the cob. During an evening meeting, children were turned loose to chase fireflies or play tag in the park, while across the street, the adults filled every seat in the assembly room of the town hall for sessions sure to include entertaining arguments, more than a few fellows emboldened by a nip or two after dinner. Should they fail to deliver, there was always Milton Garwood's thin skin and Angus MacCallum's habit of rubbing it thinner whenever he could.

Such displays of temper might have gone from theater to back alley had C. Herbert Judson not routinely intervened. He had a talent for shifting moods to the matters at hand, typically offering a joke or a run of vocabulary words that had us later scouring a dictionary. His calm voice and Mr. Johns's firm grasp of Robert's Rules of Order always managed to get the meeting back on the rails. Indeed, folks were a little disappointed each time Mr. Johns gaveled the proceedings to a close, dawdling outside the town hall or on the walk home as if reluctant to let the curtain fall on the evening's theatrics. If the meeting took place on a warm summer night, more than a few lounged on porch swings or in back yards until close to the scandalous hour of ten-thirty, drinking iced tea while discussing how Mr. Johns was a fine fellow and all, but you could be damned sure things would be run differently if *they* were in charge.

Activities started early for the second town meeting and Fremont Park was packed by five o'clock. I was there with Ma and Alex, sharing fried halibut, macaroni salad, and watermelon slices with Miss Lizzie and Fiona. My mother was more than a week into drinking Miss Lizzie's latest concoction and was uncommonly steady, joining Miss Lizzie and Fiona in a monumentally boring discussion of how much they all admired First Lady Eleanor Roosevelt. This left Alex and I no choice but to prowl about with our pals, playing tag or hanging out with Tuck Garwood and his junior high buddies, snickering as they told each other dirty jokes or lied about which base they'd gotten to with their girlfriends. We returned to retrieve Ma a little before seven o'clock.

"Stay in the park until I come back for you," I instructed my brother. "And don't go to the beach. I mean it."

"I want to come to the meeting," Alex said.

This was a surprise. I was fascinated by the little dramas that played out at a typical town meeting, but things like Milton Garwood's griping or Coach Wally Buford's bloviating had always seemed pointless to Alex.

"Why?" I asked. "It's the same old stuff. You'll hate it."

"I want to go."

I was about to give Alex a pinch when Ma butted in. "There's no reason he can't go, Connor," she said.

I shot her the sort of look parents throw at each other when they disagree about what to do with their kid.

"There isn't," Ma reiterated, her voice soft.

I sometimes argued with my mother when she overruled me about Alex. I figured I should have a say in what he did since Ma could be pretty crazy at times and I was the one who would have to get him out of the trouble she allowed him to get into. Besides, like most men, I hated to back down, even though this time Ma's eyes were clear, her voice was steady, and I was wrong.

"I just think—"

"There isn't," Ma interrupted.

"He'll be bored, Ma."

My little brother took one of Ma's hands. "You don't know what I'll be," he said.

I glared at him but offered no rebuttal, since there really was no reason he couldn't go other than my damned stubbornness. Ma and Alex were right and we all knew it.

"Fine," I muttered.

I took Ma's other hand and we led her across the street to the town hall. Inside the assembly room the usual leadership group was already seated at the front: Roger Johns the Banker, C. Herbert Judson the Lawyer, Miss Lizzie Fryberg, Fiona Littleleaf, James Throckmorton, and Coach Wally Buford. Cyrus Dinkle sat at the end of their row of chairs with his man standing a few steps away, the tall, thin fellow's expression a lugubrious blend of somnambulist and basset hound.

Ma, Alex, and I took seats in the back row and watched Coach Wally Buford make his regular pitch for the moderator's gavel. He finished up by nominating himself, his name uncharacteristically making it to the ballot when Milton Garwood impulsively seconded the nomination because Angus MacCallum told him he couldn't. Of course, Angus just wanted to stir things up and voted for Roger Johns like everyone else. Moderator Johns then asked if anyone proposed corrections to the minutes of the previous meeting. Milton Garwood, a staunch Catholic with six children and thirty-seven grandchildren, believed a request for corrections to the minutes was tantamount to a referendum on the ambergris distribution plan. He asked for another vote in favor of the per person allotment supported by his church.

"I'm just asking for approval of the minutes," Mr. Johns pointed out. Milton then provided a lengthy rebuttal, confusing parts of the Bill of Rights with the Ten Commandments. He went on to declare his dissatisfaction, specifically, with President Roosevelt and, in general, with the crooks who made up Congress back in Washington D Almighty C. Eventually, someone in the back of the room advised Milton to "run for dad-burned office if you want to give a speech." Mr. Johns followed up with a gentle suggestion that Milton save his proposal for new business following completion of the published agenda.

"You can't tell me what to do, Roger," Milton groused. "You're the moderator, not the King of Persia or something."

For once, Milton had a small group of backers, Catholic hackles still up over the previously agreed upon allotments. With Mr. Judson's help, Mr. Johns successfully gaveled them down, then got his majority vote to approve the minutes. That's when silence settled over the room, all eyes on Cyrus Dinkle. Mr. Johns introduced him and Dinkle rose from his chair. He moved across the stage, his footsteps softly echoing over the hushed assembly.

Now if Roger Johns was as inoffensive as a fellow can be, Cyrus Dinkle was the opposite—a mostly bald and thin-lipped reptilian tyrant who looked as if he had never in his life done any heavy lifting, because he hadn't. He was soft—soft belly, soft manicured hands, and soft jowls that flowed seamlessly into his soft neck. You'll recall that Dinkle's appearance on the agenda had sent small whirlwinds of gossip whipping around Tesoro like rumor-laden dust-devils. Indeed, his appearance at a town meeting, even without the promise of an offer, would have waggled tongues anyway as Dinkle disdained civic goings-on, preferring the solitude of his estate overlooking the ocean, except on those occasions when his man fired up the Duesenberg for a trip to San Francisco. Heads turned when the Duesenberg rolled through town with Dinkle in the back seat, his eyes resolutely avoiding us in favor of his *Wall Street Journal*, his purplish lips curled into a censorious sneer. "He goes to San Francisco to meet up wit' the rest of the divils runnin' this damned country," Angus MacCallum once told me. "They drink brandy and smoke cigars and try to figger oot ways they can stick it to the workin' man."

Angus's assertion might have seemed like a mean-spirited harangue from a bitter old man except that he was entirely correct. As Miss Lizzie claimed, Dinkle actually owned land and various businesses in several states, and his trips to San Francisco were spent in the company of bankers, who helped him foreclose and evict; mining company executives, who helped him figure out ways to put a maze of shafts where bears might have hibernated; lawyers, who advised him on the best way to maintain his stranglehold on water rights; and accountants, determined to make sure he paid less taxes than an Okie fruit-picker. Unlike self-made tycoons like Henry Ford, George Pullman, or Andrew Carnegie, Dinkle had not made his fortune by building something; rather he had manipulated and enticed and intimidated, moving money from someone else's ledger column to his. In that way he was a harbinger of the future, a man unable to construct a birdhouse but adept at luring the bird inside and then eating it.

Dinkle glided toward the podium, a surprisingly graceful man given his age and bulk and the stiff curl of his back. Once settled, with the full attention of the room at his command, he fashioned a smile. I had never seen him smile and expected the result to be a serpentine thing. Instead, his smile was genuine, even warm. It was a welcoming smile, an expression of approval from a man whose wealth made us believe he was somehow superior to us, the unexpectedly seductive result making Dinkle not so much likable as irresistible. He began to speak next, and his voice was not the gruff, impatient snarl he routinely flung at kids in Tesoro, but a polished, syrupy tenor that would have elicited envy from a Chautauqua preacher. I looked around the room and was astounded to discover the faces of my friends and neighbors to be as open and unguarded as lemmings approaching a cliff.

"Citizens of Tesoro, it is a privilege to be here tonight," Dinkle cooed. "It has been far too long since I shared your company and for that I beg forgiveness. I am hopeful that when you hear what I have to offer, you will pardon my absence from your lives and find it in your hearts to once again call Cyrus Dinkle your friend."

Dinkle went on, repeatedly referring to himself in the third person and invoking a lot of claptrap about God, good will, and charity, inferring that he, Cyrus Dinkle, possessed a non-stop elevator to Heaven. Of course, the opposite was true as Dinkle was Satan in saint's clothing, the devil playing to a room filled with Fausts. I kept quiet, figuring folks would know this without hearing it from a ten-year-old boy like me, but it soon became apparent that they didn't. Before long, heads began to nod approvingly, people in the audience laughing at his contrived, self-effacing asides. He was mesmerizing them with flattery and faux-amiability, a snake charmer playing his pungi, and I was reminded of Miss Lizzie Fryberg's advice: "A man who refers to himself in the third person has a big enough head for two faces. Steer clear of him."

I was contemplating her words when Dinkle unexpectedly called out my name.

"Come up here, young Connor," he boomed. "There's a good lad. Come up here and let your friends and neighbors see what a fine young man you are."

I was stunned to hear my name called, even more surprised that he knew my name at all.

"Come on now, Mister O'Halloran. Come on up," Dinkle exhorted.

"Go on, Connor," Ma whispered.

I shook my head.

"Go on," Ma repeated, giggling. "Everyone is waiting."

I stumbled to the front of the room and climbed the steps to the stage. Dinkle then led me to the podium and stationed me at his side, a hand lightly cupping the back of my neck. His hand, like his smile, confounded my expectations. It was not warm and unctuously moist, as I had always surmised, but as dry and cool as snakeskin. He began to speak again, talking about good fortune and divine benevolence, at the same time squeezing my neck until I was dizzied.

"What a lesson you've taught us, young Connor," Dinkle clucked, going on to employ a surprisingly competent repertoire of Bible verses, praising me as a combination of Jesus Christ and Tom Sawyer, and generally captivating the congregation like a magician about to levitate a volunteer from the audience. I was heartily embarrassed and wriggled out from under his hand, putting enough space between us to make certain the lightning bolt likely to crash through the roof at any moment would merely lift the hairs on the back of my neck while turning a liar like Dinkle into a spent matchstick. He issued a fatherly chuckle after I pulled away.

"That's right, boy," he said. "Steer clear of the limelight and the limelight is more likely to find you again." It was an original aphorism among a host of pirated ones, but no one was surprised. Although Dinkle disdained community events, he was a regular at that panoply of aphorisms we knew as Methodist Sunday services. He never took communion, citing an allergy to grape juice and water crackers, a claim failing to dampen the suspicion that symbolic ingestion of the blood and body of Christ would cause him to burst into flames.

"But allow me get to the point, dear friends," Dinkle went on. "You are all about to embark on a journey with which I am familiar. I, too, came from modest means, but through a combination of hard work and luck, was able to attain the measure of comfort that presently describes my station in life. You, too, have worked hard, but luck has not brightened your doors… until now. Until young Connor OHalloran parted the clouds and allowed the sun to shine through."

Dinkle smiled at me, replacing the irresistibly smarmy expression he'd evinced at the beginning of his presentation with a rabid, facial scrawl. He clearly wanted me to bite the hook that had snagged a lip on nearly everyone else in the room.

Instead, I suddenly felt like a seal already on its way down a shark's throat.

"So now luck has smiled upon you," Dinkle went on. "But I think we can all agree that luck is not a bank account. It is not a mortgage payment or a pair of new shoes or a trip to San Francisco for dinner and a moving picture show. Luck is not collateral until that pot of gold at the end of the rainbow resides in a safety deposit box at the Sonoma State Bank. Am I right?"

A hum of assents rose up, and with that, Dinkle had them. He went on to describe his offer: He would establish lines of credit for those who wished to pony up their ambergris shares as collateral. Limits would be set at $10,000, the money available upon signature to prospective borrowers as early as the next day, the interest rate, "A very reasonable 5.5 percent. Just like one of those new government FHA mortgages you've probably read about," Dinkle revealed.

"These lines of credit will allow you to enjoy your good fortune now rather than suffering through the prolonged and cumbersome negotiation process with the perfume companies," Dinkle went on. "Of course, once the ambergris is sold to a perfumer, those of you taking advantage of my offer will be free to maintain the line-of-credit or pay it off with the accrued interest and close the account. It will be entirely your choice."

I glanced at the row of town leaders sharing the stage with Dinkle and me. C. Herbert Judson and Roger Johns revealed no emotions at all. Miss Lizzie and Fiona stared at the floor, arms crossed, tight lines where their mouths should be. James Throckmorton seemed pensively interested, but Coach Wally Buford was simply agog, sporting the same grin he'd displayed after his team's last win eight years previous, an expression of glee identical to nearly everyone else in the room. Suddenly, he leapt to his feet.

"Let's hear three cheers for Cyrus Dinkle," he cried out. "Hip hip…"

"Hooray!"

"Hip hip…"

"Hooray!"

"Hip hip…"

"Hooray!"

And that was that. The ball was rolling down the hill. There would be no stopping it.

CHAPTER EIGHT

The Boops and Skitch Peterson the Hornswoggler's auto sale

Cyrus Dinkle's offer collateralized the entirety of each person's ambergris shares, but represented less than ten percent of one's total holding. "Safe as a savings bond," Dinkle assured us. He knew it would dangle more temptation in front of folks' noses than any of them could withstand, hence the long line going out the door of city hall on the morning after the second town meeting. Dinkle had spurned Roger Johns's offer to have the lines of credit administrated by the Sonoma State Bank, preferring to handle the transactions through his own lending business. Accordingly, and for purposes of enrollment, he'd brought over two of his San Francisco employees, a couple of chippies with red lips, peroxided hair, and round fannies. The two blonde Betty Boops set up folding tables in the assembly room of the town hall, opened the doors, and started gathering signatures.

After Dinkle's time at the podium the night before, the old man had quickly exited to avoid entanglement in any serious mingling. Once he was gone, Roger Johns and C. Herbert Judson cautioned people.

"It's premature," Mr. Johns told them. "We won't know how much ambergris we really have until the perfumers perform their assays."

"You should negotiate with Dinkle," C. Herbert Judson

added. "He's asking each of you to leverage your entire holding against ten thousand dollars."

Coach Wally Buford countered with his opinion that Roger Johns and C. Herbert Judson were a couple of limp-wristed milk-toasts as the ambergris would be worth far more than $10,000 per household once it was sold.

"That puts a dent of less than ten percent into its eventual value. Don't seem like much of a risk to me," Coach Wally opined. "You boys can go ahead and look a gift horse in the mouth if it suits your fancy, but I ain't gonna."

Milton Garwood then reminded everyone that neither Roger Johns nor C. Herbert Judson nor anyone else could tell him what to do. Mr. Judson followed up with advice for folks to carefully read the agreements.

"I'd be happy to look them over," he said.

"Yeah, and how much is that gonna cost us?" Milton Garwood shouted. "Roger wants us to use his bank and you want us to pay you to read something we can damned well read for ourselves. Seems to me the two of you wanna bleed us dry before we've seen even one greenback."

There was a good deal of shouting after that, about one third in attendance agreeing with Milton and two thirds expressing less than flattering opinions about his intelligence, parentage, or hygiene. Skitch Peterson the Hornswoggler and car dealer, put an end to the dispute with his announcement of a not-to-be-missed sale of used autos to begin around the time the ink was dry on the first signed line of credit agreement and ending when he ran out of cars. Skitch put some emphasis on the idea of a limit to both his inventory and his charitable disposition, suggesting folks might want to sign the damned papers and get over to the sales lot sooner than later.

Fiona and Miss Lizzie watched all this go on with frowns. Miss Lizzie's father had moved to Tesoro from San Francisco to escape the snobbery attached to his family's big money.

49

However, the big money followed him and his sole heir, Miss Lizzie, didn't need or want an advance from Dinkle. She intended to use her ambergris shares to open a bigger clinic and recruit a real doctor to Tesoro. And Fiona? She was simply too savvy to be taken in by a high-end grifter like Cyrus Dinkle. She and her aunts had a small mortgage on the mercantile and another on the Kittiwake Inn next door and could think of nothing to buy that would justify increasing their indebtedness. Besides, Fiona agreed with C. Herbert Judson and reiterated her previous warning to me. "There will be fine print in those agreements. I guarantee it. A lot of fine print."

Like much of America in 1934, Tesoro was a man's world— at least that's what women wanted them to believe. As a practical matter it meant that most of the signatures collected by the Betty Boops were men's. Dinkle, of course, had counted on this, which explained his choice of loan officers for the transactions. Betty Boop Number One was a chirpy type, distracting a mark with chatter as she lifted his wallet. "Oh, no one ever reads anything past the first and last pages," she prattled to the men in a breathy voice, arching her back as if aiming her breasts at their dilated pupils. "It's all a lot of lawyer gobbledy-gook, anyway. I just hate gobbledy-gook, don't you? It gives me a headache. Do you know what I do to get rid of a headache? I take off every stitch of clothing and get into a nice hot bubble bath. Just soak in the bath as naked as a jaybird. I love that."

Of course, the red lips and platinum hair and round fanny and talk of nakedness pretty much did it for most fellows. They filled out their names on the first page and scribbled a signature on the last one, the intervening pages given a cursory review to ensure Chirpy Boop's impression of them as sufficiently manly insofar as financial affairs were concerned. Betty Boop Number Two looked much like her partner but was a Garbo type with a Russian accent, inducing men to quickly sign before she became too bored to continue offering glimpses of her substantial cleavage and shapely legs. The Boops were a good team, and by noon, Cyrus Dinkle had leveraged most folks in Tesoro up to their eyebrows.

Not everyone in town put a foot in Dinkle's snare. I mentioned the skepticism evinced by Roger Johns and C. Herbert Judson, and of course, Miss Lizzie and Fiona were openly disdainful. Angus MacCallum merely snorted when I asked what he might buy when there was cash in his pocket. "A fool and his money are soon parted, laddie," he said, "and only a fool would pat in wit' Cyrus Dinkle." While the Boops collected signatures at the town hall, Angus occupied the day in his usual way, scanning the sea from the observation deck of his lighthouse from 4:00 a.m. until breakfast, then beachcombing and generally wasting time until it was reasonable to pour himself a glass of rye whiskey. The other person sensible enough to stand outside the epidemic of buying about to infect Tesoro was the least likely candidate for such immunity: my mother, Mary Rose O'Halloran. At first I thought Ma didn't understand Dinkle's offer. I was wrong.

"Don't be fooled by Cyrus Dinkle," she told my brother and me. "He doesn't make offers. He baits hooks."

My mother had been better since I discovered the ambergris. I wanted to credit her improved state of mind to the impending life of wealth and comfort I'd earned by outrunning Angus MacCallum to a treasure on the beach. However, I admit it was more likely attributable to the concoction Miss Lizzie had prescribed to steady Ma's nerves. Miss Lizzie had experimented with a number of nostrums over the years to treat Ma's mood swings, including St. John's Wort, saffron, ginkgo beloba, folate, and zinc. She'd driven Ma to a shabby storefront in San Francisco's Chinatown, where a fellow peppered her with needles, and had once arranged for a consultation with a psychoanalyst who claimed to have studied his craft under the famous Swiss psychiatrist Carl Jung. Some of it worked for a while but none of it for long. At times I wished Miss Lizzie would give up. However, she was the type of person who had to finish what she'd started. Her latest formulation—a disgusting blend of cucumbers, tomatoes, eggs, seaweed, lemon, sugar cane, and mineral water—was a sickening green color and Ma had been advised to choke down nearly a quart of the awful stuff every day.

"I read about it in a medical journal. It's lithium-rich," Miss Lizzie told me when she dropped off the first batch, going on to unnecessarily report the findings of the scientific article in some detail. I tried to keep up, but Miss Lizzie had a habit of giving me credit for being smarter and more mature than I was, often expounding on politics I found incomprehensible or suggesting books to read I would consider daunting even now. It's not a bad thing to overestimate a boy's ability at a tender age to take in a jumble of facts and put them in proper order. It makes him expect more of himself. However, I suspect Miss Lizzie was more impressed with my ears than my intellect as I was willing to listen quietly at a time when too many men seemed determined put her in a place that made them feel better about their own shortcomings.

"I've high hopes for this one, Connor," she'd asserted in regard to the vegetable and seaweed mixture recommended in the medical journal. And after my mother had been on the new prescription for ten days such optimism seemed warranted. Ma's behavior was now normal a good deal of the time, although she seemed a bit baffled by Alex and me. I suspect she felt as if she'd gone to sleep when Alex was a baby and I a four-year-old and woken to a pair of shaggy-haired boys who liked to wrestle in the living room, gulp milk directly from the bottle, and shout when a whisper would suffice.

Ma was the town librarian before Dad left, but when her moods became too extreme, the library committee put her on a leave of absence. No one else in Tesoro understood the Dewey Decimal Classification, and readers were subsequently forced to use an honors system as Ma was too scattered or bedridden to man the big desk between the bookshelves. That's why I was surprised when she made an announcement right after I told her about the line out the door of the town hall and the goofy-faced men signing whatever the Betty Boops put in front of them.

"Maybe I'll head down to the library for a while," she said.

I was disappointed. For years, Ma hadn't left the house without Alex or me alongside. With folks flitting about town after signing their loan agreements, frantic to spend the money before Dinkle changed his mind, the scent of not-to-be-missed pandemonium was in the air and I wanted to witness it first-hand rather than be later regaled by Webb Garwood and his blowhard, big brother Tuck. Chaperoning Ma was not part of the plan.

"Want me to take you?" I asked her with exactly the sort of enthusiasm you'd expect from someone who wanted, instead, to head over to Skitch Peterson's car lot where there was a pretty good chance that the combination of Skitch's rapacious desire to sell cars and most fellows' ravenous appetites to buy them would result in some entertaining finger-pointing and profanity.

Ma shook her head, smiling. "No, you run along. I'll be fine."

"I'm serious, Ma. I'll go with you."

She laughed. "I'll be fine, you little old man," she said. "You don't have to take care of me."

I eyed her. Ma's hair was neatly brushed, her gaze level. She seemed fine. Besides, I had just been given permission to be irresponsible.

"Okay," I said, trying hard not to sound relieved.

I collared Alex and we met up with Webb, afterward hurrying across town to Peterson Autos. We climbed to a small rise overlooking the lot and took seats on an empty, table-sized cable spool PG&E workers had abandoned when they brought electricity to Tesoro a few years earlier. From there we watched as a fervently hearty Skitch Peterson greeted James Throckmorton, owner of the Last Resort Bar & Grill. James had signed his credit contract with little more than a glance at Chirpy Boop, unaffected by her physical charms and naked jaybird chatter on account of the heavy torch he'd been carrying for my mother since elementary school. James was a steady fellow and a town leader, who typically kept his head nearer his shoulders than his rear end. Nevertheless, he'd signed one of Dinkle's credit agreements without fully reading the thing and then headed directly to Peterson Autos where Skitch manipulated him into consideration of the philosophical conundrum posed by a 1927 Oldsmobile versus a 1931 Ford. James thought he might buy both cars to avoid hurting Skitch's feelings but came to his senses at the last minute when his father, old Axel, pointed out that he was not about to learn how to drive just because his damned fool son couldn't make a decision. James didn't need either car as he had a Chevy pickup used to transport spirits and soft drinks from San Rafael to Tesoro. Still, he bought the Olds, despite a twinge of reluctance he should have heeded, as you will see.

While Skitch would have loved to hit an auto dealer's daily double by selling two unneeded cars rather than just one, his disappointment was short-lived. Once folks began to wander over from the town hall with their brand-new Dinkle Company checkbooks, it became apparent that the number of buyers outweighed Skitch's inventory. Before long, to the delight of Alex and Webb and me, fellows were frenetically skittering about the car lot like bugs on the surface of a mud puddle—shouting, waving their arms around, and behaving, in general, just as badly as we'd hoped when we showed up to watch. There were a couple of near fistfights, with one buyer locking himself inside the 1931 Ford James Throckmorton had spurned. Despite panting and sweating like a Sumo wrestler, the obstinate and very overweight fellow refused to open the windows, cracking one just enough for Skitch to insert the purchase papers. Once the car was his, the new owner seemed to go into a trance. Skitch and a few of his customers stood around for a while, analyzing the situation.

"New car euphoria," Skitch proposed. "Seen it a million times."

Eventually, the onlookers reached a consensus that the man had passed out and Miss Lizzie was called. She had James Throckmorton break one of the car's windows in order to unlock the vehicle. Afterward, James and a few others hauled the patient into Skitch's office. While Skitch called C. Herbert Judson to check out his liability in the matter, Miss Lizzie revived the fellow with smelling salts and a glass of water, afterward making clear her preference for heat and stupidity over bliss as the cause of the man's swoon.

After the excitement settled down, Miss Lizzie returned to her apothecary and the retail mayhem proceeded. By mid-afternoon Skitch had sold every auto on his lot, and that's when another problem popped up—one that could not be blamed on heat, stupidity, or the ecstasy of new vehicle ownership; rather, it was a consequence of Skitch Peterson's hornswoggling.

Skitch had a practice of siphoning gas from an auto after he acquired it, leaving just enough in the tank for a new buyer to coast into the Sinclair station, a business he also owned. He then sold them new gas at a premium rate while unloading their old gas to a trucking outfit in Oakland. However, on the day of the Great Post-Boops Auto Sale, Skitch underestimated the excitement the event would generate and about half the new car owners eased up to the Sinclair station on fumes only to discover that the pumps had run dry. Milton Garwood then proved that Skitch wasn't the only opportunist in town by offering to hitch his team of horses to any car with an empty gas tank and an owner willing to part with two bucks. He spent the rest of the day towing cars. That night, he counted his money, added it to the ten grand Dinkle had made available to him on credit, and then made a deposit to his regular account in a Hills Brothers coffee can kept hidden in his crawlspace. Afterward, Milton announced to his wife that he had always wanted to own a monkey and intended to buy one.

CHAPTER NINE

Dinkle's man

There is a story inside my story, although I confess it has been dabbed with conjecture and a splash of rumor. It is the story of Dinkle's man, Sergei Yurievsky, and I will tell it as I think he might.

Despite sharing a surname with Prince Georgy Alexandrovich Yurievsky—uncle to the last tsar of Russia—Dinkle's man was not a royal but the son of a minor Moscow government functionary, a pencil-pusher whose bloodline prohibited his only son from rising above the rank of sergeant in the Russian Imperial Army. In that respect Yurievsky was lucky, not that a sergeant needs luck. I was in the army, too, and know that sergeants make their own luck. Nevertheless, he was a commoner and fortunate to be one in 1917, the year Russia finally grew tired of tsars and tsarinas. This is neither conjecture nor rumor. It is indisputable fact.

It is a fact, as well, that in the early summer of 1934, Yurievsky spent most mornings in the garage of the Dinkle estate, washing the already spotless Duesenberg or tinkering with it. Indeed, about three weeks after Milton Garwood began monkey shopping, Yurievsky was preparing the car for his employer's weekly trip to San Francisco. The morning was hot and not for the first time Yurievsky mourned the loss of the icy days and gray skies that had distinguished his native Russia from northern California. He mourned another loss as well: his past life with Olga and their daughter, Irina. He had first met

57

Olga when she was only a bit older than Miss Littleleaf, the young woman in the village who ran the mercantile. Irina, the girl he had nicknamed *Myshka*—his little mouse—would now be the same age as the postmistress were she still alive.

Dinkle's man added polish to his rag and applied it to the fender of the Duesenberg. Something was going on in the village. Miss Littleleaf and the lawyer's wife had been in the mercantile the previous day when he retrieved the old man's mail. With his appearance, their eyes had widened, their voices becoming whispers. He was familiar with such behavior. The morning after the Mad Monk was killed, the whispers had followed Yurievsky wherever he went.

It had been eighteen years since Grand Duke Pavlovich enlisted Yurievsky—now Dinkle's man—to be the lookout in a plot to assassinate Rasputin the Mad Monk. It had not gone well. Rasputin's body had miraculously resisted the poison, and they'd been forced to shoot him, afterward pitching his body off the Bolshoi Petrovsky Bridge. The conspirators, except for Yurievsky, were officers. They were better equipped to order a job done than to actually do it. They bungled things. There was blood left on the bridge and a galosh. The body was not weighted and didn't sink. Within hours the conspirators were exposed and caught: Usupov, Grand Duke Pavlovich, the fascist Purishkevich, Lieutenant Sukhotin, and the driver of their getaway car, Lazovert.

Pavlovich was exiled to the Persian Front. He took his aide, Yurievsky, with him. Olga and four-year-old Irina remained behind in St. Petersburg, waving from the train platform, their figures slowly enshrouded in steam as the cars pulled away from the station. "Things will settle down and I'll return," Yurievsky assured his wife and daughter. But then came October and the Revolution. Yurievsky was inextricably linked to Pavlovich and the aristocracy. He could not return. One more letter came from Olga. *It is chaos here*, she wrote. *We will try for Paris. If not, we will go east.* And then they disappeared.

After the Revolution and the end of the Great War, he went with Pavlovich to Paris and then London. They parted ways. Yurievsky heard that many Russians were in New York City. He booked passage, found one of the other conspirators—Lazovert, the doctor. "The Bolsheviks killed or exiled everyone even remotely connected to the Romanov's," Lazovert told him. Some were in America, but not Olga and Irina. "They might be in China," the doctor thought, "...or Siberia."

For nearly twenty years Yurievsky had been searching: London, Paris, Istanbul, New York. He slipped back into Russia through its Georgian underbelly and followed breadcrumbs to Moscow and St. Petersburg before trekking eastward to Siberia and China. He met a great-niece to Grand Duke Mikhailovich in Harbin who thought she recognized the faces in the tattered photo. Shanghai, she thought, or perhaps Peking. His money was gone by then. He became a mercenary, serving first as a soldier and then an assassin for a Chinese warlord. He worked as an enforcer for a Filipino strongman, a bodyguard for a British businessman in Hong Kong.

The years passed and he almost gave up. And then a whore in Macao thought one of the faces was familiar. "I once saw a woman who looked like the child in this photo," she told him. "It was in Vladivostok. She wanted to go to Shanghai. She was a prostitute like me." Eventually, Yurievsky followed the clues to San Francisco, where he answered an ad for a fellow who might combine the roles of valet, butler, and chauffeur into a single position. He was hired, and by the time our ambergris washed up on the beach, the former soldier had resided in the apartment over the garage of the Dinkle estate for almost six years, no longer Sergeant Sergei Yurievsky of the Russian Imperial Army but Dinkle's man.

Yurievsky finished polishing the Duesenberg and drove it to the front of the main house. The small white stones of the driveway crunched beneath the tires, the sound reminiscent of boots on crusted snow. The old man came out and crawled into the back seat, immediately burying his face in a newspaper. He was alone, for which Yurievsky was grateful. Dinkle was often accompanied by the two female vipers from San Francisco. One was Russian. She spoke little and always in English, as if ashamed of her native language. The other was such a chatterbox that it took great restraint for Yurievsky not to strangle her. This morning the two men would mercifully traverse the thirty miles to San Francisco without company or the exchange of a single word, sharing their affection for silence. They shared nothing else.

Dinkle's man steered the Duesenberg through the open gate of the estate and then along a narrow unpaved road. They traversed the mile to the main body of the village and then slowly drove past the dark-windowed bar & grill, the tourist shops, and the mercantile. Fiona Littleleaf stood outside her store. She lifted a hand as they passed. Dinkle ignored her, but Yurievsky glanced over and nodded, a formal and stylized gesture he had learned from Grand Duke Pavlovich, the nuanced movement both conveying respect and suggesting intimacy.

They drove on to the city where he dropped off his employer in front of a building on Market Street. The old man went inside and Yurievsky drove to Fisherman's Wharf where he bought a bold coffee from one of the street vendors and then sat on a splintered dock, watching the sea lions bellow. He figured the old man wouldn't need him for at least two hours, free time the tall Russian might previously have used to visit three or four Barbary coast whorehouses along a section of Pacific Avenue between Chinatown and North Beach. It had been a routine part of his early days in San Francisco, a time when he had yet to become Dinkle's man. The women in the houses had enthusiastically accepted his money, both curious and grateful that he desired merely answers. Each time he had stepped into one of the stale, carnally decorated parlors, he'd prayed that he might find Olga; prayed perhaps harder that he wouldn't.

He no longer visited the houses, the women quickly learning that fabricated clues and real ones paid the same. Nevertheless, Yurievsky had yet to give up. He might yet uncover a new trail—perhaps with the old man's help. Dinkle's tendrils were long and reached dark places. *Perhaps,* Yurievsky mused as one of the sea lions issued a great bark and then slipped off the dock and into the water. *Perhaps.*

CHAPTER TEN

The Zenith Stratosphere, a monkey, and a jeweled commode

After the Great Post-Boops Auto Sale and Gasoline Scam, Milton Garwood's monkey aspirations were temporarily confounded as he wasn't sure how to go about purchasing one. He first consulted the *Montgomery Ward* catalog. It proved to be woefully monkey-deficient as did *Sears, Roebuck and Company*, a lapse in customer service that might have put him in a sour mood had he not run across an ad in the *San Francisco Chronicle* for the new Zenith Stratosphere Model 1000Z, the finest radio of its day and one that saw a mere 350 models roll off the production line. Temporarily placing his monkey shopping on hold Milton determined to acquire one of Stratospheres as quickly as possible, figuring he would blast the speakers at peak volume to make sure everyone in town knew he had it.

"It ain't just a radio," he claimed to a group of fellows loitering around at the Last Resort. "It's both a work of art and a workhorse...More than four feet high with a wood veneer cabinet, walnut inlay, top-notch speakers, and fifty watts of output. It'll cost me seven hundred fifty dollars, but mark my words, by 1950 that radio will be worth twice that if not more."

Milton didn't have a radio; indeed, he knew nothing about them despite his regurgitation of the Stratosphere's ad copy. He'd only listened to a couple of programs—*Death Valley Days* and *The Jack Benny Show*—favorites of neighbor C. Herbert Judson, who made a habit of leaving his den window open most evenings. However, Milton had reached the sixth decade of his life and was beginning to wonder if it had all been worth it. He figured a Stratosphere could provide exactly the sort of testimonial that would shout, "Milton Garwood was here," to those unimpressed with his years of service as the town blacksmith and welder. Not long thereafter Angus MacCallum popped a hole in Milton's crankcase by opining that no radio was worth seven hundred fifty dollars as a person could buy an entire house in a dustbowl state like Oklahoma for the exact same amount. "Besides, we git a radio signal here in Tesoro aboot a quarter of the time, if that. Yer wastin' your money, Garwood. I'd nae be doin' it if I were ye," he told Milton.

I have previously established that no one, in general, could tell Milton Garwood *what* to do and Angus MacCallum, specifically, was not invited to advise him what he *should* do. However, as Angus was a prudent penny-pincher of some renown, Milton was uneasy enough to seek out an alternative vendor who might mitigate his investment risk. After checking around it turned out that Skitch Peterson knew a fellow in Oakland with some fell-off-the-back-of-a-truck contacts who thought he might lay his hands on a Stratosphere for five hundred dollars plus ten percent for his trouble. So, Milton convinced James Throck-morton to test out his recently purchased 1927 Olds with a trip to Oakland where our town blacksmith vetted the discounter, determining that he seemed legitimate. James later reported that the man had heavily pomaded hair, a tonsorial feature most in Tesoro equated with disingenuousness. However, Milton had the Stratosphere bit in his teeth by then and wrote the fellow a check from his line of credit for the full amount. That was the last he heard in regard to both the check, which was cashed, and the black-market Zenith Stratosphere Model 1000Z, which was never delivered. From that day forward Milton Garwood began each morning by driving his buckboard and its team of horses to the street fronting Skitch's house, waiting until the horses had dropped their business on Skitch's lawn jockey before moving on. The swindle also leap-frogged "New Monkey" back to the top of Milton's wish list.

The next day Milton popped into the mercantile to see if Fiona Littleleaf's produce supplier could add a monkey to his regular delivery. "He brings bananas," he reasoned. "I figure that where there's bananas, there's likely to be monkeys." Fiona had little patience for such nonsense and shooed him out. Milton next went to the library where he was surprised but quite happy to see Ma behind the big desk.

"What monkeys make good pets?" he asked her.

Ma spent a little time going through the card catalogues before leading Milton to a back section of the library where they found a monograph on Capuchin "organ-grinder's" monkeys. On the cover was a picture of a tiny, dark-furred creature with a halo of blonde hair wreathing its baby face. Milton was delighted.

"This is perfect," he told Ma. "I'll walk around town with one of these little bastards on my shoulder and people will say, 'There goes Milton Garwood and his trained monkey.' And I will train him, too. I'll teach him how to retrieve my newspaper and open beer bottles and play the harmonica. It'll be better than having a Zenith Stratosphere."

He grinned at Ma. "So, where can I get one?"

"I don't know," Ma answered. "A pet store?"

There were no pet stores in Tesoro and Milton couldn't buy a new car to drive to San Francisco as his now-bitter enemy, Skitch Peterson, was the only dealer in town and Milton didn't know how to drive, anyway, still relying on the horse-drawn wagon he'd inherited from his father. However, James Throckmorton went into the city for the afternoon every week or two to see the minor-league San Francisco Seals play baseball, and he agreed to let Milton hitch a ride on his next trip. Not long thereafter, Milton had his monkey, a creature he named Mr. Sprinkles.

A buying frenzy had gripped Tesoro. Remember that the carrot on Dinkle's stick was dangled during the Great Depression, a terrible time at least partly to blame for my father running out on us, given his already inconsistent acquaintance with a regular paycheck. I didn't know Seamus O'Halloran well. He left when I was four. I've seen pictures and know he was handsome; his hair dark and thick and curly, the end of his nose round like a little ball. The only other memory I have is of someone who was very tall.

Angus MacCallum once described him for me as, "a fella unwillin' to do the work that connect a long reach wit' a short grasp." That probably explains why he tried on so many jobs but never found one that fit. At various times Dad was a salesman, a journalist, a novelist, an actor, a prospector, a bookkeeper, a beekeeper, and a barkeeper. He wasn't much of a father, although I remain amazed that he didn't catch the scent of treasure in the air when I discovered the ambergris on the beach, returning to lay claim to his old chair at the head of a much more solvent table than the one he deserted after Alex was born.

As far as that goes, people in Tesoro had not only caught the scent of treasure; indeed, Dinkle's lines of credit now threatened to asphyxiate them in a cloud of cupidity. They wrote checks for clothes and jewelry and appliances. They bought sofas and mattresses and china and knick-knacks and knick-knack shelves. One woman ordered a chandelier with globes shaped like the heads of Presidents Washington, Jefferson, Lincoln, and Theodore Roosevelt, another an entire Craftsman house kit from *Sears, Roebuck and Company*. James Throckmorton's father, Axel, had been widowed for more than a decade, and although he'd sworn never to consort with another woman after his beloved Lillian died, years of going to sleep in an otherwise empty bed joined to a line of credit from Cyrus Dinkle was simply too much enticement.

"I'm gettin' me a mail-order bride," he announced to his son, owner of the Last Resort Bar & Grill. "I'm tired of being alone. I ain't got that many years left and I'd like to have someone warm my feet under the covers."

After Coach Wally Buford's wife, Judy, packed their house full of so much furniture they had to squeeze through it all sideways, she sent off for a porcelain commode with a jeweled seat cover. "You can't get one of these from Sears or Montgomery Ward," she told her friends. "It's a special order, custom-made item. Definitely not pedestrian." Judy had received a Word-of-the-Day calendar from Coach Wally on her last birthday and "pedestrian" happened to land on the same date she ordered her commode. Of course, hardly anyone in Tesoro understood Judy's use of the word in that context, but the more perplexing question attached to her purchase was the lack of a sewer system in our town.

A few of the wealthier folks—Cyrus Dinkle, Miss Lizzie, Roger Johns the Banker, and C. Herbert Judson the Lawyer—had septic tanks and indoor sewer plumbing, but the rest of us, including the Bufords, trudged to an outhouse each morning after arising and just before retiring at night. Judy was undeterred, figuring a septic tank was in the Buford future once their ambergris ship came in, and she filled out the order form for the commode, wrote a check from the line of credit Dinkle had set up for them, and then spent several days making certain that everyone in Tesoro knew what was coming and how much it cost.

The plumbing fixture arrived in Oakland on a Thursday and Coach Wally drove over to pick it up. A sizable crowd was on his front walk when he returned, anxious to *ooh* and *aah* when the thing was uncrated. Judy and Coach Wally happily accommodated the looky-loo's and before long the toilet sat white and gleaming atop its palette like a king about to be crowned. Wally attached the wooden oval seat and then unveiled the coronet: a cover encrusted in fake rubies, emeralds, and sapphires. He held it up for the crowd to behold, like a boxer displaying his championship belt, and then fastened it in place, afterward puffing out his chest and squeezing Judy's hand as they basked in the chorus of "Well, I nevers" and "Don't that beat alls" that poured out of the assembled onlookers. After the hubbub settled down, Coach Wally had a couple of his high school football players haul the commode inside where he and Judy contemplated the dilemma of where to put it in a house without indoor sewer plumbing.

"Eventually, we'll have a real, big-city lavatory," Judy asserted, "so we should put it where we think a proper bathroom might go." The Buford residence was a nice little house but had only enough space for a couple of bedrooms, a living room, dining room, and kitchen, so they put the commode under the stairs while Judy worked on design plans. She took over the kitchen table with a pad of paper and a newly sharpened pencil. A day or so later the pencil and its eraser were nubs and the kitchen floor was littered with crumpled balls of rejected lavatory drawings. "There's no place to put a bathroom," she complained to her husband. "We'll have to add on."

Coach Wally was a creature of habit and ordinarily blew a gasket if even a scent of change in his routine was in the air. However, he kept his cool when Judy apprised him of her conclusion because he never listened to his wife, and with his tacit consent, she set about planning the renovation. In the meantime, however, Judy felt the commode deserved a more prominent position in the Buford furniture hierarchy.

She first made Coach Wally haul it into the living room where she tested out several locations before ordering him to place it next to the sofa. A day or so later she had him move it to the head of the dining table, and then to the kitchen where the coach put his foot down. "That's it," he told Judy. "This damned thing weighs a ton. I ain't movin' it again. I didn't want it to begin with." Still, once the commode had settled into Coach Wally's favorite room, he managed to look past his initial disdain. Indeed, he eventually took a real shine to the thing, perching on it when he had his morning coffee and read the paper, anticipating its special purpose by doing so with the jeweled lid up and his underwear down to his ankles, a bathrobe tastefully shielding Judy from unnecessary glimpses of his manhood.

Now, I can promise you that when a fellow adopts such a position for an extended period of time his physiology will begin to advance some pretty insistent mandates, and it wasn't long before Coach Wally was reading the sports section or cheating on his crossword puzzle while filling the air around him with gas that made the disgusting, black coating of the ambergris I'd discovered on the beach smell like lavender. Eventually, Judy ordered her husband to take his coffee on the porch, but Coach Wally had fallen deeply in love with the jeweled commode by then and refused to budge unless the toilet went with him. That's how it ended up on their front porch with Coach Wally atop the thing each morning, his coffee and a cigarette always in hand, a bathrobe making certain that passers-by would be titillated by nothing more provocative than a set of hairless and veiny ankles.

It had been one month since I discovered the ambergris on the beach and Tesoro had changed from a sleepy little seaside village to a bastion of consumerism, home to a commode with a jeweled seat cover and an organ-grinder's monkey named Mr. Sprinkles. It would soon change again.

CHAPTER ELEVEN

Mr. and Mrs. C. Herbert Judson

Our ambergris came to reside in C. Herbert Judson's boathouse after Angus MacCallum suggested that exposure to salt water might transform more of the foul, black-gray crust and its brown, waxy undercoat to sweet, lucrative ambergris. The boathouse—a floating, wood-frame garage with a tin roof—had once been painted red, but weather and the sea had beaten the siding into the dull pink-gray of the Tesoro sky at dawn. Inside were narrow walkways and a spider's web of ropes and pulleys used to lift Mr. Judson's boat out of the water should the hull need to be scraped or repainted. There was a single door on the landward side of the structure with double doors on the seaward side, allowing the *C. Breeze* to be put out or docked without leaving the water. Before the ambergris was relocated, the place smelled of salt water and barnacles with a hint of rot, the lower edges of the wood siding dark and ragged from years of exposure to the sea. Afterward, it smelled like the worst outhouse one can imagine.

Guards from a list of volunteers had been posted around the clock in twelve-hour shifts since moving the ambergris from the beach to the boathouse. It was tedious duty, particularly at night, and most of the assigned guards were dozing when I rode my bicycle past the place around 6:00 a.m. every day. I delivered papers for the *San Francisco Chronicle*, the newspaper that would eventually employ me as a writer. I had a large route, a significant number of folks in Tesoro relying on a big city paper to keep them abreast of which politician in Sacramento or Washington D Almighty C deserved to be shot as well as the latest goings-on with *Dick Tracy* and the *Katzenjammer Kids*. I also carried for our own *Tesoro Town Crier*, a weekly publication devoted to local issues and happenings.

It was mid-July, the summer half over, and Ma was back at the library full-time, her moods so smoothed by Miss Lizzie's nauseating potion that she seemed tantalizingly normal. Unfortunately, as Ma became more clear-headed, the rest of Tesoro went crazier. Once people wearied of buying things they began to consider how money might help them settle family squabbles or disputes with neighbors. There were a couple of petitions for separation and so many lawsuits that C. Herbert Judson was no longer able to shutter his office and go sailing whenever he pleased.

Mr. Judson was a subscriber to the *Chronicle* and my first delivery each day. Before the ambergris turned up on the beach, his windows were dark each morning and I quietly slipped his paper under the mat rather than toss it against the front door. However, with the promiscuous proliferation of lawsuits, more often than not I now found him sitting on his porch swing, reading a document, contemplating the sunrise, or just staring at the immaculately painted floorboards. "Top of the morning, Connor," he always said.

Sometimes his wife, Mrs. C. Herbert Judson, sat with him, a hand stroking the back of his neck, her legs curled up beneath a fuzzy bathrobe so oversized it must surely have been her husband's. She was a handsome woman although I thought her ancient, a callous and immature appraisal that now amuses me. In 1934, Mrs. C. Herbert Judson was probably in her early fifties—far from ancient—and second only to Fiona Littleleaf as the most beautiful woman in Tesoro. She and her husband were very much in love and had given the tongue-waggers a workout when they arrived from San Francisco, walking about town hand-in-hand and occasionally kissing each other full on the mouth right out in the open where anyone could see them.

C. Herbert Judson had been a big deal lawyer in the city, a founding partner in his firm and a man with photos on his office wall that showed him hobnobbing with some impressively famous people of the early twentieth century: Teddy Roosevelt, Woodrow Wilson, Thomas Edison, Stanford White. A vigorous man with hair more the color of ash than charcoal, he was not young and yet I remember him as youthful. Mrs. C. Herbert Judson had been a prominent socialite in the city, chairperson of organizations populated by photogenic women with rich husbands. She was as charming as she was beautiful and had been a favorite at the various theater, symphony, and ballet openings, always in the latest fashion from New York or Paris.

That the Judsons appeared at all in Tesoro was a surprise. Mr. Judson, an avid sailor, claimed to have heeded a call from the sea. Mrs. C. Herbert Judson was less enthusiastic about sailing—prone to seasickness and fearful of underwater creatures. She loved her husband but generally spurned the pitch and sway of his twenty-eight-foot sloop, the *C. Breeze,* in favor of tea with Fiona and Miss Lizzie or an excursion to San Francisco.

There were no Judson children for reasons I suspect to have been biological, as both Mr. and Mrs. Judson liked children a great deal—dressing in costumes for Halloween, leading caroling parties at Christmas, and opening their spacious lawn for Easter egg hunts. They cheered for the Tesoro High Seagulls, attended school plays and concerts that featured other people's kids, and organized beach weenie roasts in the fall. It might seem Mr. Judson's sailing left his wife too much on her own inside their huge Victorian at the landward edge of town, but they were blessed with a decent number of nieces and nephews as well as a good many friends from San Francisco and elsewhere, their four stylishly appointed guestrooms rarely unoccupied.

Upon moving to Tesoro, C. Herbert Judson's pedigree had been immediately joined to the fact that anyone from San Francisco whose name began with an initial was automatically enveloped in a cachet of respect and dignity. This installed him as a town leader, a trust he subsequently justified, offering sound advice in a calm manner. Unlike Coach Wally Buford, who seemed determined to engage in a pissing contest with the rest of the town leaders, Mr. Judson was never overbearing, unfailingly polite, and would have been just as likeable as Roger Johns the Banker had we not all been a little daunted by his unpretentious use of words like "estop" and "subrogate."

A week after the Fourth of July, I was up earlier than usual, unable to sleep on a night that lacked its typical cooling breeze from the sea. I picked up my papers at the Sinclair station—the drop-off used by the fellow from the *Chronicle* who serviced most of the coastal villages and towns north of the bay—then pedaled off, reaching C. Herbert Judson's house by 5:30 a.m. Mr. Judson sat on the porch swing, reading from a sheaf of papers in the pale light of early morning, a cup of coffee in one hand, a stack of files on the wooden porch floor. Unlike many men who reach their fifties with a bald pate and substantial belly, he had remained fit with all his hair and a complexion healthily bronzed by sun and saltwater spray.

"Top of the morning, Connor," he called out.

"Hi, Mister Judson," I answered. I hopped off my bike, climbed the steps, and took a seat next to him on the swing. From there I could easily read the print at the top of his document:

Axel Throckmorton v. Harvey Fu Chang

I wasn't surprised. Given the epidemic of litiginitis that had infected Tesoro, it was predictable that old Axel would end up suing the fellow who had sold him his mail-order bride.

The notion of buying a wife likely seems old-fashioned and quite odd in today's world with its steady diet of unmarried folks carrying on with one another on cable television. But I can assure you that it was already old-fashioned and odd in my day, too, given that such transactions were already in the sunset of their time in 1934. Keep in mind, however, that old Axel was in the sunset of his own time, too, figuring he lacked both the stamina and the timeline for an extended courtship. Thus, a few days after signing his line of credit agreement with the Boop who looked like Garbo and spoke with a Russian accent, Axel had caught a ride with his son to San Francisco where James cheered on the baseball Seals, giving the old man plenty of time to canvass restaurants and shops in Chinatown. After being thrown out of several establishments, the evictions accompanied by a good deal of mixed Chinese-English profanity, Axel came across Harvey Fu Chang, a fellow who traded in imports, exports, opium, and mail-order brides. Harvey and Axel struck a deal, and a week or so later, a fiancée named Mei Ling was scheduled for delivery.

On the night the transaction was to be completed, James accompanied his father. He was opposed to old Axel's engagement but was even more opposed to the idea of a contract finalized at midnight in the shadows of a dimly lit Chinatown alley. So he fired up his recently acquired 1927 Olds, and the two men made it into the city shortly before the appointed time. They found the designated alley just off Grant and Clay with about five minutes to spare and eased up to the rear of the importer's store. Axel had donned a suit and tie for the occasion and carried a bouquet of roses for his new fiancée. However, the flowers threatened to wilt as visibly as the old man's expression when sixteen-year-old Mei Ling stepped out of the shadows and into the pale halo of light provided by a single, forlorn bulb on the rear face of the fellow's establishment.

"Why, she ain't but a kid!" Axel exclaimed. He glared at the mail-order bride vendor, Harvey Fu Chang. "You were supposed to get me a woman fit for marriage. This one's young enough to be my granddaughter."

Axel and Harvey then engaged in a heated discussion, the savvy Chinese fellow suddenly losing his grasp of the same English language he'd grasped pretty darned well a few minutes earlier. Regardless, both men seemed to fully understand one another, with Axel making clear that he didn't appreciate being hornswoggled and Harvey conveying his No Exchange-No Return policy. The discussion came to an end when Harvey produced a windstorm of profanity in perfect English along with a pistol. James promptly grabbed his father with one hand and the girl with the other, dragging the pair of them back to his car. Minutes later they were on the way to Tesoro with old Axel in the front seat and Mei Ling in the back. Once there, they woke up Miss Lizzie. She answered the door in her bathrobe, a shotgun in one hand.

"Axel…James! What on earth are you thinking? Do you know what time it is?"

She likely had more to say but went mute when Mei Ling emerged from the back of James's car, the young woman's eyes dark and a trifle fierce, her face otherwise expressionless.

"Oh, my goodness," Miss Lizzie whispered.

Like everyone else in town she had figured Axel's impending mail-order nuptials would be a May-December arrangement. However, neither Miss Lizzie nor an obviously disappointed Axel had expected fifty years in age to separate bride and groom—the May end of the relationship well into the twentieth century while the December side was about three decades into the back end of the nineteenth.

"I ain't gonna engage in no connubial bliss with a child," Axel huffed.

"I should think not," Miss Lizzie answered.

She agreed to take the girl off their hands until Axel figured out what to do. So far, suing the broker was as far as he'd gotten, hence the document *Axel Throckmorton v. Harvey Fu Chang* that occupied C. Herbert Judson when I joined him on the porch.

Mr. Judson set aside Axel's petition to the court and took the newspaper I'd brought him. He glanced at the headline.

"You're up early," he said, at the same time turning to the sports page. "What's going on?"

"Couldn't sleep," I told him.

"Me neither," he said. "Too hot."

We sat together. I listened to the trill and rustle of birds in the trees that populated Mr. Judson's yard. He scanned the newspaper, leafing through its pages quickly as the last of the night crept off and morning took over. After a few minutes, he put the paper aside, then selected a new file from the stack on the porch floor. He read silently for only a few seconds before closing the folder.

"Money changes people, Connor," he said, sighing.

I nodded.

"I'm not supposed to tell you this...attorney-client privilege and all that," he said, gesturing with the folder, "but here's a man suing his wife for grinding her teeth and keeping him awake. I had just about convinced him to drop the whole darned thing when she found some ambulance chaser in the city who filed a countersuit claiming that her husband is so annoying, she's ground her teeth to nubs from the aggravation of living with him."

He sighed again. "What's wrong with people?" he said.

I remained quiet. I was only ten years old but recognized a rhetorical question when it came my way. Mr. Judson looked at me and smiled. "You're a good man, Connor O'Halloran."

"Thanks," I said.

"What do you want to be when you grow up?"

"I don't know. I like newspapers. Maybe I'll work for the

Chronicle…Take over for the guy who drops off my papers at the Sinclair station."

Mr. Judson laughed.

"I think you'll do better than that," he said.

I didn't answer and was suddenly very uncomfortable as I sensed some wisdom or life lesson about to be tossed at me. I liked Mr. Judson, but he offered a lot of advice—a professional hazard, I suspect, given that he was in the advice-offering business. A good deal of what he suggested remains with me even now. However, at ten years old such perspicacity tended to remind me of how little time was left before I was thrust into the world of paystubs and taxes and mouths to feed. After all, it was my summer vacation.

"I guess I'd better go now," I said, climbing off the porch swing. I moved toward the steps as quickly as I could, but it was too late.

"Just be a man people can count on, Connor," Mr. Judson said.

"Okay, I will," I answered. I kept moving.

"And find yourself a good woman," he added.

"Yes, sir."

The screen door to the house opened and Mrs. C. Herbert Judson appeared. She wore her husband's huge, fuzzy bathrobe with no evidence of pajamas or a nightgown beneath it. Her feet were bare and her hair tousled in the way a woman's hair gets tousled behind a bedroom door. She was devoid of makeup and quite beautiful, rendering me suddenly and very unexpectedly stupefied. I have no idea what expression was on my face, although the amusement on hers makes me suspect mine to have been equal parts bedazzled and electrocuted.

"Good morning, Connor," she said, smiling. "Have you had breakfast? Would you like something?" She seemed anxious to entertain a guest, even a ten-year-old one. I didn't answer. I couldn't.

"Connor? Are you okay?"

She moved to the swing and sat next to her husband, one leg tucked beneath her, the other dangling provocatively below the edge of her robe. Her skin was smooth, her cheekbones high, her eyes alternately green and hazel. For the first time, but not the last, I was aware that Mrs. C. Herbert Judson was a knockout.

"Are you okay, Connor?" she repeated, her lips curled into the tiniest wisp of a smile—the sort a woman gets when a young fellow looks as if he's taken too many rides on a roller coaster and can't decide if he's delirious with excitement or just flat-out delirious. I hastily raked fingers through hair I knew to be a tangled wad of yarn, wishing I hadn't scrambled from bed and dashed out to deliver papers before running a comb through it.

"I'm fine," I managed. "I have to get going."

I stumbled down the walk, climbed onto my bicycle, and headed off, pondering mail-order brides and the case of *Axel Throckmorton v. Harvey Fu Chang* and Mr. Judson's advice. Before turning the corner at the end of the block, I looked back. Mrs. C. Herbert Judson sat next to her husband on the porch swing, a hand along the back of his neck. Even now I think it one of the most intimate things I have ever seen, and I determined more than ever to someday put myself on a porch swing with Fiona Littleleaf's hand stroking the back of my neck.

CHAPTER TWELVE

The Allegheny Chemicals Corporation

Mr. Sprinkles turned out to be a disappointment for Milton Garwood, displaying little interest in retrieving his newspaper, opening his beer bottles, or playing the harmonica. He preferred to urinate and defecate all over the Garwood house, repeatedly demonstrating a particular affection for the commemorative bowl Mrs. Garwood had acquired during the 1915 Panama-Pacific International Exposition in San Francisco. Prominently displayed on the dining room table, the bowl's potpourri was now routinely mixed with less delicately scented organic material, considerably diminishing the luster of monkey ownership for Milton's wife. Eventually, she encouraged Mr. Sprinkles to escape with a broom and an open door. He quickly turned feral, foraging for food in compost piles and overturning trashcans.

His predilection for demonstrative evacuation of his bowels continued and he took a liking to the commode on Coach Wally Buford's front porch, expertly flipping up the jeweled seat cover in order to leave a prize selected especially for the coach and his wife. The Bufords quite reasonably were not excited to put their commode to its foreordained use before a septic tank had been installed, and after they filed a lawsuit against the Garwoods, Milton used an orange to lure Mr. Sprinkles back into his cage, eventually giving the monkey to a woman who maintained an exotic animal preserve in Petaluma.

Meanwhile, the negotiating committee for our ambergris—

Roger Johns the Banker, C. Herbert Judson the Lawyer, and Miss Lizzie Fryberg—had been in discussion with several perfume makers, including Chanel, Guerlain's, Dana, and Jean Patou. All four companies had made bids—dependent on confirmation of the purity of our ambergris—although none wanted the entire specimen, and it appeared we would have to apportion it among the competitors. "The perfumers know this and their bids are a bit lower as a result," Mr. Johns reported in a letter to the ambergris stockholders. Still, our agents anticipated a yield between $1200 and $1500 per ounce, a handsome set of offers and well above the credit limits Dinkle had established for those who signed papers for the Betty Boops. The committee was about to schedule visits for the perfumery analysts when a letter arrived at C. Herbert Judson's office.

22 JULY 1934

DEAR MESSRS. JOHNS AND JUDSON, MISS FRYBERG, AND TESORO AMBERGRIS STOCKHOLDERS:

WE ARE MOST INTERESTED IN PROCURING YOUR ENTIRE INVENTORY OF AMBERGRIS AND WISH TO SCHEDULE AN APPOINTMENT TO ALLOW OUR ANALYST, MR. EVERSON DEXTER, TO CONDUCT AN ASSAY. WE ARE PREPARED TO PAY $2845 PER OUNCE, PENDING MR. DEXTER'S ANALYSIS OF YOUR SPECIMEN.

SINCERELY,
J. PIEDMONT BELL
PRESIDENT, ALLEGHENY CHEMICALS CORP.

"They must want it pretty bad, to bid it up like that," Milton Garwood suggested to the boys at the Last Resort.

I was there, collecting for my paper route from the owner, James Throckmorton. Like most newsboys I didn't like collections. My older customers forced me to come in and look over their stamp collections or family heirlooms, the younger ones had to be chased down at work, and of course, I had my share of weasels who refused to answer the door, peeking out through a crack in the blinds until sure I had given up and left. James Throckmorton always paid on time. Better yet, he let me hang out at the Last Resort and listen to the talk, so long as it wasn't too salty. I loved the Last Resort with its massive, polished bar, dim lighting, and tantalizing odor of sizzling hamburgers, grilled onions, and spilled beer. James seemed to like having me around, too, peppering me with questions about Ma: *How is she? Does she like being back at the library? Is she doing anything for fun?* Back in high school he and my mother had been sewn to each other's hips, spooning in the back seat of James's car and making the promises teenagers make to one another. After they graduated Ma went off to college, leaving James in Tesoro, and as happens with young love, the promises burned for a time and then didn't.

I sat at the bar and listened to Milton Garwood carry on, nursing an RC Cola I'd poured into a glass, adding salted peanuts to give it a thick foam collar like the beers James tapped off for his other customers. I liked to listen to the men talk at the Last Resort as I had been mostly raised by women to that point—Ma and Miss Lizzie and Fiona—and figured I needed to learn how to cuss and spit and authoritatively hold forth on things I knew little about. James kept the cussing and spitting to a minimum when I was around, but there was plenty of holding forth, a lot of it from regulars Milton Garwood, Angus MacCallum, and James's father, old Axel Throckmorton. The mysterious letter and offer from the Allegheny Chemicals Corporation were the topics of that day.

"Seems to me they ain't paying that kind of money to make perfume," Milton speculated. "Maybe ambergris works like them rhinoceros horns."

As you might expect there weren't any rhinocerologists in the bar and Milton's theory was met with blank expressions.

"It could be one of those…what do you call 'em…marital aids," Milton explained. "Lots of rich fellas like Injun rajahs and Arab sheiks and whatnot love them marital aids. They'll pay a pretty penny for stuff like that, especially rhinoceros horns. They grind them into powder and take it like snuff. It makes them…you know…bigger."

This provoked a generous round of hooting and guffawing and then some jokes so raw James made them stop.

"Sorry, Connor," he said to me. "You're a little young for this sort of talk."

"I know about boners," I said, setting off the guffawers again. I scowled at them. I was ten years old and thought I knew plenty about boners. James came out from behind the bar and steered me to the door with a hand on my shoulder.

"How's your mother these days?" he asked, handing me a few coins to cover his *Chronicle* subscription. "Seems like she's getting on better."

"She is," I said. "She's been drinking this awful green stuff Miss Lizzie gave her. It's helping."

"Say hello for me," he said. James hesitated and then went on. "Maybe I'll stop by one of these days."

I liked James and it was okay with me if he liked Ma. I just wasn't ready for him or any man to *like* her. So, I sassed him.

"What for?" I asked, even though I damned well knew what for.

James's face wrinkled into a frown, one that dads give their sons just before reaching for their belts. For a moment I thought he might give me a dressing down, but then he sighed in a way that seemed to expel his frustration. At the same time his face softened.

"For crying out loud, could you please just tell her, Connor?" he said.

৵

All over town folks were talking about the offer from the

Allegheny Chemicals Corporation. No one had heard of the company, although C. Herbert Judson—who personally knew Henry Dow and had met two of the Duponts—claimed to have read an article in the *Wall Street Journal* about its president, J. Piedmont Bell. I now showed up at Mr. Judson's house around 5:30 a.m. every day so we could talk for a while before I finished my route. Not long after receiving the letter from the Allegheny Chemicals Corporation, we sat on his porch swing as the hazy gray of dawn was burned off by full-on sunrise. Mr. Judson was on his second cup of coffee, while I sipped hot chocolate Mrs. Judson had given me in a mug proclaiming its user to be the "World's Best Husband."

"Allegheny Chemicals isn't a public company," Mr. Judson told me as if I cared. "That's why it's hard to get their particulars." He seemed uncharacteristically nervous, his usually steady gaze flitting from me to the front door of his house to the rose trellis and back again. "They're not Dow or Monsanto. Those boys are chemical giants and they're public so you can get information about them." He went on to explain the newly formed Securities and Exchange Commission in Washington D Almighty C, a body created to provide the sort of oversight sadly lacking when the stock market crashed five years earlier. "Public companies must provide regular reports to the SEC and make their businesses transparent to stockholders," he droned as I pretended to be interested. "They're a necessary watchdog in the fight against…"

There was more, but I stopped listening. I knew there was a lot to learn from Mr. Judson, but if there was anything more boring than a discussion of the Securities and Exchange Commission I didn't know what it was. I still don't. Besides, he seemed determined to paint the Allegheny Chemicals Corporation in a peachy color and it wasn't necessary. Frankly, I no longer cared about the ambergris. No amount of money could outshine the fact that Ma was better. She had been drinking

Miss Lizzie's concoction for several weeks by then without a single day spent in bed hidden under a blanket or gadding about like a hummingbird flitting from flower to flower.

"I have to get going," I interrupted. "Coach Buford will complain if he doesn't get his paper pretty soon."

I finished my route and stopped at the mercantile to see Fiona. Her adoptive twin maiden aunts, Rosie and Roxy Littleleaf, were talented bakers and Fiona kept a large selection of their delicious scones, cinnamon rolls, and croissants in a basket on the front counter. She offered me a scone along with some warm milk that had a little coffee in it. Like Mr. Judson she was behaving suspiciously.

"Did you ride past the boathouse this morning?" she asked.

I did every morning and said so.

"Was the guard awake?"

I nodded and it suddenly occurred to me that for the past ten days the same four fellows—Roger Johns, C. Herbert Judson, Angus MacCallum, and James Throckmorton—had rotated the duty. Previously, the guard roster had numbered at least two dozen men from around town. I asked Fiona about it, but she was conveniently engrossed in her account book, something that occupied her until Mrs. C. Herbert Judson showed up to look over some new hats from Chicago.

"They're in back. I haven't unpacked them yet," Fiona informed her. Her voice was affected—a bit too loud while at once both wooden and falsely expressive—reminding me not only of the amateur actors in the recent Tesoro Community Theater production of *A Little Bit of Fluff* but of Mr. Judson's calculated earnestness earlier that morning.

"I could come back," Mrs. C. Herbert Judson replied, her own delivery almost believable. She was a better actress.

"That's okay. Follow me," Fiona said, glancing my way. "Stay here, Connor," she added.

They retired to the storeroom at the rear where they

compounded my suspicion by speaking in whispers until Mrs. Judson came out alone.

"You take care, Connor," she said and the way she said it and the look on her face reminded me of recently ended Prohibition days, when a fellow had to sneak into the back room of the Last Resort to enjoy a snort or two.

"What were you talking about?" I asked Fiona after Mrs. Judson was gone.

"You should probably run along now," she replied. "I've a million things to do."

Fiona typically kept busy when I was there, pausing occasionally to look at me. Her eyes, like the rest of her, were lovely—almost teal, almost sapphire—but she gave up little of them while rather obviously trying to get rid of me. I didn't take the bait, instead watching as her gaze wandered uncomfortably from the figures in her account book to the clock on the wall to the front door of the mercantile. Suddenly, she looked at me as if about to confess, her expression less a sinner slipping into the confessional than the chagrined wife who has rear-ended someone while trying to simultaneously drive and apply her makeup.

"Connor…"

She didn't finish.

"What's going on?" I pressed.

"Nothing," she said. "Nothing's going on."

"That's not true. You're being weird. Mrs. Judson is being weird. I was at Mr. Judson's this morning and he was weird, too. And the same four guys have been guarding the boathouse all week. Why aren't the other men helping? What's that about?"

Fiona didn't look at me, instead directing her gaze to the stockroom door, peering at it as if words flowed across its surface; words, I thought, for the briefest moment, she was about to share with me. She didn't.

"I have to go to the back," she said. "You should run along."

She made for the stockroom, disappearing inside for a few minutes before returning with a large box. I was still there, eliciting a sigh from Fiona that she hid poorly.

"Wouldn't you rather be off with Alex or your friends doing something fun?" she asked, feigning nonchalant cheerfulness that made me mad. The woman I loved was hiding something from me.

"Wouldn't you?" I retorted.

Fiona shot me a peeved look and then headed down one of the mercantile's three broad aisles. Halfway along it she stopped and began to unpack her box, placing indigo-and-ruby tins of Quaker oatmeal on a shelf already filled with them. I joined her.

"Connor, I'm really swamped today," she said without looking at me. "Lots to unpack and stock."

"I can stay and help."

"It's summer. It's your vacation. I can't make you work on summer vacation."

"I don't mind."

This back-and-forth went on for a while until Fiona became cross.

"Connor, you have to go. I've a lot to do."

She had never kicked me out of the mercantile and I must have suddenly looked like a wet dog to her—half mad, half miserable. Her expression softened.

"I'm sorry," she said. "I didn't mean hurt your feelings. It's been a tough week."

Now this was the place where a smart fellow who has been around the track with women a couple of times knows to keep his mouth shut, offering an understanding nod of his head, the tight line of his mouth providing the only evidence that a woman has dented his fender. I was a boy and not that smart.

"Yeah? What's been so tough about it?" I muttered.

Fiona frowned and now it was her fender being dented.

"Mind your manners, young man," she scolded. "If I need someone to speak to me like that, I'll find myself a husband."

I didn't grasp the irony of her remark until I was much older. It wouldn't have mattered if I did. She clearly didn't trust me and I was pissed off.

"I gotta go," I said, tossing more words over my shoulder as I headed for the door. "You're not the only one with a lot to do."

I was behaving badly and knew it. But I wasn't lying. I had plenty to do. I was determined to find out what was going on inside C. Herbert Judson's boathouse.

CHAPTER THIRTEEN

Dinkle's mousetrap

It should not be surprising that a man like Cyrus Dinkle had both a fondness for mousetraps and a talent for inventing new ways to attract and catch a mouse. Back in the Indian Territories he'd garnered cheese for his traps by providing Indians with guns and then convincing the U.S. Army that Indians with guns were best disarmed and forcibly removed from land Dinkle then claimed as his own. He subsequently divided his vast holdings into small parcels he sold to homesteaders from the east. Once they were settled, he cut off their water supply until the hardscrabble pilgrims were forced out, their meager savings in Dinkle's pocket, the land once again made available as bait for the next mouse. From there he expanded into banking, railroads, and oil. Along the way he collected a wife, a beautiful meatpacker's daughter who saw him as a chance to escape marriage to someone exactly like her father. The marriage ended in divorce after only a few years and Dinkle's ex-spouse was now more than grateful to be a meatpacker's wife back on Omaha's South Side.

No one knew where Dinkle had been raised. He had a patrician way of speaking suggestive of Philadelphia or the Upper East Side in New York City, but Miss Lizzie always thought she detected something more raw and brutal. "South Boston, maybe, or Chicago," she opined. "He hides it well…makes people think he's pheasant under glass or filet mignon…but there's corned beef and cabbage in there somewhere."

While I made my way to C. Herbert Judson's boathouse, Dinkle was actually enjoying a corned beef on rye his cook had prepared. He ate in the mansion's cavernous dining room, alone as usual. Dinkle liked being alone. He knew the mealy little nobodies who made up the population of Tesoro viewed his solitude with both fear and pity. He relished their fear, disdained their pity. "They need, need, need. None of them could stand alone like I did in the Indian Territories," he often bragged to his man. "They spend their days scratching out an existence and their nights clinging to each other against sounds in the darkness. Pathetic! They make me ill. They fear the world will crush them if they let go of one another. Well, I say they deserve to be crushed. They were born to it."

Dinkle ripped a bite from his sandwich just as one of the Boops, the chirpy one, appeared in the arched doorway of the dining room, followed a moment later by the Russian Boop. He pursed his lips approvingly. Although the Russian girl was fully dressed for the day, Chirpy Boop wore a lacy thing that didn't much tax a fellow's imagination. It was about half of a usual nightgown, its lower edge fluttering just below her hips.

"That's what you're having for breakfast?" she said. "Corned beef?"

"This is lunch. I had breakfast hours ago," Dinkle growled.

Dinkle had hired the Boops to work in a San Francisco house of ill-repute that he owned, immediately appreciating a mature shrewdness and absence of scruples despite their youth— neither girl more than twenty-two years old at the time. The establishment's madam was near the end of her active career, preferring the company of a bottle to that of revenue-generating men, and it hadn't taken much time for the chatty hooker and her Russian friend to take over the books and day-to-day operations. From there Dinkle set them up in an office on New Montgomery in the Financial District, where they now managed one of his money laundering operations. They'd given him no reason to regret his decision. Chirpy Boop and her Russian cohort quickly exceeded his expectations, earning generous raises to their salaries despite shameless skimming of company proceeds. He didn't mind their thievery. Duplicity was comforting to him, an utterly predictable slice of human nature. Indeed, Dinkle preferred doing business with crooks as he considered honest men to be annoyingly fickle, their consciences too often getting in the way of opportunity. Besides, even though the Russian Boop was a bit regal for his taste, Chirpy Boop offered additional services he occasionally enjoyed, even at his age.

"We have to get back to San Francisco this afternoon," Chirpy Boop told him. "We'll need your man to drive us."

"That's fine," Dinkle said.

"Also, we realize the foreclosures are set to execute after ninety days but thought perhaps we could get our end now. We've been thinking it would be nice to travel a bit. Maybe Cuba...or Europe."

The foreclosures she referenced were in the small print Fiona had warned me about. Between the first and last pages of the credit agreements the bewitched Tesoro men had signed was a tiny clause requiring the borrower to indicate in writing by ninety days an intention to renew the terms of the contract. Otherwise, the loan balance—or the collateral if the money wasn't paid—would be due in full on the ninety-first day. It was Dinkle's mousetrap. No one read the clause on the day the agreement was signed. No one would read it until he called in the loans. Not a single borrower would be capable of fulfilling the obligation. They would all default and he would take not just ten percent but the entirety of their ambergris shares— two million invested in the lines of credit neatly turned into more than thirty million dollars. A nice summer's work.

"Are you listening, Cy?" Chirpy Boop pressed when Dinkle didn't answer. "How about giving us our end now?"

Dinkle scowled. "You know the policy. I don't give advances."

After entering the dining room, the Russian Boop had poured herself a coffee and now sat at the opposite end of the huge table, using a file to smooth a ragged fingernail. She typically allowed her friend to do the talking, but the old man's response made her look up.

"Is not advance," she pouted defiantly. "Is our take."

Dinkle glowered at her. Like his valet-chauffeur, Yurievsky, the Russian Boop was tall, solemn, and subtly menacing, a thinly veiled air of foreboding about her that unsettled the ex-gunrunner.

"Is our take," the Russian Boop repeated. "Is not given. We earn. You owe."

Dinkle slammed his hand on the table, causing Chirpy Boop to startle so violently, her flimsy nightgown nearly fell off.

"Stop begging!" he shouted. "You'll get paid when I pay you! Understand? Not a goddamned minute sooner."

Unlike her talkative friend, the Russian Boop was unaffected by Dinkle's outburst. She remained silent and motionless, her eyes so icy and defiant they might have murdered him on the spot were eyes capable of homicide. Meanwhile, Chirpy Boop fashioned a single crocodile tear, managing to fully expose one breast in the process. The tear had no effect on Dinkle, but his affection for women's breasts, in general, and Chirpy Boop's, specifically, softened his tone.

"I don't even know how much the stuff is worth," he said. "There's an analyst coming from back East. If things check out, we can talk about an advance."

Chirpy Boop smiled wanly, using the hem of her nightgown to wipe away the solitary tear, an absence of undergarments offering further evidence of her inducements.

"Okay, Cy honey," she said, shushing her friend with a glance. "We understand."

There were 197 households in Tesoro with around 800

residents among them. Not counting Dinkle, one hundred ninety had signed the Boops' papers. None had read the fine print. Thus, as I pedaled my bicycle across town toward the marina and the boathouse, only Roger Johns, C. Herbert Judson, Miss Lizzie Fryberg, Fiona Littleleaf, Angus MacCallum, and I, by way of my mother, had failed to nibble the bait in Dinkle's mousetrap.

CHAPTER FOURTEEN

I discover the truth

Tesoro had no police force. We were under the authority of the county sheriff who occasionally sent a deputy our way—a stringy, pigeon-chested fellow with a pencil-thin moustache, a slight paunch, and enough slack in the seat of his pants to make one wonder if he had any buttocks at all. He followed the same routine: Cruise the main drag through town two or three times, then park in front of the mercantile and go inside where he tried to sell Fiona on the notion that a man with a badge was a bit of a catch. Fiona wasn't buying. "One of my friends over in Stinson Beach went out with him," she reported to Ma one day. "He's a little too handy, if you know what I mean."

Our lack of resident police protection had prompted round-the-clock guards at the boathouse, the sleepless nights quickly unpopular for fellows accustomed to days that ended with eight or ten hours of uninterrupted snoring. Thus, as I pedaled toward the boathouse, I couldn't help wondering if attrition had shrunk the regiment down to the four men who had taken over the duty for the last week or so.

Mr. Johns was at his post when I rode up. Miss Lizzie was with him, firing off words like bullets and waving her finger about as if trying to direct the billowy, overhead clouds into a swirl. I have previously suggested that Miss Lizzie was the smartest person in Tesoro and this is no exaggeration. "She's playin' two-deck canasta whiles the rest of us be stook on crazy eights," Angus MacCallum once claimed. Miss Lizzie's intelligence was mostly a virtue, but she could be snappish when confronted by a something she found stupid, and had long ago stopped disguising her disdain in such instances.

"I can stand a watch, Roger. I'm quite accustomed to being up at night," she was saying as I climbed off my bicycle and approached. "Most babies are born after dark, a good many after midnight. I probably do more night duty in a month than you men will do in your lifetimes."

"It's not about sleep, Miss Lizzie," Mr. Johns contended. "Let's face it, men are physically stronger than women. If fisticuffs or some such were necessary, we men are simply better equipped to fend off a ne'er-do-well."

Miss Lizzie pulled herself up to her full height—a substantial pull as she was quite tall. It fashioned a posture that caused Mr. Johns to recoil slightly as Miss Lizzie was a daunting figure in any circumstance, but when stretched out and ready to fire words, could be a considerable force. I've often wondered why she spent her life in our little village. She was too big for Tesoro, too smart, too able. She never married and had no children. Maybe that's what we were: her children. She liked solving our problems and was remarkably good at it, making her indispensable to us. Being indispensable is a powerful drug for a person who likes to be counted on. As for marriage, some of the snarks in town postulated that she preferred the company of women, but I suspect her spinsterhood was a matter of choice regardless of preferences. She was simply unwilling to kowtow in the way a marriage requires. She certainly wasn't about to kowtow to Mr. Johns.

"When was the last time you were in a fight, Roger?" she barked. "Have you *ever* been in a fight? I have. I've held down a hysterical woman with one hand and flipped a breech baby with the other. Fisticuffs, for God's sake! Fisticuffs? Ne'er-do-well? What's that about? Have you been reading Jane Austen? Fisticuffs! I'll show you some fisticuffs right now if you like."

This went on for a while with Mr. Johns slowly backing up until he was pinned against the wall of the boathouse by the finger Miss Lizzie threatened to shove up his nose. Finally he noticed me, the look of relief on his face that of a man reprieved on the gallows.

"Connor! What brings you here this morning?"

His question temporarily put a cork in Miss Lizzie's spout and halted her waggling finger, although she kept it pointed at him lest he try to escape. She followed his eyes to me.

"At last…a real man," she said, lowering her finger. She faced me. "What took you so long? I expected you to figure this out days ago."

I knew Miss Lizzie preferred for people to get to the point. And so, I did.

"I want to look inside the boathouse," I said.

Miss Lizzie didn't answer, instead leading me along a floating wooden dock to the double doors that marked the seaward entrance. There was a latch with a padlock. Miss Lizzie extracted a key from her pocket and inserted it into the lock. Moments later we stood inside the dark boathouse, with the doors once again closed. Slowly, my eyes adjusted to the dim light as I struggled not to vomit. The smell was overpowering.

"Hold this," she said, handing me a jar of eczema remedy compounded from camphor and sandalwood. She pulled off the lid and dipped a finger into the ointment, afterward putting a generous amount just under her nose. I did the same and the pungent salve suppressed the stench of the boathouse just enough to calm my stomach.

I had been in Mr. Judson's boathouse before. He had taken me sailing on his *C. Breeze* a few times. I loved being on his boat, scampering over the polished deck or ducking under the boom as it swung about on a tack. He'd even let me man the tiller on occasion. This time there was no sight of the *C. Breeze* inside the boathouse, the sloop temporarily relocated to an open slip to make way for our ambergris. However, there was no evidence of the ambergris, either. The huge mass originally had been placed on a tarp that was then attached to the boat hoist and lowered into the water with the hope that the brine would convert more of the exterior crust to pure ambergris. The boat hoist and tarp remained there. However, the blob I'd discovered on the beach nearly two months earlier was merely a greasy sludge on the surface of the water. A small orange crate sat on one of the interior walkways. Miss Lizzie pointed to it.

"Take a look in there," she said.

I did and found a large egg-shaped object about the size of a football. It was whitish and hard to the touch. Scars remained from where Angus MacCallum had shaved off a few slivers. I looked at Miss Lizzie.

"What happened to our ambergris?"

She smiled grimly, a humorless thing that filled me with unease.

"It wasn't ambergris, Connor. We think most of what you found came from the sewage tank of some ship. They must have dumped it overboard."

"What's this?" I asked, indicating the egg.

"That's real ambergris. It was stuck inside whatever they threw off the ship. When Angus scraped off the crust he just happened to hit the ambergris by chance. It was luck...dumb luck."

People are funny. Even when confronted by circumstances that can't possibly lead to anything good, a person will cling to the thinnest shred of hope—the egg stain on a necktie might not be noticeable; the bank might honor an overdraft; the firing squad might miss their target. I'm no different. I felt as if I were staring into a phalanx of gun barrels but wasn't quite ready to accept what now seemed inevitable.

"But we'll still get a lot of money, right?" I asked. "There's enough real ambergris to make everyone rich, isn't there?"

Miss Lizzie shook her head.

"No," she answered. "We're not rich. Far from it."

I confess that Miss Lizzie's revelation nearly made me swoon. It was as if hope was suddenly and inexorably draining from my body like blood from an open vein, a fluid level physically appreciable as it descended from forehead to chest to thighs to toes, indeed, a hemorrhaging of hope that threatened to bleed me lifeless. I had entered the boathouse as a town hero, a Jack returning from his climb up the beanstalk with a golden egg. By the time the last of my essence had drained from me, I had become a goat, the boy with a whitish egg to share that was far from golden. Miss Lizzie knew me well and sensed my despair, pulling me into her embrace, my head against her bosom.

"I'm sorry, my dear little man," she said.

We went back outside where I slumped against one of the dock pilings, while Miss Lizzie and Roger Johns explained what had happened.

"No one checked inside the boathouse for the longest time because of the smell," Mr. Johns told me. "A couple of weeks ago Angus was on duty and got curious. He went inside and found the ambergris egg. It's amazing it didn't float off. It was about a foot underwater, deep enough to wash under the doors. The rest of the ambergris—or what we thought was ambergris—had mostly dissolved."

"Angus woke us up," Miss Lizzie revealed, "Fiona, Herb, Roger, and me…and we went to the Last Resort to get a look at one of Dinkle's loan contracts."

I knew James Throckmorton had taken out a line of credit with the Boops, afterward making his way to Skitch Peterson's car lot where he took a 1927 Olds off the master salesman's hands. From Miss Lizzie and Mr. Johns, I learned that he had since been in the uneasy throes of buyer's regret and wasn't surprised by a middle-of-the-night knock on the door of his apartment above the bar. "I shoulda known better," he'd said ruefully when apprised of Angus's discovery. Afterward, he retrieved his credit agreement, handed it over to Mr. Judson, and then retired to the bar's kitchen to make coffee.

"Herb explained to us how Dinkle never had any intention of entering into a traditional loan arrangement," Miss Lizzie disclosed. "The old scoundrel wrote the contracts with the specific intent of stealing everyone's ambergris shares." After reviewing James Throckmorton's contract, Mr. Judson had dolefully deciphered the small print Fiona warned me about. "Any borrower failing to renew the terms of the contract in writing on or before ninety days is liable for the entire amount on the ninety-first day," he'd told the small group. "That means their collateral is sacrificed."

"We didn't know what to do," Mr. Johns said. "Should we tell everyone the truth, that there was hardly any real ambergris? Should we tell Dinkle? It was a mess."

Miss Lizzie scowled. "It wasn't a mess, Roger. It was a problem."

"But a big one."

Miss Lizzie aimed a narrow eye at the banker. She was a problem-solver by nature, whereas Mr. Johns, for all his likeability and waxy handsomeness, had a bit of hysterical teenager in him when confronted by turmoil. I liked him and knew him to be a stalwart fellow if accurate account balances were at stake. However, he could be a hand-wringer if the fish on the end of a ten-pound line was ten pounds and one ounce.

"Roger, be quiet and let me finish the story," Miss Lizzie said. She reiterated for me the provision that notice be given in writing. "Verbal notice results in default," she said, her face grim.

Their talk of defaults and liability and collateral were confusing to me and my expression likely reflected it. Miss Lizzie appreciated this, offering further explanation.

"Here's the thing, Connor," she summarized. "If Dinkle

discovers our ton of ambergris is really just a couple of pounds of the stuff, he'll claim he was defrauded, that his borrowers knew their collateral was no good. He'll be able to seize homes, businesses, cars, clothes, jewelry...You name it. Dinkle will take everything. He'll financially ruin most of the town."

I didn't understand how a piece of paper with an imprudent signature allowed Cyrus Dinkle to commit robbery. "Why not tell everyone except Mister Dinkle?" I asked. "People could return all the stuff they bought, get their money back, and pay him off."

Mr. Johns sighed. "That's the problem. They borrowed too much and most of it can't be returned. There's a Depression going on. Folks won't be able to sell their stuff. There won't be any buyers, not at retail prices anyway. They'd be lucky to get half of what they originally paid."

I thought about some of the purchases made over the summer and had to admit that the demand for disobedient monkeys, under-aged mail-order brides, and slightly used jeweled commodes was likely to be a meager one.

"Maybe people could pay off what they owe a little at a time," I offered. I knew Fiona ran tabs for her customers at the mercantile as did James Throckmorton at the Last Resort.

"Without the ambergris money, people couldn't afford to make payments on a loan balance of that size," Miss Lizzie said. "Besides, we don't want them to make payments."

"You don't want people to pay back the money they owe? I don't get it. You said they'd lose everything."

"We want Dinkle to call in the loans," Miss Lizzie explained. "Think of it this way. If Dinkle doesn't get paid, he takes his collateral—the ambergris—and the borrowers owe him nothing more. He thinks millions are there for the taking, but he'll be stuck with whatever he can get for our little dinosaur egg... or at least his share of it. Those of us who didn't borrow money from him get part of it, too."

I considered what Miss Lizzie and Mr. Johns had told me. It was a big secret in a small town, the sort of place where secrets are an endangered species.

"Who knows about this?" I asked.

"Just a few of us," Miss Lizzie said. "Herb Judson and his wife, Fiona, James, Angus, Roger, me." She smiled. "And now you."

"What about Coach Buford?" I asked. I thought his exclusion conspicuous, if not foolhardy. He was a notorious buttinski and had been known to evince some monumental toots over far less than being excluded from a secret this big. Miss Lizzie set me straight, making the face of someone who has bitten into a piece of uncooked liver.

"Wally Buford never met a secret he wasn't immediately willing to release into the wild," Miss Lizzie said. "I'd sooner publish it on the front page of the *San Francisco Chronicle* than tell him. As far as that goes, no one else needs to know. Especially those who borrowed money from Dinkle. As long as they believe there's a thousand pounds of ambergris in this boathouse, they're not lying. There's no fraud on their part. Besides, the more people who know, the bigger the chance Dinkle will find out what he's accepted as collateral."

According to Miss Lizzie and Mr. Johns, after the wee hours meeting at the Last Resort, the group had disbanded and five of the six participants went home. Angus returned to the boathouse to finish his guard tour. He was the only one required to remain awake, but none of them slept that night. The next morning the conspirators met at the boathouse. A new member had been added: Mrs. C. Herbert Judson.

"She was involved with theater groups in San Francisco," Miss Lizzie told me. "She knows a lot of actors. She knew one who might help us."

I should have been skeptical. After all, this was a matter comprised of contracts and figures, deadlines and defaults. We needed a lawyer like Mr. Judson or a banker like Mr. Johns to sort it out, not someone who pretended to be a lawyer or a banker. On the other hand, I had never met a real actor and must confess that the prospect rendered me a bit star-struck, able to repress the threat posed to the town by Dinkle in favor of an actor's ability to rescue us.

"Is he famous?" I asked. "Is he in moving pictures?"

Miss Lizzie shook her head. "No," she answered. "He works on stage, in live theater. And he's not famous. He's hardly known at all. But that's why he's perfect. He's more or less anonymous."

"So, he's not in moving pictures?"

"He's been in one moving picture."

"Which one? Maybe I saw it. I would remember his name if I heard it. Tell me his name."

Miss Lizzie exchanged looks with Mr. Johns and then leveled gray eyes on me. "This is not to go any further, Connor. You tell no one. Not your brother, not your mother. No one. Understand?" I nodded.

"His name...at least the name he'll use," Miss Lizzie told me, "is Everson Dexter."

She went on, taking me back-stage for a play that would be staged for the edification of Mr. Cyrus Dinkle. I learned that there was no Allegheny Chemicals Corporation, no analyst named Everson Dexter. They were both fakes—part of a sham invented to counter Dinkle's sham, the trickster being tricked. According to Miss Lizzie and Mr. Johns, if we could keep the old bandit in the dark about the ambergris in the boathouse until the ninety-first day of the loan contracts, the borrowers would default and he would take their shares. However, no one would have to pay back the $10,000 the ex-gunrunner had given them.

"Do you understand?" Miss Lizzie asked me.

I nodded. It was a poker game and the fictional Allegheny

Chemicals Corporation and equally fictional Everson Dexter were parts of a bluff. Miss Lizzie and her fellow card sharks had outbid the legitimate perfumers, hoping they might fold before one or more of them sent a real analyst to Tesoro. It was a bluff that had to hold up for no more than one second past ninety days.

Miss Lizzie solemnly reconfirmed that the only people in town aware of what was really inside C. Herbert Judson's boathouse included she and Mr. Johns, Mr. and Mrs. Judson, Fiona Littleleaf, James Throckmorton, and Angus MacCallum. Now I knew, too. Among the eight of us, only James had signed a line of credit agreement, using it to buy the 1927 Olds that no longer graced his garage. Once apprised of the empty boathouse he had quietly sold the car in San Rafael at a small loss, dipped into his savings account at the Sonoma State Bank for the difference, and paid Dinkle. His line of credit balance was now zero. He was no longer encumbered. Thus, members of the unlikely cabal that dreamed up the Allegheny Chemicals Corporation and hatched the plan to bring the fictitious Everson Dexter to Tesoro owed not a penny to Cyrus Dinkle. They were not at risk. Nevertheless, they were about to imperil both their reputations and their freedom—not for themselves but for their friends and neighbors. It was an utterly dishonest act plotted by perhaps the most honest and honorable people I have ever known. It was also a conspiracy worthy of Arthur Conan Doyle or Robert Louis Stevenson.

And I was to be part of it!

CHAPTER FIFTEEN

The falcon spots the field mouse

On my way to the boathouse I had encountered Dinkle's man on the narrow, sand-and-gravel road linking Tesoro to his boss's estate. We passed within feet of one another, but even from a distance I'd have recognized him by his military gait. He didn't so much walk as march—head up, shoulders back, elbows locked as his arms swung like pendulums through precise arcs. He'd nodded at me, an elegant gesture that made me feel as if I should salute. I didn't. Years later, when I was in uniform, such a response became instinctive. But in 1934 I was ten years old with armies and war and salutes far off. Hence, I merely lifted my chin, scarcely slowing as I pedaled on to the boathouse. Meanwhile, Dinkle's man negotiated the last quarter mile to the mercantile and went inside, the bell dangling from the door handle announcing his entry. Fiona Littleleaf was behind the counter, sorting mail with her back to the door. She turned and greeted him with a smile.

She is lovely, Yurievsky thought, a woman the Grand Duke might have pursued. He instinctively scowled. He had seen too many old men of the Russian Imperial Army, officers all, made silly by attempts to recapture their youth with someone's niece or daughter. Yurievsky had no such inclinations. Olga might turn up one day, expecting faithfulness even after so many years. Should that miracle come about, he did not wish to disappoint his wife. She had suffered enough disappointment; left alone to raise Irina, his sweet *Myshka*, for months at a time when he was off soldiering, his returns marked by moodiness and troubled sleep.

Fiona—the young woman Irina might have become—waited for him to approach the counter, framed by the cash register and a basket filled with pastries. She wore no makeup, and was quite beautiful despite little effort to make herself so. Yurievsky admired her disdain for pretension, her subtlety. It stood in sharp contrast to Dinkle's Chirpy Boop, a woman who wore her carnality like jewelry. Behind the mercantile proprietor was a den of cubbyholes, the top row reachable by a ladder that slanted against the shelving. Most of the compartments were empty, a few filled with a letter or two. Names were below each box. Yurievsky recognized only a few. None would have recognized his name; indeed, the young mercantile proprietor, the lawyer, the tall midwife, and the crazy woman's son were the only people in the village who spoke to him at all.

"Good morning, Mister Yurievsky," Fiona said.

"Miss Littleleaf," Yurievsky replied, his dignified manner worthy of a knight addressing his queen.

She cocked her head, offering a wry expression.

"When will you start calling me Fiona?"

Yurievsky shrugged. "Perhaps tomorrow," he said.

She laughed. "I'm going to hold you to it."

Fiona turned away to retrieve Dinkle's mail from one of the open cubicles. Unlike the villagers' boxes, there was a good deal of mail for the old man: business envelopes with impressively embossed return addresses, a couple of thick Manila packets. She took a few moments to bind the correspondence with twine, uncharacteristically prattling as she did so. "Big goings on around here these days," she finished up, handing over the bundle. "I imagine you've heard about the letter we received from back east."

"I did."

"They've offered so much money. It's hard to believe."

Yurievsky didn't answer. It was part of the game they played. Fiona tried to pull words from him; he resisted. She offered him pastries; he declined. She teased; he allowed merely a smile. An outsider might have thought her too kind for such a stone-faced fellow, but there was lightheartedness and familiarity in their exchanges, even affection. Yurievsky had once played similar games with Irina, always ending with his daughter's arms around him, her lips pressed against his cheek, her whisper in his ear: "*Ya ochen' lyublyu tebya, Papa.*" *I love you ever so much, Papa.*

His response had been equally scripted: "*I ya tebya, moya sladkaya Myshka.*" *And I, you, my sweet little mouse.*

Fiona suddenly interrupted his thoughts.

"I bet Miss Lizzie I could get more than two words at a time out of you, Mister Yurievsky," she said.

Yurievsky took Dinkle's mail from her outstretched hand, the unmistakable trace of a smile gracing his lips.

"You lose," he said.

He turned to go, her laughter trailing him.

"See you tomorrow," she called out as he opened the door and stepped into the sunlight.

Yurievsky headed back toward the estate, unable to shake the feeling that something was amiss. Fiona's demeanor had been too breezy, too casual. A woman typically efficient with words, her idle chatter was unusual, the pitch of her voice too high, the flow of words too rapid. Indeed, her behavior had seemed altogether affected; perhaps calculated. Yurievsky had a nose for such things. One of his previous employers—a notable Manila gangster—had more than once sent him to gather information from someone not inclined to provide it. The unfortunate fellows always began with lies but ended up telling Yurievsky the truth. Their voices, like Fiona's, had been high-pitched, words tumbling from their lips, their attempts at nonchalance exposing them as liars. The young mercantile proprietor and postmistress had not told him a lie, but there had been artifice in her manner and his curiosity was piqued. Worse, he was suspicious and Yurievsky did not want to be suspicious of her. He had spent decades at the mercy of his suspicions. There had been little peace attending such vigilance and he wanted desperately to believe that Fiona Littleleaf was guileless, a true innocent.

Yurievsky approached the gated entry to the estate and stopped. To the west, he could hear the waves of the Pacific Ocean as they slammed onto the beach at high tide. The sound was comforting, and for a moment, he was convinced that his suspicion was unwarranted. At the same time, a falcon dove earthward from overhead, sweeping close to the ground and then soaring upward, a field mouse in its beak, the poor thing's tail whipping about like a streamer. Yurievsky sighed. *She has something to hide*, he thought, the nervous pitch and rhythm of Fiona's voice too fresh a memory. *Something she wants hidden from me...and from Dinkle.*

CHAPTER SIXTEEN

James Throckmorton makes his play

Axel Throckmorton's mail-order bride, Mei Ling, did not go back to China but remained with Miss Lizzie. Our long-time town medical officer could well afford to feed another mouth, but Axel felt obligated to provide a small measure of financial support and gave Mei Ling two dollars in nickels each week. "I gotta keep her happy. She's evidence in my lawsuit against the sonuvabitch who sold her to me," he told people. Axel was an honest man who never cheated at cards, watered down the whiskey bottles at the Last Resort, or concocted a whopper unrelated to the size of a fish. However, his two dollars per week were less a legal strategy than a way to ease the guilt he felt for spiriting Mei Ling across an ocean in anticipation of marriage only to be confronted by an intended older than one of the Pliocene-era moon snail fossils we occasionally found on our town beach.

"The girl come from China expecting a husband and connubial bliss, and I ain't gonna be the one to see her go wanting on either count," he told his son, James. "I was prepared to keep up my end of the bargain as far as warming the bed goes, but I just ain't up to the connubial blissing somebody that young is looking for." Axel reckoned it would take a while to get a court date for his lawsuit and determined to put the time to use finding Mei Ling a husband nearer her own age. Miss Lizzie put an end to the nonsense after discovering Axel, Milton Garwood, and Angus MacCallum compiling a list of groom candidates over beers at the Last Resort.

"Mei Ling is sixteen years old," Miss Lizzie scolded. "She's too young to marry anyone."

Miss Lizzie further contended that, when the time came, the young Chinese girl would be more than capable of determining who tickled her fancy without help from three dried-up old coots whose fancy-tickling days were far behind them.

Meanwhile, Mei Ling was quickly adapting to life in America. She had been predictably suspicious at first, her mother cautioning that her daughter's new American husband would likely connubially bliss her morning, noon, and night for a while. "You'll have to put up with it until he tires out," her mother advised. "Then you can start squeezing his balls." However, a little time with Miss Lizzie had provoked a rather remarkable transformation and Mei Ling now seemed less interested in connubial bliss than learning English and spending Axel's two dollars on movie magazines and bubble gum.

Mei Ling wasn't the only addition to Tesoro. The village was now filled with treasure seekers, the story of my discovery on the beach eventually making it into the *San Francisco Chronicle*. This inspired a gold rush of sorts, an army of people with dollar signs in their eyes streaming into town and then setting up Hoovervilles on the beach below the lighthouse, and around the edges of the Dinkle estate. The reporter who incited the ambergris prospectors, a small fellow with a bow tie and virtually no chin, was particularly taken with my decision to share the treasure with the entire town. Ten-year-old Santa comes early to Tesoro, California the headline read when his story appeared on page five, sparking attention I enjoyed at first. Ma and Miss Lizzie and Fiona were proud of me and showed it. Girls looked at me in a different way, too, particularly a brown-haired cutie with an upturned nose who would eventually become my wife, Marjory.

However, after the treasure hunters began to pile into town, overrunning the village like cockroaches, the nature of the attention shifted. People don't like change and strangers clearing the shelves at Fiona's mercantile, or parking their heaps until the only road in and out of town was turned into a one-lane tractor path, or sneaking into someone's outhouse to do their business was a good deal of unwanted change. Someone needed to be blamed for such nonsense and the kid who had stumbled upon a stinking, viscous mass on the beach was as good a target as any.

As the sons of a crazy woman and the bounder who abandoned her, Alex and I were accustomed to a bit of talk from behind someone's hand. However, the Ambergris Rush, as I like to remember it, put a barb on tongues I'd always thought fairly blunt. Milton Garwood the Misanthrope was in the thick of it, the stinger on his tongue as poisonous as a scorpion's tail. He and Angus MacCallum nearly came to blows when Milton suggested that Ma and Alex and I ought to pay a surtax to cover the cost of clearing up refuse the ambergris prospectors left piled up in Fremont Park and on the beaches, the debate fueled by a few beers and whiskey chasers over at the Last Resort.

"No one taxed ye extra when yer damned monkey ran aroond town crappin' up a storm," Angus growled. "I think mibbie ya oughta start savin' up to pay the tax on dunderheeds. Yers is gonna be bloody steep."

The two old men then carried on a discussion of the various flaws each possessed that might be taxable. Eventually, James Throckmorton broke it up by kicking them both out of the bar. Outside, Milton and Angus found the street deserted, and as is often the case, the absence of onlookers cooled off the combatants. Neither apologized, but they did share a conciliatory nip from Angus's flask before stumbling off in opposite directions. Angus headed toward the lighthouse while Milton made for the cottage where Ma and Alex and I were about to turn in.

Ma was still drinking Miss Lizzie's remedy every day and was calm when she answered the knock on the door. Milton was half-drunk and acting about one quarter crazy, which seemed to calm her even further.

"What do you want, Milton?" she demanded.

Her question, a straightforward request, was unintentionally philosophical from Milton's point of view. It rendered him momentarily flummoxed.

"What do I want, what do I want?" he sputtered, adding after a moment's pause, "I don't know. What the hell *do* I want?"

His ambergris shares had provided at least one of many things Milton felt was lacking in his life: a lot of money. However, a fat bank account had failed to fulfill its end of the bargain with the Zenith Stratosphere Model 1000Z nowhere in evidence and Mr. Sprinkles now urinating and defecating at the exotic animal preserve in Petaluma. His wife had managed to exhaust most of their remaining line of credit with stuff he didn't care about, filling their house with so much junk he couldn't walk from the kitchen to the bedroom without climbing over a sofa, squeezing past an icebox, or tripping over one of several whale-replica doorstops. Worst of all, after agreeing to make his outhouse available to any of the ambergris prospectors who had both an urge and a nickel, he could no longer enjoy his morning bowel movement in peace, instead waiting in line with a bunch of strangers who were rapidly using up his catalog pages.

"What do I want?" Milton said, echoing Ma's question one last time. "I'll tell you what I want, Mary Rose. I want things to go back to the way they were."

The inconveniences imposed by the Ambergris Rush partly gave way to excitement over the impending visit from Everson Dexter, the analyst from the Allegheny Chemicals Corporation. Every new stranger in town was looked over from eyeball to toenail, making the ambergris prospectors justifiably nervous. A few of them turned tail and ran in the face of such scrutiny, but a good many stayed. "Too damned many," Angus MacCallum growled as the driftwood he had once carved into mermaids and gnomes was scavenged by the prospectors for use as tent poles and firewood.

Some folks in Tesoro worried that Mr. Dexter might not find the town at all as someone was removing the road signs pointing motorists in our direction. In early August, James Throckmorton went to San Francisco to see the Seals play baseball and reported no shortage of billboards advertising Burma Shave or Coca Cola or Vicks cough drops. However, there was a complete absence of anything to help someone find Tesoro. The culprit who had pilfered the signs was a mystery and remains one even now—travelers wishing to visit Tesoro today still must do so sans the benefit of signs to guide them.

I had begun to see a good deal of James Throckmorton. As I previously revealed, he had been sweet on Ma for a long time; indeed, they'd known each other from kindergarten, at the same elementary school Alex and I attended, to graduation from Tesoro High School in 1918. "Them two was quite the lovebirds," Angus MacCallum often told me. "No offense, but she shoulda married James instead of tha' no-good bastard da of yers." Ma had gone off to Cal, returning to Tesoro four years later with a degree in library science and a no-good bastard husband. James Throckmorton stayed in town and remained a bachelor.

I've been told James came around for a time after my father left us. I don't remember it, but I guess Ma's illness drove him off. She wanted no part of anyone when depressed and her up moods could test the bounds of a man's ability to be a gentleman. Alex and I stayed with Miss Lizzie or Fiona during such times, with Angus MacCallum standing guard over Ma to make sure she didn't run off to a roadhouse somewhere to offer up something she shouldn't. James might have taken advantage of such moods but didn't, and I remain grateful to him for being a good man when being a bad one would have been so easy.

James was as happy as Alex and me when Miss Lizzie's latest treatment started to work, and once Ma returned to her job at the library, our town tavern-keeper unearthed a previously concealed affection for reading. Before long he began to turn over the Last Resort to his father, old Axel, in order to spend his afternoons thumbing through magazines or scanning western novels from a table conspicuously close to Ma's desk. She didn't seem to mind having him around, recruiting his help to re-shelve books while offering glances and little asides as she moved through the stacks, putting the musty, old place back in order after so many years away. James was partial to *True Detective* and Zane Grey novels although Ma convinced him to give *Robinson Crusoe* and *The Count of Monte Cristo* a try. It didn't take a genius to figure out that she could have asked him to spout nursery rhymes in his underwear from atop the gazebo in Fremont Park and he would have done it. He was still crazy about her and Miss Lizzie's concoction had opened a door he'd long thought closed. I soon learned that it had opened for Ma, too.

"James Throckmorton is coming for dinner," she told my brother and me one afternoon. Alex had his nose in a book about airplanes and simply nodded. I wasn't pleased. I knew James liked her and I thought he was okay, too, but the job of looking after Ma and Alex had been mine for a long time. I wasn't ready to be replaced. Besides, Ma's even temperament was too novel. I was enjoying it and wanted to keep her attention solely on Alex and me for as long as possible.

"Why is he coming over?" I griped. "He owns a bar. He can cook for himself."

"Don't be like that, Connor."

"I'm not being like anything. I just don't get it."

"He's not coming because he wants dinner. He'd just like to spend a little time with us."

"Why?"

"He likes us, I guess. I don't know. He wants to be our friend. Let that be reason enough, okay?"

"Why can't he find his own friends?"

I confess this recollection to be one I find embarrassing. Despite her improvement in mood, Ma was still fragile, my peevishness causing her to become increasingly flustered, the skin on her neck suddenly splotchy and red, her hands anxiously patting down invisible wrinkles on her dress. Alex could see it, too.

"Stop," he mouthed silently.

I wanted to smack him. Brothers are supposed to put a knot in each other's ropes once in a while, but I'd always had the decency to do it in time-honored fashion: peeing in his bath water while he was still in it, or seasoning his peanut butter sandwich with snot. Alex didn't fight fair. He pestered me with perfect reason and unassailable virtue, qualities I would come to admire and emulate, but absolutely infuriating when I was ten.

"Stop," he repeated, this time aloud.

He might have said more. He might have reminded me that we'd known James Throckmorton all our lives, that James was a decent fellow and Ma obviously liked him even though he was nothing special to look at, his hair thinning, his belly fighting his belt. I went to Ma and gave her a hug.

"Sorry," I said.

Ma sighed, unconvinced. I don't blame her, my apology flavored with the same enthusiasm I displayed when she tried to persuade Alex and me that Methodist Sunday services were a better idea than playing baseball or lying around doing nothing.

"Please, Connor," she said.

"It's fine," I pouted, my voice making clear that it was nowhere near fine.

"Connor—"

"I said I was sorry. I'm glad he's coming."

But I didn't sound like it and I wasn't.

That night Ma wore a dress borrowed from Fiona and had her hair nicely made up in a style I'd not seen before, her face worked over with some of Miss Lizzie's face pastes and creams. She looked very pretty and James said so. Repeatedly. Over a dinner of fried salmon patties with peas and a milk salad, he paid a lot of attention to Alex and me, too, insisting that we call him "James" instead of "Mr. Throckmorton" and talking to us about baseball. He was a big fan of the San Francisco Seals and regaled us with stories about Vince and Joe DiMaggio. "You heard it here first, boys," he told us. "Joe DiMaggio is going to be the greatest player who ever lived." He promised to take us to a game. I wanted to hate him, but James had a pleasing manner. Tall and broad-shouldered with big hands and thick wrists, he was a bit like a tamed bear—strong and powerful but also gentle and protective.

After dinner James went outside with Alex and me to throw a ball around. I was a decent player, but Alex was an absolute marvel. At six years old, he leapt and dived for balls I could hardly reach, never failing to snag a throw anywhere near him. He had a good arm, too, putting some zip on the ball that made it pop when it hit my glove or James's. "You've a little brother who'll be a pitcher someday, Connor," James said. "Let's teach you to be a catcher." And he did. He taught me all about framing a pitch to fool the umpire and firing a ball to second base from my knees and blocking the plate against a runner bearing in on home. Of course, most of that would come later. That night—the night of the first dinner—we just played catch. Eventually, James sent Alex inside to check on Ma, giving us a chance to talk in private.

"Have you told your mother about the boathouse?" he asked. I scowled.

"Of course, I haven't told anyone," I snapped. "I'm not stupid."

This sort of sass is commonplace these days. My great-grand-kids mouth off to their parents as if they're pals. In my time, kids were kids and grown-ups were grown-ups, the difference between us reinforced with an occasional swat on the backside. Fortunately for me, James was still on probation with Ma and not anxious to get on her bad side by paddling me. He laughed.

"Sorry, Connor," he said.

"I can keep a secret."

"I know."

"Maybe you should worry about yourself. Have *you* told any-one?"

James frowned. "Ease up, young man," he said.

He didn't have to say it again. I had seen James tell men at the Last Resort to ease up, always after a few drinks had provoked a disagreement about what was ruining the damned country or who could strike out who blindfolded. Such disputes occasion-ally evolved into chest-thumping and wildly thrown haymakers, forcing James to break it up. In most cases, it took merely a warning and a grim expression as James was a great bear of a fellow, as I've already pointed out. Drunk or sober, fellows around town weren't anxious to replace his customarily affable disposition with one that might get them tossed out of the Last Resort as easily as my brother Alex flung a baseball into my glove. I certainly wasn't about to challenge him. Besides, de-spite the competition between us for Ma's attention, I couldn't help liking him and suddenly realized that I wanted him to like me back.

"I'm sorry, James," I said.

This time I meant it.

That night Alex and I lay in the bed we shared. I couldn't sleep. I wanted to tell my brother about the boathouse and Everson Dexter and the fictitious Allegheny Chemicals Corpo-ration. But a secret was a secret.

"I like James," Alex said.

"He's okay," I said.

I could see the shine of my brother's eyes in the dark. He studied the ceiling as if the uneven plaster held secrets of its own.

"Will he marry Ma?"

"I don't know."

"If he does marry her, he'll be our dad."

"I guess."

Alex was quiet for a long time, so long that I felt certain he'd fallen asleep. When he again spoke, I was both terrified and grateful.

"What's going on in the boathouse?" he said.

CHAPTER SEVENTEEN

The Ambergrisians and Axel Throckmorton's fiancée

I knew Alex to be trustworthy. But I had promised Miss Lizzie and Mr. Johns to keep our secret.

"What's going on in the boathouse?" he repeated in the dark of the room we shared.

"I can't tell you," I answered.

My voice made clear that further discussion was off limits and Alex didn't argue, merely shrugging and then rolling over. A couple of minutes later, his breathing coarsened and I knew he was asleep. I wasn't surprised that he'd given up so easily. Alex rarely argued with anyone, virtually never with me. We got on pretty well. We both felt responsible to keep Ma on high ground as much as possible and enjoyed throwing a ball back and forth. We shared headphones when listening to programs on my crystal radio, enjoyed skinny-dipping in the ocean, and I cannot ever remember either of us throwing a punch at the other. Since I mostly let him hang out with Webb Garwood and me, those rare occasions when he was excluded tended to provoke a challenge and some language we'd both picked up from the men at the Last Resort. Otherwise, Alex was like a Buddhist monk in a kid suit, an affect that made many folks around town think him strange. He was, I guess. Patience is often seen as strange, given that most folks have little of it. And Alex was patient. He would not remain in the dark about the boathouse forever and he knew it. He was satisfied to wait.

116

Alex did not ask again about the boathouse, indeed, seemed to know what was inside without being told. I remained uneasy for a time, worried others might have suspicions, as well, but then the summer went on and I was carried off with it. Over eighty years have passed since then, but I don't think boys have changed. Once the final school bell rings in June, with the next one three months off, it isn't possible to worry about consequences for long, especially when the days are warm, the afternoon rains soft, and the breezes cool at eventide. I delivered my papers, splashed about in the brisk northern California ocean until my teeth chattered, played pick-up baseball, and laughed at the ambergris prospectors who waded about in the surf, casting out nets or dipping pole-hooks into the water.

For the first two weeks after the newspaper article about my discovery was published, a steady stream of fortune-hunters piled into Tesoro. They prowled the beach at first, but when no ambergris washed up, the prospectors began to venture into the water where they were mostly knocked down by incoming waves, their efforts unrewarded by even an ounce of ambergris. The Pacific Ocean in our part of the world was pretty chilly year-round and it didn't take long for the pilgrims to lose heart, their numbers steadily dwindling until only a few of the more determined fellows remained in town, waddling into hip-deep water each morning only to waddle back empty-handed at the end of the day.

It had been sixty-one days since the Boops garnered signatures on Dinkle's lines-of-credit and nearly every household in Tesoro—save those belonging to a group I had dubbed the Ambergrisians: Angus MacCallum, Fiona, Miss Lizzie, Mr. Johns, Mr. Judson, James Throckmorton, and me—was deeply in debt to Cyrus Dinkle, in hock up to their earlobes with compendia of unneeded or useless stuff wedged into every corner of their homes. Fortunately, their potential salvation in the form of Everson Dexter of the Allegheny Chemicals

Corporation was fast approaching, with the Ambergrisians concluding that our actor should make his appearance as near the ninety-day deadline as possible.

"Once our charlatan has set the honey pot, we don't want to give Dinkle too much time to think about it," Mr. Judson advised. "He's too good at sizing up the angles on a deal." He hoped Allegheny's outrageously tantalizing bid of $2845 per ounce—certainly well above anything the legitimate companies like Chanel or Jean Patou would match—might encourage Dinkle to execute the default feature on his loan contracts without much scrutiny. "With millions more than he originally thought at stake, I'm hoping the old scoundrel's greed will override his judgment," Mr. Judson told us. In the meantime, we figured Dinkle wouldn't be anxious to call attention to either side of the loan agreements, given that his half was as much a Trojan horse as ours.

Most of the Ambergrisians worried that the savvy former Indian Territories trader might push for one of the legitimate perfumers to conduct an assay before our fake analyst made his appearance. "Maybe," Mr. Judson told them, "but it's to Dinkle's advantage to drag things out until we hit the ninety-day mark." If all went well, he told us, the deadline would pass and Dinkle would claim the ambergris shares as planned. The town would be made whole and our unsuspecting dupe would discover the collateralized one thousand pounds of ambergris to be no more than two pounds of the precious compound, along with whatever sludge continued to float on the surface of the water inside the boathouse.

The Ambergrisians met about once per week, after-midnight affairs at the Last Resort. The points discussed were always the same and there seemed to be little reason to gather. I was too young to truly grasp the danger we faced. For me, it was a great adventure. However, I now suspect the secret sessions were a way for the others to make certain the twine binding the conspiracy wasn't coming undone. Even if the scheme worked, a world of ruin could still await us, and in my old age, I have often wondered if the true purpose of our clandestine gatherings was to see if anyone was ready to talk some sense into the others.

"Isn't this fraud? Won't the sheriff eventually get involved, anyway?" Mr. Johns worried one night to his fellow conspirators. It was a never-ending concern for him, the nosy bank examiners and FDIC compliance officers that haunted his day job heavily coloring his view of a financial shenanigan like the one we had concocted. It was two o'clock in the morning and the Ambergrisians were gathered around a table at the Last Resort. I was there, too, after slipping out the window of my bedroom and then darting from shadow to shadow as I made my way across town. My covert movements were part of a charade, of course, a game of cloak-and-dagger acted out alone as no one else was likely to be awake at that hour other than the Ambergrisians and Alex. He'd said nothing as I made good my escape, his eyes gleaming in the dark.

"It's not fraud for the borrowers," Mr. Judson patiently reasoned for Mr. Johns. He had addressed the banker's worry several times in the past, but if annoyed by his co-conspirator's chronic fretting, it didn't show. His voice was steady, his face relaxed. "None of them know that the amount of actual ambergris in the boathouse is far less than originally thought," the lawyer went on. "As for us, we have no legal obligation to tell Dinkle anything. It's his responsibility to appraise the collateral he's accepted. Not ours."

Mr. Judson's face grew solemn.

"But let's face it. For those of us in this room, it is fraud. Unadulterated fraud. It's a crime. If Dinkle finds out that Dexter is a fake, we could all go to jail."

This was a revelation neither surprising nor welcome. For several weeks the Ambergrisians had done an excellent job of avoiding the truth, casting our line into the water with the idea that mackerel and cod were the only fish under the surface. Mr. Judson's words reminded us that a tug on the line might come from a shark and his candor gave way to silence in the moments that followed. Eventually, he took a deep breath and went on.

"I want you all to be my clients. That includes you, Connor. I'll prepare the papers and bring them around. If there's an investigation, you were advised by your attorney to keep quiet. That's the story. At the same time, I won't be able to tell what I know without breaching attorney-client privilege. We'll cancel each other out for a while…Buy some time. I know a bit about Dinkle's affairs. Maybe enough to convince to him to make a deal with us instead of going to the sheriff."

He laughed.

"Of course, we can always make a run for it. How's everyone feel about sailing with me to South America?"

No one else laughed and Mr. Judson's expression once again sobered. He looked at me.

"Connor, you'll have to figure out a way to get your mother's signature without telling her what's going on. I know it seems she's turned a corner, but if she goes back to the way things were…"

He didn't have to finish. Ma was better, but her even temperament was still novel enough to make us uneasy about handing her a secret. If she abruptly soared into one of her up moods, she would be unable to stop talking. No secret would be safe.

"I understand, Mr. Judson," I said.

After the meeting broke up I headed home, this time making no effort to conceal myself as I walked through the center of town. It was warm and the streets were deserted, the night given over to crickets and bullfrogs. I added my own chirping to their songs, whistling softly as I walked, confident I could dance a jig and sing "A Long Way to Tipperary" all the way home and still escape detection.

At the center of Tesoro was Fremont Park with its splintered benches and unfinished cedar picnic tables. There was a gazebo, as well, the site of weddings, award presentations, and occasional speechifying—Coach Wally Buford or Milton Garwood not infrequently feeling the urge to unload a few of the opinions that would otherwise constipate their brains. None of these things transpired after midnight and I expected the gazebo to be deserted as I approached, its dark silhouette as rigid and lifeless as the exoskeleton of a cicada. It wasn't. The moon was only mid-month, but the sky was cloudless, allowing more than enough light to make out something that might have caused me to levitate entirely over that damned gazebo had such a thing been possible. A solitary figure sat inside the open-sided structure—a woman, her hair pulled into a single, long braid. She looked directly at me, and even in the dim moonlight, I easily recognized her. It was Axel Throckmorton's erstwhile fiancée, Mei Ling.

People who traipse about alone at three o'clock in the morning are usually up to no good, and I figured Mei Ling would likely see it that way—maybe size me up as a burglar, or worse yet, a window peeper. An explanation was needed, one I neither had nor was able to conjure despite frantically mining the remotest parts of my mind. Nevertheless, I headed for the gazebo. "If ye get caught wit' yer breeches doon, act like ye means it to be tha' way," Angus MacCallum once advised me. I later shared his counsel with Miss Lizzie who disagreed. "Typical man's point of view," she snorted. "Try keeping your pants on to begin with."

Of course, Miss Lizzie was right, but sound advice isn't much help to a fellow who has already forgotten his belt, so I abandoned any notion of sneaking off and made directly for the gazebo. I reached it and strode inside, behaving as if I thought myself expected. I'm not much of an actor now and likely wasn't any better then. Thus, I probably came off as exactly what I was: A ten-year-old kid skulking about town in the wee hours.

"Nice night," I said, cursing the involuntary squeak in my voice.

Mei Ling was not beautiful in the way of Fiona Littleleaf or Mrs. C. Herbert Judson—her face broad, her build a bit stocky, a faint spray of acne on her cheeks—but she was a pleasant-looking girl. I'd only seen her from a distance since her arrival in Tesoro. From afar she'd seemed a grown woman. Close up, she looked younger than her sixteen years. I took the seat next to her.

"What's going on with you?" I asked. "Why aren't you home in bed?"

Mei Ling didn't answer, instead looking past me to a sundial a few yards away, the device useless at that hour of the night. She knew little English, but well understood one of the words I'd used.

"Home," she said, "...Day."

I relaxed. Miss Lizzie had explained the International Date Line to Alex and me. It was three o'clock in the morning where we sat in the gazebo, but folks in the place Mei Ling still called home were sitting down to dinner at 6:00 p.m. the next day.

"You," Mei Ling said, the feathery hint of a smile on her face, "Treasure Boy."

"That's me," I said.

Mei Ling turned away, tipping her head to look at a moon more than halfway through its nocturnal arc. Even in the dark I could see that her face was filled with longing, her eyes moist. I understood. For a long time I had sent messages for the moon to pass along to my father, wherever he was. I suspect Mei Ling might have been doing the same, sending greetings for the moon to carry to her family on the other side of the planet. Her loneliness was palpable and I suddenly wanted to rescue her from it.

At ten I possessed the inclination to be a hero, particularly one capable of coming to the aid of a pretty girl who has slipped into that mysterious and ethereal region where only teenagers reside. However, the wherewithal accompanying such an inclination is too often sadly lacking, particularly for those of a tender age like mine at the time. I possessed neither great strength nor prowess with weaponry, but then, Mei Ling's predicament did not require muscle or sword, did it? It called for a fellow with sharp wits, and for the minutes that followed, I somehow found a way to be that fellow.

"The treasure isn't real," I said, divulging the secret I'd pledged to withhold. Mei Ling cocked her head, obviously curious, and I blurted out everything: the blob on the beach that became a dinosaur egg, Cyrus Dinkle's mousetrap, the Ambergrisians, the Allegheny Chemicals Corporation, Everson Dexter. All of it. At first, she appraised me as one does a lunatic, her expression a mixture of nervousness and fear. However, she was soon rapt as I acted out the parts: Angus MacCallum's crab-like gait, Miss Lizzie's clipped, no-nonsense voice, the hale affect of Roger Johns, Mr. Judson's measured tones, Fiona's spit and vinegar, James Throckmorton's broad-shouldered presence, the paunch and sneer of Cyrus Dinkle. Before long the moisture in her eyes glistened with amusement, and when I impersonated Dinkle's man as a stiff-backed incarnation of film star Bela Lugosi, she laughed aloud.

"Treasure Boy...funny," she said.

Of course, Mei Ling hadn't understood more than a few words, but I was quite certain she could recognize beans being spilt as they tumbled out of the can. I think she was grateful; at least it seemed so. Her face was less shadowed, her eyes brighter. She wasn't alone any more. She was now in on a secret, part of something on our side of the world.

"Don't tell anyone," I instructed. She grinned.

I grinned back and then bade her good night before heading

home. She remained in the gazebo. After reaching our cottage, I scrambled noiselessly through the window of my bedroom. Alex lay on his back in our bed. His eyes were closed, his breathing steady. I slipped in next to him and lay awake. It had been a relief to tell someone and I wanted to tell Alex and Ma, too. Secrets have a way of oozing out of whatever jar one puts them in, and I'd been struggling to keep the lid on mine for weeks. I remained awake until it was time to head for the Sinclair station to pick up that morning's editions of the *Chronicle*. I passed Fremont Park on the way to the station. The gazebo was deserted.

CHAPTER EIGHTEEN

Welcome to Fort Buford

I returned from delivering papers and went back to bed, sleeping until early afternoon. I awoke rested and ready to face facts: Other than secret meetings with the Ambergrisians in the wee hours and my charade for Mei Ling, the part I had thus far played in the scheme to fool Dinkle had been utterly disappointing. When it began I had fancied myself as a Jim Hawkins sort. We had both become involved by accident—Jim made privy to the pirates' plan in *Treasure Island* because he wanted an apple from the ship's barrel, me stumbling upon the truth about the ambergris because my paper route took me past the boathouse each morning. However, Jim had gone on to fight pirates while my only job thus far had been to keep my mouth shut. It was not a satisfying assignment, and I decided to stop pining for adventure. It was time to get back to the rest of my summer vacation. After all, one week in August was already behind us and the air was filled with the ominous smell of new pencils, lined tablets, and the freshly applied floor wax that wafted from the open windows of the Tesoro Elementary School.

Mr. Judson wanted to get on with things, as well. "No point staring at a clock when the wind is good," he told me. He and Mrs. Judson had taken a shine to Alex and me, the Judsons having no children of their own, and as folks' appetites to sue their neighbors abated, we spent more and more time on his boat. In the beginning my brother and I were useless—shinnying up the mast, dangling from the bowsprit where ocean spray could hit us in the face, riding the boom as it swung about on a tack. But as the days passed, Mr. Judson taught us more and more about seamanship, showing us how to raise and lower the sails without tangling the lines, how to bring the boat about without turning her over, and when to hoist the jib. Before long he had me, and then Alex, at the tiller. I loved it and later taught my kids and grandkids how to sail on my own boat. I'd have taught the great-grandkids, as well, if my balance was better and my hips less creaky.

Sometimes, when the wind was down, we lowered the sails and just floated. Mr. Judson did most of the talking on those occasions while Alex and I wolfed down crab salad sandwiches or the ginger snap cookies Mrs. Judson always packed for us. Mr. Judson occasionally let me have a sip of beer or a puff on his pipe, promising Alex similar favor when his age was in double digits. "I'm a bad influence on you boys," he said, but he wasn't. He talked about the importance of a firm handshake and looking a fellow in the eye, how ignoring a pile of trouble simply makes the pile bigger, and how to talk to girls so they don't realize you're an idiot until they've convinced themselves that you're not one.

While Alex and I negotiated the high seas with Mr. Judson, more than a few folks back in Tesoro were beginning to bend under the onerous weight of consumerism Dinkle's lines of credit had shoved down their throats. "There's only so much crap you can buy," Milton Garwood griped, and if anyone could appreciate that wisdom, it was Milton. His house was still filled with furniture he and Mrs. Garwood didn't need, and teak miniatures they needed even less, and the glass cats his wife used to like before she had about a hundred of them, and ships in a bottle, and an aquarium filled with dead fish, and a set of encyclopedias that were still in the box, and a newfangled electric bread toaster he'd already broken, and, of course, all the doorstops shaped like whales that had seemed like a grand idea at the time. He also had Mr. Sprinkles back after reclaiming him from the exotic animal preserve in Petaluma.

Milton decided he hadn't given the little fellow a decent chance the first time around and figured to try a different approach, giving him a collar and putting him on a leash. It turns out that organ-grinders' monkeys don't have a natural affinity for either collars or leashes, but Mr. Sprinkles didn't scratch or bite as you might expect. Instead, he turned ironic and was willing to be led about on a leash if he could occasionally drape himself across the old man's bald head until it appeared Milton was wearing a toupee with arms. The little fellow also became territorial, screeching and hurling himself at the screen door when anyone stepped onto the Garwood porch. While this unfortunately sent Milton's spinster cousin from Stinson Beach to the hospital after she fainted and hit her head on a whale doorstop, it also helped him close his waste disposal service.

Long before the ambergris rush died off on its own, Milton grew tired of standing in a line of strangers to use his outhouse and decided to close up shop—nickel be damned—a change in business policy that proved unpopular. "You can't fight the call of nature, you old fart," one of the ambergris prospectors yelled when Milton ran him off. Milton put a bell on his outhouse door and stood guard with a shotgun as much as he could, but a good many former depositors still managed to sneak inside and conduct their transactions. Eventually, Milton turned Mr. Sprinkles loose on them. "It was outstanding," he told the boys at the Last Resort. "The little bastard started right in to shrieking and spitting and pissing and throwing turds. Them boys scattered like turkeys on Thanksgiving Day. I woulda kissed the little sonuvabitch, but I'm scared he might bite my lips off."

Meanwhile, Coach Wally Buford had decided to use some of his line of credit for investment purposes. "We need to grow our money," he told wife Judy. "That's how Dinkle got rich. He invested his money and it grew." His wife was no fan of Dinkle and pointed out that conniving had likely produced a much higher rate of return than investing for the old gunrunner. Coach Wally was undeterred and made an appointment with Dinkle to ask for advice. While waiting in the old man's study, he snooped around. There were the usual things a man with big money and a need to appear dignified might have: a massive desk, a couple of deep leather chairs, a huge globe, and lots of unread books by Greek and Roman philosophers. Two handwritten letters had been carefully framed and hung near the fireplace.

"Those are letters written by George Washington himself," Dinkle told Coach Wally after joining him in the study. "I bought them both for a hundred dollars. Together, they're worth at least two thousand now."

"Who are they written to...them letters?" the coach asked.

"One is to a stable owner in Philadelphia," Dinkle reported. "Something about buying a horse. The other one is to Washington's overseer at Mount Vernon, instructing him to switch their crop from tobacco to grains."

"Wow," Coach Wally said, adding an appreciative whistle that had less to do with his admiration for the impressive majuscules, minuscules, and flourishes of Washington's signature than Dinkle's claim of a twenty-fold return on investment. Once home the coach made an announcement to his wife. "Rare documents are as precious as diamonds these days," he said. "I'm gonna find me some rare documents to buy."

It turned out that rare documents were even tougher to come across than monkeys, but Coach Wally finally established a dialogue with a pawnbroker in Reno who claimed to have letters exchanged between legendary frontiersman Kit Carson and Sioux chief Sitting Bull of Little Big Horn fame. The fellow was willing to part with the letters for one thousand dollars. Judy Buford was skeptical, her suspicion warranted as any historian worth his salt can tell you that Sitting Bull and Kit Carson were both illiterate, neither able to differentiate the English alphabet from Egyptian hieroglyphs.

"Could Sitting Bull read and write?" she asked. "Could Kit Carson, for that matter?"

"Oh, don't be like that," Coach Wally scolded her. "These are really rare documents. In a few years they'll be worth at least fifty times what we're paying. Now this fellow in Reno, he's a little reluctant to hand them over as he'd planned to auction them off to the highest bidder, but he likes me, and since I'm a newcomer to rare document collecting and all, he figures to cut me a break."

Judy was unconvinced but believed it worth a thousand dollars to see her husband look stupid and eat crow at some point down the line. She conceded without further argument and a delighted Coach Wally cut a check to the rare documents man in Reno. A few days later a parcel was hand-delivered to the Buford residence. Inside was a velvet pouch that held two manila envelopes. One of them contained the Carson letter:

DEAR CHIEF SITTING BULL,

I TRUST THIS DAY FINDS YOU HALE AND HEARTY AND SEND MY DEEPEST REGARDS. I WRITE TO ENCOURAGE YOU TO GIVE YOURSELF OVER TO THE LOCAL FORT. THEY'LL TREAT YOU SQUARE AND THAT WAY I WON'T HAVE TO HUNT YOU DOWN AND PUT A BULLET IN YOU.

SINCERELY,
KIT CARSON

The second letter was Sitting Bull's reply:

DEAR CARSON,

ME HOPE YOU WELL AND SEND REGARD BACK.

Me can't give up. Great Father tell Sitting
Bull to stay in Badlands. Me put arrow in
eye you come here, so don't.

Sincerely,
Sitting Bull

Coach Wally immediately invited his football players over to
see the letters. They went home and told their parents who
then told their friends, and before long, there was a line of people at the Buford door hankering to get a look at a couple of
honest-to-God rare documents. Coach Wally was proud of his
new acquisitions and happily accommodated the thrill-seekers,
letting people gander willy-nilly until Milton Garwood suggested that pawing over rare documents could reduce their value by
contaminating them with spit or dirty fingerprints. Moreover,
he wondered if a rare document's luster might be diminished
by too much exposure. "The more people see stuff like this,
the less interested they are in seeing it again," Milton opined.
"If it were me, I'd put them in a vault. Rich fellas all have
vaults big enough to hold their paintings and jewelry and stat-
ues and rare documents and whatnot along with a gold-plated
easy chair and a wet bar. Some of them never sell any of it.
They just go inside their vaults once in a while and look over
their crap and drink brandy. But the ones that wanna sell get a
lot more if not too many folks have seen whatever it is they're
selling. Now I'm no rare documents man, mind you, but I'm
betting you can get more money for one of them letters if less
eyeballs have crossed paths with it."

Coach Wally ordinarily was about as interested in being told
what to do as Milton Garwood was, but he thought a vault for
his rare documents was a grand idea. He went straight to the
Montgomery Ward and *Sears, Roebuck and Company* catalogs, quickly discovering that their pickings were as slim for bank vaults
as they had been for rare documents and monkeys. Both listed

safes of various sizes. However, neither retailer sold a vault that would hold a gold-plated easy chair and wet bar, items Coach Wally had to admit might come in handy if several hours were needed to soak up whatever satisfaction a rare document had to offer. He asked Mr. Johns where they'd found the vault at his branch of the Sonoma State Bank. Mr. Johns gave him the name of a company in Oakland and Coach Wally immediately drove over.

The salesman at Alameda Safes & Security hadn't previously entertained a request for a bank vault, other than from a bank, and pointed out that such an item would likely be too large to fit into the Buford residence, particularly in latter's present state of furniture and doodad gluttony. "You really just need a vault door on your house," the salesman told Coach Wally. "You could put one in front and one in back. Throw some bars on your windows, and she-bang…you're as secure as the Bank of London."

It turned out that converting the Buford residence into the Bank of London would cost just over twelve hundred dollars, but Coach Wally had only $1154.89 remaining in his line of credit. A bit of haggling ensued and the salesman was eventually satisfied with $857.00 plus the two Blue Vermont Marble tombstones the coach had purchased from the Bras & Mattos Monument Company. "Who needs 'em?" Coach Wally told people. "By the time me and Judy are ready to kick the bucket, my rare documents will have made us even richer than the ambergris did. Hell, I'll buy us a whole damned mausoleum and still have enough left over to put an eternal flame in front or maybe even a water feature."

It had been around two months since the arrival of the Buford's jeweled commode, the buzz surrounding it having diminished to a hum, and so the coach and his wife were pleased when folks gathered on the sidewalk outside their residence to watch the installers from Alameda Safes & Security replace

Coach Wally's thin wooden doors with a pair of dense iron ones. The faces of the vault doors each had a numbered combination dial and a polished brass turn-handle resembling a small ship's wheel. To prevent the Bufords from being locked in, an operating dial and handle were on the inside as well. The workers set the locks so the same combination would open both the front and back doors and then installed thick iron bars on the windows of the house. By four o'clock they were on their way back to Oakland, leaving behind an edifice that amused onlookers had already dubbed "Fort Buford."

CHAPTER NINETEEN

I meet a real actor and learn about sex

It was nearing Labor Day of 1934. Summer was almost over. The time rapidly approached when Dinkle would spring his mousetrap—and we would spring ours—and the old bastard had yet to suspect that the cheese he sniffed was bait. The game was afoot. And, amazingly, it seemed to those of us who comprised the Ambergrisians that we might actually pull it off. Mr. Judson recommended that Everson Dexter arrive on the Tuesday following Labor Day.

"He could stay with Mrs. Judson and me," he offered during one of our after-midnight meetings, "but it might be less suspicious if he were at the Kittiwake."

"I've already set aside a room," Fiona said.

"Fine," Miss Lizzie said. "That's settled. Once he's checked in, Mister Dexter can retrieve a sample of ambergris from the boathouse and use my laboratory for his assay." She went on, even though it was unnecessary. We all knew the plan and had gone over it so many times the steps were as committed to memory as the Pledge of Allegiance. Dexter would muck about Miss Lizzie's lab, occupying the better part of an afternoon in order to convince folks he was as analytical as an analyst from the Allegheny Chemicals Corporation ought to be. He would deliver the fake good news to everyone at a town meeting the next day and then exit stage left on his way back to San Francisco and the footlights of a legitimate theater. "The less time he spends in Tesoro, the lower the chances someone will peg him as a charlatan," C. Herbert Judson reasoned.

Everson Dexter was not our imposter's real name nor was the name "Leslie Carrington" listed under his picture on theater playbills. His real name was Harold Lester Huffaker, and he was not from New York City, as asserted in the biography he provided to producers; rather, Hal Huffaker hailed from Delphic Oracle, Nebraska, a small place at the confluence of the Platte, Missouri, and Loup River Valleys. I don't know who came up with "Everson Dexter." Probably the actor himself. Actors are drawn to names no one would ever use, disdaining "Bill" or "Joe" in favor of "Cary" or "Randolph" or "Everson Dexter." Even now, that name seems like a blaring foghorn to me, a name Dinkle should have thought as thin as the rest of our pretender's backstory.

I have become more jaded about fame and celebrity as I age, but at ten years old, I was quite excited by the prospect of meeting a real actor. The rest of Tesoro was excited, too, albeit for a different reason, anticipating that the representative of an exalted eastern company like the Allegheny Chemicals Corporation was certain to make their reaches equal to their grasps. In Scene I of our play, Mr. and Mrs. Judson were to travel to San Francisco where, supposedly, they would meet Mr. Dexter's train from Philadelphia and then show him a night on the town, driving to Tesoro the following morning. Mr. and Mrs. Judson, indeed, had a night on the town in the wonderful City by the Bay, afterward staying at the elegant Fairmont Hotel on Nob Hill. However, Dexter was neither on a train from Philadelphia nor in their company, instead acquitting himself as "Mr. Grantham" in the closing night performance of *The Bishop Misbehaves* at the Victoria. The next morning he exited his somewhat dowdy Mission Street hotel, hopped into the Judson's Chrysler Imperial town car, and they headed for Tesoro.

I had a picture in my head of Mr. Everson Dexter as someone like Clark Gable. James only recently had taken Ma and Alex and me to see the wildly popular *It Happened One Night* in San Rafael. In the movie Claudette Colbert played a runaway heiress with Gable as the cynical reporter who goes on the road with her. The square-jawed actor was everything I thought a real man should be: wide-shouldered, voice tinged with gravel, a wisecrack always at the ready, hat pushed back on his head in that I-don't-give-a-damn way a lot of women seem to love. However, the Everson Dexter who stepped out of C. Herbert Judson's Chrysler was more like Miss Colbert than Mr. Gable.

He was handsome—I had to give him that—but not the hacksaw sort of handsome I'd expected. Rather, Everson Dexter was nearly as beautiful as Fiona Littleleaf and Mrs. C. Herbert Judson, his features utterly proportional, his skin flawless, his wavy brown hair flecked with blond highlights and tousled in a way that made it seem simultaneously perfect and careless. Watching him glide as gracefully as a dancer from the car to the front door of the Kittiwake Inn, I was struck by the contrast between he and Clark Gable. Gable was a warship, Dexter a Yankee Clipper; Gable a stained undershirt, Dexter a velvet smoking jacket. Watching Gable onscreen, one could almost smell the tobacco and whiskey and sweat, whereas Everson Dexter seemed like a fellow who never perspired.

His appearance in Tesoro had an immediate effect. Dexter checked into his room at the Kittiwake Inn as planned, but upon entering the main parlor, was greeted by the single largest horde of gussied-up women Tesoro had ever gathered together in one spot.

"Well," he said, displaying a smile likely capable of separating most in the room from their undergarments, "if only I had a glass slipper."

There was a good deal of lady-like tittering after that and then Judy Buford stood and recited the poem "How Do I Love Thee?" by Elizabeth Barrett Browning, followed by an invitation from Milton Garwood's wife for Dexter to come

135

have a look at Mr. Sprinkles. This provoked an avalanche of invitations that might well have ended with some clawing and handbag-swinging had Mr. and Mrs. C. Herbert Judson not reminded everyone of their guest's foreordained mandate to carry out the business of making them all rich.

"Ah, duty calls…sadly, I will confess," Dexter told them with a slight bow that made a good many of the women in the room weak-kneed. Then he and the Judsons were off to the boathouse to meet the rest of the Ambergrisians and raise the curtain on Scene II: The Fake Analysis.

At the boathouse Mrs. Judson waited on the dock while the remaining Ambergrisians followed Everson Dexter inside. The night guard, Angus MacCallum, had kept the seaward doors open all night, closing them and securing the padlock at dawn, but the stench remained more than robust, almost instantly transforming Everson Dexter's flawless tan from bronze to gray. Fortunately, Miss Lizzie had a jar of her camphor-sandalwood ointment at the ready. She smeared a dab under his nose, afterward passing the jar around, and Dexter's color slowly improved until he was merely ashen.

"How long do we have to stay in here?" he asked, his nose so wrinkled with disgust that his nostrils nearly turned into dimples.

"A few minutes," Miss Lizzie answered. "Enough time for you to take a sample. I see you have your case. Open it."

Dexter had brought along a doctor's bag filled with test tubes, vials of variously colored liquids, cotton swabs, glass pipettes, an eyedropper, a scoopula, and a small mortar and pestle—all of it provided by Miss Lizzie. He opened the bag but then hesitated, staring at the laboratory equipment as if the items were symbols in the runic alphabet.

"Now what?" he asked.

Miss Lizzie took over. The dinosaur egg that was our only true ambergris remained in an orange crate a few feet away.

She used the scoopula to scrape off a bit of the hard, whitish material and transferred it to a test tube. She then capped the tube with a rubber stopper.

"Take this," she said to Dexter. "We'll go back to my lab to finish."

Upon re-emergence from the boathouse a sizable crowd awaited us. They perked up at the sight of Miss Lizzie and me and our fellow Ambergrisians, then began to instinctively cheer and clap when Dexter appeared, something that instantaneously eased his biliousness—applause for a ham actor apparently equivalent to smelling salts for a cock-eyed boxer. To his credit he resisted the temptation to bow, merely lifting a hand to acknowledge the adoration flung his way, afterward pasting on a dignified expression as he strode up the gangplank to the road above the boathouse. Except for James, who took over the guard duty, we then walked to Miss Lizzie's with Dexter leading the way and the rest of the crowd trailing. The day was already warm and the men removed their jackets as we hiked along the road while many of the women dabbed at their underarms with handkerchiefs. As I had suspected might be the case, Everson Dexter did not sweat at all.

Back at Miss Lizzie's, our imposter improvised a bit. After climbing the steps to the porch, he turned to the crowd.

"Good citizens of Tesoro," he began in a voice resonant, theatrical, and decidedly un-analyst-like. "I shall need several hours to complete my assay. However, rest assured I shall provide a report to you as expeditiously as possible."

This earned Dexter another round of applause, and with his craving for approbation not yet sated, he was about to stray even further from the script when Miss Lizzie took one arm and Fiona the other, pulling our analyst off-stage before he could lift the backdrop from our little drama and thus reveal an alarming lack of any substantive ambergris in the wings. Mr. Johns and C. Herbert Judson stayed outside where they attempted to disperse the crowd. I followed Dexter inside, keeping a close eye on him, as his first glimpse of Fiona that morning had elicited a predatory expression. Unfortunately, as the day wore on, I discovered that Fiona had a predatory look of her own.

The details of Everson Dexter's actions in Miss Lizzie's lab are unimportant. Had he been a real chemical analyst, his expertise would have been far beyond what I can convey, given my fourth-grade education at the time and my present lack of enthusiasm for anything requiring familiarity with the periodic table. But then, he wasn't a chemical analyst at all, was he? Hence, adding a red liquid to the ambergris shavings Miss Lizzie had dropped into one of his test tubes and then pouring the red liquid into a green one followed by a yellow one—the whole mess afterward heated up over a Bunsen burner—was really just a basket of actor's tricks.

I concede that he was a good actor. Donning a white knee-length coat and horn-rimmed glasses, he carried out his activities with cool professionalism, punctuating each step with, "Ah, yes," or "Hmmm," or "By Jove, this looks promising." The day was warm and Miss Lizzie had the window sashes up—the sills all around, as well as the open doorway to her small laboratory, populated by as many eyes and ears as could find space. Dexter's dramatics served our scheme well and not a single person in town evidenced suspicion that the envoy from the Allegheny Chemicals Corporation was as phony as a carnival fortune-teller.

Of course, the Ambergrisians knew the man was a walking wooden nickel, which is why I was astounded that Fiona seemed so beguiled by him. During his performance he offered up maddeningly intimate asides she found entirely too wry or amusing, our fake chemist demonstrating one implausible finding after another for her sole enlightenment, each causing her to lean against him or gaze into his face as if he were the amalgamated reincarnation of Louis Pasteur and Ronald Colman. I was embarrassed for her. The Fiona I loved did not fawn over a man. Men fawned over her. Besides, it seemed to me that such shameless flirting might well unlid the magician's box of our little plot and thus reveal to everyone that the lady inside wasn't really sawn in half. I left before the play was over, offering up a good bit of huffing and foot-stomping for Fiona's benefit. She was oblivious to it. I brushed past Mei Ling on my way out. She, too, seemed captivated by Everson Dexter but at least offered a goodbye of sorts. "Treasure Boy," she said, "...Funny."

I went home to sulk, an exercise that lasted through the evening despite the efforts of Ma and James to cheer me up. Alex joined them, pleading with me to toss the baseball around or head over to the lighthouse where we could sneak up on Angus and startle him, afterward listening to him cuss in a Gaelic dialect we found inexplicably hilarious. It was no use. I was irretrievable and ignored them all until fitful sleep claimed me.

The next morning I picked up my stack of *Chronicles* from the Sinclair station and made my first stop at C. Herbert Judson's house. I was still in a black mood.

"Who kicked your dog this morning, Connor?" Mr. Judson teased.

"I don't own a dog," I grumbled, my impudent tone provoking a bemused look that made me even more irritable. Mr. Judson tried to pull me out of the dark hole I'd fallen into, but I merely growled responses until he went back to his newspaper. Eventually I left, muttering a goodbye before furiously pedaling off. I then purposely threw the next few papers on my route onto the roofs of my customers.

I finished my route before making my usual stop at Fiona's mercantile for a scone and a cup of milk with a little coffee in it. Roxy Littleleaf, one of Fiona's twin maiden aunts, was at the counter.

"Why are you here? Where's Fiona?" I demanded.

Roxy was tongue-tied, offering the face of one who has

walked off the edge of a cliff and only just realized it. This was not too far afield of her usual expression, given that Roxy always behaved as if she thought a piano about to fall on her. She and her sister, Rosie, had been briefly conjoined at birth, a fleshy rope connecting their abdomens. The midwife, Miss Lizzie's predecessor, had tied off their common tether at either end and excised the rest. However, before severing the tenuous bond, an exchange of essences had occurred that gave Rosie a stiff backbone and Roxy a limp one. Hence, as was her shy way, poor Roxy didn't answer me; instead, she pointed toward the Kittiwake Inn next door, her complexion as red as Fiona's should have been when I discovered her exiting Everson Dexter's room with hair tousled in the same way as Mrs. C. Herbert Judson's the morning she sat on the front porch swing next to her husband wearing nothing but a fuzzy oversized bathrobe and an enigmatic smile.

Every boy has a friend with an older brother happy to introduce an innocent younger sibling and his pals to pornography. Mine was Webb Garwood, whose brother Tuck had already initiated our education with a library of postcard photos depicting Rubenesque women and hairy men engaged in naked Greco-Roman wrestling. Thus, I believed myself to have more than a nodding acquaintance with what went on behind a bedroom door and was incensed with Fiona. My indignation might seem silly in today's world, but I assert with some confidence that it is difficult to stumble across a bigger prude than a ten-year-old boy in 1934. Thus, I was profoundly ashamed of Fiona as well as frightened by the prospects a liaison with Everson Dexter had put in her future. I knew sex resulted in babies, rejecting the claim of Judy Buford, my fourth-grade teacher, who had solemnly informed our class that childbirth was a result of marriage, prayer, and a good night's sleep. "You pray very hard, and when you wake up, you're pregnant," Mrs. Buford told us. So, I hope it's understandable that what I next said to Fiona was a product of my worldliness, when compared to Mrs. Buford, and the distress attending Fiona's decision to become a fallen woman before I was old enough to fell her.

"Now you're gonna get pregnant!" I shouted.

I ran off and went to the beach below the lighthouse, firing sand dollars into the surf until my arm ached. Then I sat on the damp sand, muttering curses I'd heard the men use at the Last Resort, all the while plotting various ways to make Fiona sorry she'd chosen Everson Dexter over me. The air was filled with the smell of the sea, and although it was a scent I usually found invigorating, it now seemed dank and rotten, redolent of brackish tide pools and decay. My mood, already sour, grew more bitter. And then, in the way of all spurned lovers, anger drifted into despondence, self-pity rolling over me like the low, gentle waves curling relentlessly onto the beach, the thin rim of foam at their crests like the tears clinging to my eyelashes. I was heartbroken; indeed, it was my first broken heart.

I had nearly worked up the courage to drown myself when James showed up.

"Nice day," he said, sitting next to me.

"Leave me the heck alone, James," I said. "I don't want to talk about it." He didn't make me and we spent a couple of minutes in silence. Of course, I did want to talk about it, but when I at last chose to speak, my voice was little more than a whisper.

"Is Fiona a whore now?" I asked him.

James frowned. "You watch your tongue, young man," he scolded, his tone making clear that there was only one adult on the beach and he'd be sure to let me know when there were two. "Fiona Littleleaf has been really good to you and your brother. She loves you and you love her. You don't put names like the one you just used on someone you love."

I wrapped my arms around my knees and leaned forward, burying my face in the nest made by the crooks of my elbows.

"Fiona's not your usual woman," James said, putting a hand on my shoulder. "She's not a plow-horse. She's a bit of wild mustang. No one man will ever put a saddle on her." He went on to describe Fiona in various ways, trying to unravel her mystery for me. I would much later understand that my first love was not a nineteenth-century harlot but a modern woman, one who didn't allow herself to be hamstrung by convention or what others thought to be shameful. James went on for a while, attempting to decode Fiona's liberated nature for me. I listened, the pitch and timbre of his calm, steady voice almost hypnotic. I might have fallen asleep had my heartbreak not been suddenly swept aside by the image of Tuck Garwood's postcards…and curiosity.

You see, once I was able to put the pictures of Fiona and Everson Dexter out of my mind, it seemed I had a safe opportunity to figure out the sex business once and for all. Tuck had described sex for his brother Webb and me based on diligent study of the lewd postcards and a single romantic encounter he had observed between his family's Rottweiler and a couch pillow. It seemed to me that James, despite his bachelorhood, was likely to have a firmer grasp on the real thing and I pressed him for information. He was briefly taken aback, but after a moment, bravely forged ahead.

James had no experience as a father or wisdom to draw from; his own father, old Axel, was a devoted disciple of the philosophy that sex education was best obtained in the back seat of a car or the hay loft of a barn. However, James acquitted himself nicely and I resurrected much of his approach years later with my own sons. He began by getting the engineering out of the way, making sure I understood what tab went where. Afterward, he focused on what he called the "psychological particulars."

"No matter what the older boys tell you, Connor," he finished up, "remember that there are two voices in the bedroom and you'll do well to listen to the one other than your own."

I didn't entirely understand what he meant. Still, I felt better. That was the thing about James. He had a way about him that I found comforting.

"Are you gonna marry Ma?" I asked on our way back to the village.

James wasn't surprised.

"Would that be okay with you?" he asked.

I stopped and appraised him. I have previously asserted that James was a big man and he was. Fully four inches over six feet tall, he was likely two hundred fifty pounds, bone dry, with curly hair thinning over the crown of his head and the start of a second chin to match the slight belly he carried about. He was not rugged like Clark Gable or as handsome as Everson Dexter. However, standing on the beach, I could see how a woman might be drawn to a fellow like James. His eyes were steady and warm, his lips always slightly upturned. When he put his hand on my shoulder it reminded me of how he grazed Ma's hand when we went to the movies, or leaned against her when they stood next to the sink and washed dishes, or touched the small of her back to help guide her through a door he'd just opened. He was a gentleman, and along with C. Herbert Judson, Mr. Johns, and even old Angus MacCallum, more of a man than either Everson Dexter or Gable's wisecracking reporter could ever be.

The prospect of James as my father suddenly seemed quite all right, although the still vivid memory of Tuck Garwood's scandalous postcards was disturbing. The pornographic images had shown a limited variety of positions, most of them involving the man rutting about atop the woman. James, as I have pointed out, was large, and my mother of average size at best.

"You won't crush her, will you?" I asked.

James pulled his lips inward, swallowing an urge to laugh—an impressive display of self-restraint that I didn't fully appreciate until years later.

"I won't," he said. "I promise."

CHAPTER TWENTY

The third town meeting

The third town meeting to hear to the results of Everson Dexter's analysis was scheduled for three o'clock in the afternoon. Before the meeting Alex and I dropped by the library to pick up Ma. Alex immediately disappeared into an alcove in the back where a huge atlas and various other maps were housed. He had developed a fondness for geography, determining to learn the names of every country in the world. Eventually he did, too. Ma had a basket of books to re-shelve, and I followed her as she moved among the stacks.

She had been drinking Miss Lizzie's disgusting green remedy for three months, her transformation from madwoman to mother quite remarkable. She still had periods when I could see her eyes darken as she teetered on some precipice in her mind or dart about nervously if her mood was about to scatter like dry leaves in the wind. James helped at such times, wrapping his arms around her if she was about to fall or providing an anchor with a hand on hers when she threatened to fly away. Indeed, even before he educated me about sex, I had stopped competing with him. It had simply become too easy to hand Ma's reins over to James so I could enjoy the last days of perhaps the best summer of my life; one I'd spent hanging out with Alex and my friends, sailing with Mr. Judson, and sneaking out at night to conspire with the Ambergrisians.

Ma finished shelving books and sat at one of the heavy tables in the Fiction section of the library.

"Sit down," she said and I did. Her hands were in her lap and she studied them as if words were written there. After a few moments she looked up and fashioned an expression that unnerved me. I'd not been the target of such a thing, although my friends had described a "mom's look" for me enough times that I recognized one when I saw it. My wife, Marjory, had a mom's look she regularly used on our children, a face that snatches a lie out of the air and then dangles it in front of a kid, provoking an unsolicited admission of guilt in the same way a tendon hammer causes a knee to jerk.

Had she heard me sneak out? Did Alex tattle? Did Mei Ling under-stand more English than I thought?

I was about to break down and confess my role in the plot to scam Dinkle when Ma spoke.

"I want to talk to you about James," she said.

My relief must have been palpable and she hesitated, head cocked in the way of someone who has opened a secret door only to find an even more secret door inside.

"Is there something you want to tell me, Connor?" she said.

There was, but I didn't.

"James has asked me to marry him," she went on after a moment. Ma spoke as if requesting my permission, as if I were the parent. It made me uncomfortable. After my talk with James that morning her announcement wasn't a surprise, but I tried to pretend it was, resurrecting my respect for the skill of a real actor like Everson Dexter. Our thespian from San Fran-cisco was capable of lying with both credence and flair, while my wooden performance for Ma was about as convincing as a pickpocket's claim of innocence after you've discovered his hand inside your coat. Nevertheless, she bought it, probably because she had expected some push-back and wanted desper-ately to believe it had been that easy to tell me. Her relief was unmistakable, her eyes watery as she went on.

"Things will be different...better, I think," Ma said. "You

boys need a father." Her voice was fluttery and thin as tears spilled over and began to trail down her cheeks. "Lord knows I've been a terrible mother."

For the second time that day my heart genuinely ached. Her despair and my contribution to it by being born brought tears to my own eyes. I reached out and took her hand. "You aren't a terrible mother," I said.

I wasn't lying. I'd never viewed Ma as a terrible mother, probably because Angus McCallum had explained to me that parenting is a tag-team wrestling match. "Yer mither done 'er best, boys," Angus had once told Alex and me, "but she gotta slap hands wit' other folk noo' n' then or get 'erself pinned to the canvas."

I continued to hold Ma's hand as she dabbed at her eyes with a handkerchief.

"My goodness, look at me. Who's the grown-up here?" she said. She mustered up a brave smile. "And you...When did you get so smart and so old?"

I was neither but didn't argue the point as she appeared to have already made up her mind about it. Besides, I liked feeling both smart and old.

"I love you, Ma," I said.

It took her a few minutes to compose herself, but after a trip to the library's restroom, she reappeared with both her makeup and her outlook refreshed. We collected Alex and headed for the town hall with my brother veering off at Fremont Park to run with his pals while Ma and I went across the street and entered the assembly room.

As the discoverer of the ambergris, I was expected to preside with the town leaders during Everson Dexter's climactic presentation. I got Ma safely settled between Rosie and Roxy Littleleaf about three rows from the front, then made my way to the line of seats on the stage where I took a chair as far from Fiona as possible. I made a great show of ignoring her, although lavishing her with attention would have elicited the same response. She ignored me right back, taken up in hushed conversation with Everson Dexter. I wanted to scream at the pair of them, exposing him as a phony and a philanderer and Fiona as the fallen woman who had allowed herself to be despoiled by such a villain. I might have done exactly that if not for James. From his seat on the stage he recognized my fidgeting as a pot about to boil and brought me back to a simmer with an almost imperceptible shake of his head.

Shortly thereafter Mr. Johns called the meeting to order and requested nominations for moderator. Coach Wally Buford then spent five minutes campaigning for the position, this time with a set of hand-drawn pie charts and several whoppers exaggerating both his leadership experience and the authority naturally conferred upon anyone in possession of genuine rare documents. Over the years I've learned that a lie confirming what folks want to believe, especially when delivered with conviction, can be alarmingly convincing. However, Coach Wally had spent a lifetime showing folks his warts, because he was under the mistaken impression that one man's warts were another's garlands. Thus, the good citizens of Tesoro weren't about to let him turn their heads with a pie chart of questionable validity. Still, the coach was nothing if not gung-ho and made a pretty good run at the moderator's job until Milton Garwood interrupted from the back of the room.

"Try again when your boys have actually won a game and maybe we'll give you a shot," he shouted, reminding the congregation that it had been eight years since the coach's leadership produced a winning score for the Tesoro High Seagulls. This provoked a lot of laughter, most of it not particularly good-natured, as folks were impatient to find out how rich they were. After the hubbub provoked by Milton's remark died down, Mr. Johns was elected moderator and the meeting proceeded with an introduction of Everson Dexter. The handsome actor glided to the podium, accompanied by cacophonous cheering and clapping. He waited for the applause to subside, the tiniest hint of a smile on his face, then launched into his presentation.

In sharp contrast to the impromptu flamboyance of his "Good citizens" greeting the previous day, he spoke in a monotone. "Thallium was evidenced at four parts per million; calcium carbonate at sixteen parts per million; silica, basalt, and mica at two, seven, and fifteen grams, respectively," Dexter droned, "with common seaweed in various stages of decomposition representing fifteen percent of the total mass."

He went on like this for two or three minutes, his report making about as much sense to the assembled townsfolk as algebra to Milton Garwood's monkey. Slowly, the room began to fill with the sounds of shoes shuffling against the hardwood floor, nervous coughs, impatient sighs, and hoarse whispers. Finally, Milton Garwood had had enough.

"How much is the damned stuff worth?" he shouted.

This opened the door to a chorus of similar inquiries and Dexter lowered his report to the podium, fashioning a provocative smile that muted the men and made most of the women want to leave their husbands. He added a theatrical pause, the subsequent hush that settled over the assembly captivating his audience and putting them completely at his mercy. Once again, I marveled at his talent. He was an excellent actor, his voice and the manner in which he used it as nuanced and intentional as the notes played by a concert violinist. I hated him for usurping Fiona's affection with so little effort and yet found myself mesmerized along with the others while awaiting a verdict I already knew to be unadulterated balderdash.

"The final figure shows nine hundred fourteen pounds and seven ounces of ambergris at a purity of ninety percent," he said. "I have consulted with my superiors at the Allegheny Chemicals Corporation and they are prepared to make good on their original offer for that portion of your specimen that is pure. It calculates to just over eight hundred twenty-two pounds." Dexter then gave the final figure attached to the alleged sale: $37,444,752 or just to the north of $191,000 per Tesoro household.

The public declaration of an amount of money representing the national treasuries of a few small countries led to a good deal of whooping and leaping about. A few folks dissolved into a bizarre mélange of laughter and sobbing. One woman swooned. Milton Garwood had brought Mr. Sprinkles, absent his leash, and the little fellow was so unsettled by the range of emotions buffeted about the room that he began to screech and spit, eventually abandoning his post atop Milton's head in favor of one of the four ceiling fans. Once there, the slow rotation of the fan, along with Mr. Sprinkles' capricious decision to relieve himself, caused a considerable number of those packed into the chamber to be sprayed in a shower of monkey urine.

Now, when I think of that day, I recall a documentary film I once saw that followed jungle primates engaged in behaviors meant to establish dominance or encourage mating. There was a lot of screaming and arm-flinging in the film with the whole lot of excited chimps occasionally dashing about willy-nilly with no apparent purpose or destination in mind. This is more or less exactly what the good citizens of Tesoro did in those several minutes following Everson Dexter's announcement, and with all the dancing and shouting and weeping and monkey urine dodging, I suspect Mr. Sprinkles, taking it in from his perch atop the ceiling fan, must have felt right at home.

Once things settled down, the crowd peppered Dexter with questions—all variations of when, where, and how the money would find its way into their pockets. Eventually, the expected question was posed, although its author was entirely unexpected. He had entered after the meeting was already in progress and then listened to the presentation from the back of the room, a tall, gaunt fellow whose English was flavored with a Russian accent.

"Your employers pay much more than other bidders. Why?" Dinkle's man asked.

For a few moments the room was noiseless save the sound of the ceiling fans moving the air about and the window blinds gently clattering against their jambs. Not many folks around town had ever heard the fellow's voice; indeed, more than a few thought he might be an apparition incapable of speech that did not involve ghostly screeching or howling. About half in attendance turned to look at him, the rest bowing their heads, as if expecting icy fingers might suddenly jerk them from their seats and into the bowels of hell.

Everson Dexter was the first to recover. He had been to enough auditions to know the difference between a dilettante funding his first play and a producer with some actual juice. Dinkle's man had a serious way about him and Dexter fashioned an expression sober enough to evince proper respect.

"Ah, the question of the day," he said. "I've been wondering when it might come. However, before I answer, perhaps the ladies in the room might wish to powder their noses." He glanced at me. "The children, too."

No one moved. You see, folks back then had just as healthy a craving for titillation as they do now and Everson Dexter's suggestion that an impropriety was in store for those who stayed was a bit like waving bacon in front of a dog's nose and then asking him to be satisfied with an old shoe.

"I see," Dexter said when he saw every butt in the room still firmly glued to a chair. "Very well, then."

It turned out that Milton Garwood had been correct, or so Everson Dexter wanted folks to believe. According to the fiction he foisted upon the assembly, the Allegheny Chemicals Corporation had discovered that ambergris possessed male enhancement properties far outweighing its commercial value as a perfume fixative. He delivered this utter claptrap in terms so couched they might well have been spoken in Latin. Nevertheless, everyone got the point, the men snickering, the women blushing and dabbing at their lips with handkerchiefs. I was the only kid in the room and a few nervous eyes were cast my way, particularly from Judy Buford who was clearly afraid that her "marriage, prayer, and a good night's sleep" explanation of how babies were conceived was about to be debunked.

As nearly as I could tell, Dinkle's man neither believed nor disbelieved the explanation Dexter offered. He listened impassively and then exited as noiselessly as he had entered. The meeting broke up shortly thereafter with a good many attendees heading over to the Last Resort where they took turns buying drinks for each other to celebrate their forthcoming lives of wealth and comfort. Old Axel Throckmorton had no way to know that the tabs building up had little chance of ever being paid off and kept pouring while his son confabbed with the rest of the Ambergrisians on the stage of the assembly room.

"In two days there will be a lot of angry people in this town," James suggested to us.

"Not as angry as they'd be if Dinkle turned them out of their homes," Miss Lizzie countered.

No one else spoke for a few moments because there was nothing else to say. Frankly, we had discussed and rehashed our plan and its possible outcomes so many times it had become a worn-out shoe with a hole in its sole and the heel worn down. Mr. Judson, like many lawyers, was ill at ease with blank spaces in a conversation and eventually broke the silence.

"The ninetieth day is less than forty-eight hours away," he summarized. "I'm sure Dinkle already has his foreclosure notices ready to send out. Once people start opening the letters, I'll have a line at my office door in short order."

He exhaled sharply, as if already exhausted by the task ahead.

"It's not going to be pretty," he said. "I'll let everyone down as easily as I can, but we can expect a rough time of it until they find out what's really in the boathouse."

The plan was to do nothing in that regard, allowing Dinkle to discover the dinosaur egg on his own. Of course, the old gunrunner would be apoplectic, threatening all sorts of legal action. However, Mr. Judson once again assured us that the argument would have no merit before a judge insofar as the lines of credit were concerned.

"As long as the borrowers had no knowledge of what was actually in the boathouse, they're safe," he reiterated. "It was Dinkle's decision to accept their ambergris shares as collateral and it was his responsibility to determine the value of that collateral. Of course, if he finds out about our part in all this…"

Mr. Judson eyed each of us in turn. He didn't have to finish. We understood what would happen if Dinkle broke our egg before it was hatched: scandal, lawsuits, jail for the adult Ambergrisians, reform school for me. Indeed, there was little to reassure us. If our scheme worked, we were liars. If it didn't, we would be criminals. It was a sobering comparison, and for the first time, I wondered which of those two hats would be the hardest to wear. No one spoke until Everson Dexter interrupted the silence.

"Well, I guess it's time to bring down the curtain on my part in all this," he said. He stood and moved away from Fiona, fracturing the intimacy they'd shared at the beginning of the town meeting. I hated him. *The bastard is leaving her*, I thought and he was. I had yet to erase from my mind the disturbing image of Fiona sneaking from his room at the Kittiwake Inn, but she was my friend, and the idea that some morally bereft scalawag from San Francisco was about to dump her—just as my father had dumped my mother—made me want to defend what was left of her honor. I was about to take a poke at him when Dinkle's man interrupted us a second time.

Once again, the phantasmagorical fellow did not so much enter as materialize, the doorway at the back of the room empty one moment, then framing his tall figure the next. He came down the center aisle, seeming almost to float. Upon reaching us, he handed Dexter an envelope, at the same time glancing at Fiona as if to say: *You can do better than this man.*

"Dinner," he said, eyeing our imposter as if he could unmask him with merely his gaze. "...Eight o'clock."

Dexter glanced at the card inside the envelope. He was nervous, the ghostly aspect of Dinkle's man temporarily putting him off his game. A moment later he recovered, although apparently still anxious as he inexplicably spoke with a slight English accent.

"Thanks so much, old chap," he said. "But I must take my leave. Train tickets and all. You understand." He offered Dinkle's man a weak smile that had the same effect a canary might have upon a cobra. "Regrets," he added.

Dinkle's man gave Dexter the same stony consideration once shown impertinent new recruits to the Russian Imperial Army.

"I bring car at seven forty-five," he said.

"Look, old boy, that simply won't work. I've a train to catch in San Francisco."

"Seven forty-five," Dinkle's man repeated, and with that, we all knew Everson Dexter would not be leaving. The curtain was not about to come down. Before we got to Act II in our play, there would be a final scene in Act I.

Dinkle's man left without another word, acknowledging only Fiona with a polite nod. After he had gone, Mr. Judson turned to Dexter. "Are you up for this?" he asked the actor.

Dexter had been unsettled by the unexpected appearance of Dinkle's man and remained so—his color less robust, his eyes blinking a bit too much.

"Not to worry," he said in a way unconvincing enough to make us worry even more. "I can handle it."

"Can he do this?" Miss Lizzie asked Mr. Judson, ignoring the fact that Dexter hadn't moved from his chair.

"I said I could handle it," Dexter reiterated, his attempt at indignance more prissy than reassuring.

"Dinkle is savvy, Hal," Mr. Judson said, using Dexter's real name for the first time. "He may suspect you and us already. That may be what this invitation is about. If so, you'll have to be on top of your game or Dinkle will ferret out the truth… Either he or that walking corpse of his."

"Maybe you and Miss Lizzie can go with him," Mr. Johns suggested, eyeing our actor. "Or you, Fiona. You know…in case Mister Dexter wavers…Strength in numbers and all that."

"I don't need anyone else to go," Dexter snapped. "I can handle it. How many times do I have to tell you?"

Mr. Judson ended the dispute. "No one else is going," he said, his voice resolute. "Nothing will raise the hairs on Dinkle's neck more than one of us showing up uninvited." He shifted his gaze to Dexter. "It's on you, Hal."

Dexter gave manly squaring of his shoulders a shot, an effort that once again was more reminiscent of Claudette Colbert than Clark Gable. At the same time he laughed, although the sound was both hollow and humorless. He delivered his next line with the excessive bravado typical of a comic melodrama. "Hal? Who's Hal? The name is Dexter…Everson Dexter of the Allegheny Chemicals Corporation."

It was an attempt at humor, but no one laughed. I later knew some self-appointed comedians in the army who would not have given up before embarrassing themselves, but Dexter was experienced enough to accept our flat-eyed response as his cue to leave. He strode up the center aisle to the rear entry of the assembly room, hesitating at the exit to offer us a grin and a jazzy two-fingered salute. His last-ditch effort to win us over fell as flat as his joke, and he formed a petulant frown, then left in a bit of huff. Once he was gone, Fiona sighed loudly.

"God help us," she breathed.

The group broke up then and everyone headed home. On

our way out Mr. Johns expressed what we were all thinking. "I'd love to be a fly on the wall of that dining room tonight," he mused. His comment was met by nodding heads and a low murmur of agreement. And that's when I knew what had to be done.

CHAPTER TWENTY-ONE

Dinkle's man squeezes the potato

Yurievsky walked the mile back to the Dinkle estate and went directly to his quarters above the garage. He carefully cleaned the road dust from his boots and applied fresh polish, recalling advice his mother had given him when he was a boy. "Always squeeze a potato before you eat it, Sergei," she'd told him more than once. "If you find a soft spot, the potato has gone bad. Don't trust the skin. The potato may look normal, but soft spots tell you it isn't."

When his boots once again shone, Yurievsky donned his butler's garb and started for the main house to give the old man a report. He was late. Dinkle would be displeased. Like officers in the former Russian Imperial Army, the old man was patient with himself, allowing ample time to arrive at a decision of what order to give, but impatient for results once it was given. He would want confirmation that his demand had been met. *And despite wearing the mask of invitation*, Yurievsky mused, *it was a demand.*

As he entered the main house Yurievsky mulled over how much he should reveal to his employer. The ex-soldier had known his share of scientific types and engineers. They were a dry lot and far less attentive to their personal appearances than the villagers' handsome expert with the dashing name. Yurievsky's wife, Olga, had loved the theater in St. Petersburg, and her circle of friends had included many actors. Everson Dexter had seemed more like one of Olga's friends than a

156

chemist, his speech theatrically articulated, his hair perfectly coiffed, his eyes instinctively searching for a reflection of his own image in the windows of the assembly room. His testimony had seemed false as well, the collection of chemical terms populating his report reminiscent of a random sampling from the glossary of a textbook, rather than anything cohesive and logical. All told, Everson Dexter was a potato with soft spots.

As a sergeant in the Russian Imperial Army and an aide to Grand Duke Pavlovich, Yurievsky had learned to keep his opinions to himself. It was a habit he'd sustained in his present employment as Dinkle preferred it that way as well. The former gunrunner had secrets of his own, as Yurievsky well knew after carefully reading every document the old man entrusted to him for delivery to San Francisco bankers and brokers and lawyers and accountants. Yurievsky was no thief but had been around enough of them to recognize one, even when disguised in spats and a three-piece suit. He knew Dinkle to be less a businessman than a privateer, the papers shared with his cohorts revealing a pirate's plunder in the form of tax evasion, insider trading, land grabs, and a very large toe dipped into a pool of water populated by the ruthless men who made their living as purveyors of illegal gambling and prostitution.

Yurievsky knocked on the door to the study. A moment later Dinkle's bark sounded from the other side. The tall Russian hesitated, his hand on the doorknob. The old man would want a succinct report, but perhaps there was more to tell...something of greater value. Dinkle had contacts in the same dark world inhabited by the whore in Macao, the woman who had recognized a face in the only photo Yurievsky had of his wife and daughter. The old man occasionally tossed out a rumor or possible sighting by one of the crooks in his underworld network. In the beginning Yurievsky had followed up on each lead. He no longer bothered. They were all fabrications, tantalizing clues offered to shorten the leash that kept close

Dinkle's most valuable servant. It was the old man's way. The former Indian Territories trader disdained kindnesses or favors, contending that business and personal transactions were mismatched socks. What he couldn't steal had to be obtained through barter. *I don't agree*, Yurievsky often mused. *Everything in life is personal. Robbery makes one man richer and able to buy food, another poorer and starving. Murder leaves a man dead, his murderer alive. The men I've killed for money did not see it as commerce. They took it personally, just as I took it personally when other men tried to kill me.*

Even though Dinkle's informants had thus far provided nothing, Yurievsky allowed his boss to believe that allegiance had been acquired via a proper trade. *The bastard might one day unearth the right potato. One without soft spots when squeezed.* Besides, the tall Russian told himself, it was useful for Dinkle to believe loyalty had been purchased, given the old man's distrust of unencumbered faithfulness.

He entered Dinkle's study. His employer was at the window. It was open and the ex-gunrunner looked out on a sea made choppy and loud by late afternoon westerlies. The old man held a glass with a single finger of scotch, swirling it gently as if dancing with the distant whitecaps. When Yurievsky didn't speak, Dinkle looked over, his face simmering with expectation and incipient rage.

"Well?" he snarled.

Yurievsky recalled the serious faces of the visiting chemist and village leaders. Their voices had been hushed as he entered, then abruptly silent when they looked up and saw him. He remembered similar voices, those of Usupov, Grand Duke Pavlovich, and the others on the night before the Mad Monk was dispatched. The villagers—the lawyer, the banker, the midwife, the bartender, and the old lighthouse keeper; the young woman Irina might have become; the boy—all of them evidenced more than surprise when he spoke from the back of the room at the town meeting.

What frightened them…me?

Dinkle's man quietly closed the door and then faced his employer.

"Well?" Dinkle demanded again. "Is he coming?"

Yurievsky's head was suddenly filled with images: the too-handsome chemist, the startled village leaders, the boy who had no good reason to be there, and finally, Olga and Irina.

Fear of me? No…fear of discovery.

"Yes," the former Russian soldier said, "he is coming."

CHAPTER TWENTY-TWO

I enter the lair

Following the adjournment of the third town meeting, I determined to sneak onto the Dinkle estate, something my friends and I had done many times. It had always been great sport for us, crawling up the dunes from the ocean side or picking our way through rows of grapevines on the acres bordering the town. To be sure, it was most often done after Dinkle's man had driven his boss through the village on their way to San Francisco, but Alex and I had more than once explored the buildings when Dinkle was at home, once hiding directly under the bay window of his study and eavesdropping on a telephone conversation. This time would be different. This time when I entered the lair the wolf would be inside.

I relished a chance to test my grit as Jim Hawkins had done with the pirates on Treasure Island, and as far as I was concerned, Mr. Johns had given me my marching orders. I was to be his fly on the wall, the spy who would secretly observe the meeting between Cyrus Dinkle and Everson Dexter, afterward reporting back to headquarters. Of course, I was a self-proclaimed spy. There were no marching orders, no headquarters. I was no more sanctioned than a stowaway. Mr. Johns had done nothing more than express idle curiosity. However, these were trifling details to a ten-year-old boy thirsting for adventure, and I wasn't about to let them deter me.

I considered taking Alex along as he had proven himself an adept cohort during previous forays onto Dinkle's estate.

Ultimately I rejected the idea, reasoning that one of us had to remain alive to help James take care of Ma. This might sound melodramatic, but Webb Garwood's older brother Tuck insisted that Dinkle's man kept an icebox on the estate filled with the body parts of boys. "He's got him a compost pile, too, for the livers and lungs and whatnot he ain't gonna eat," Tuck claimed. It was an absurd notion, but I was ten and inclined to ignore the shortage of missing boys from our small village in favor of a scary story told over a midnight campfire by someone's older brother.

Dinkle's estate occupied around one hundred acres, including a lengthy stretch of beach along the Pacific Ocean. Dunes protected the compound on the west with a few rolling acres of grapevines on the east and north. A stone wall had been erected along the southern exposure, the driveway in and out of the grounds guarded by an iron gate. Just inside the gate was a low building with six apartments—servants' quarters unoccupied since the former Mrs. Dinkle took her leave. A circular drive led to the front entry of the main house, a huge edifice fashioned after the staid English country estates the old man admired. What had once been a stable—now a garage—was to the west of the mansion, set at a right angle with its rear face exposed to the evening sun. A large guesthouse was at the back of the property. It, too, was empty with only Dinkle, his man, and the occasional Boop in residence within the compound at night.

My friends and I had explored the guesthouse and servants' quarters from attic to crawlspace many times, slipping through an unlocked window and then skulking about the deserted rooms, pretending to be spies on a mission or commandos sent to kidnap a king. One window or another was predictably unsecured, although not always the same one. I speculated that the cook or one of the housekeepers were part of our game, rotating the means of entry to add mystery and adventure.

Neither Dinkle nor his man seemed capable of such whimsy, and if captured, I figured to face the same fate as a fly on flypaper. And his man? If Tuck Garwood was right, the tall, spectral fellow subsisted on a diet of snake venom and slow children. Were a village boy to fall into his clutches we felt certain the doomed captive would be seasoned with basil and rosemary and eaten for dinner with a bottle of the bad wine Dinkle produced from the grapes on his estate.

A few of my friends claimed to have breached the brick walls of the main house. I didn't believe them. Within a perimeter of twenty yards around Dinkle's manor, there was nary a bush nor tree nor unruly tuft of grass to provide cover. Alex and I had once made it as far as the recess beneath the bay window of the former gunrunner's study, but only after sprinting across the lawn in full view of anyone looking out one of the mansion's many windows, afterward crawling on our bellies along the foundation until we reached the ocean side of the house. My mission would require similar pluck. Even with Labor Day behind us, the eight o'clock dinner engagement predicted sufficient twilight to expose an intruder dashing across open ground. Night would have taken over by dinner's end, and with the moon a modest crescent at quarter month, I knew escape would be easier.

To get out for the evening, I concocted a fiction for Ma about crabbing with Webb Garwood. "Don't wait up," I told her. "I'll be late."

Most mothers would have wrung the truth out of me in seconds, but Ma was still new to the job after several years in the throes of madness. She was susceptible to a decently told lie, particularly with James unintentionally abetting my duplicity. He now had dinner with us every evening, with he and Ma afterward getting googly-eyed over one another, something that made them quite proficient at courting but rank amateurs as parents. Once they married, Ma and James became a competent team, but on the night I broke into Dinkle's stronghold, Alex was the only one in our house with any suspicions.

"Where are you going?" he asked as I pulled on my sneakers.

"I told you. Crabbing with Webb."

"You're lying. Where are you really going? I want to go."

"You can't."

"Why not?"

"Because. You're not invited. You can't go. Now shut up."

Alex rarely argued and didn't this time, although he displayed a rare bit of cheek. "Prick," he said. Had he known what would happen that night, my little brother might have chosen a different word: *Fool.*

With no further protest from Alex, I exited our cottage and made my way across town, passing Miss Lizzie's house along the way. Mei Ling was on the front porch, curled into a wicker settee, her omnipresent stack of movie magazines nearby. I waved and she giggled in reply, holding a finger to her lips as if to tell me that our secret at the gazebo remained just ours. Afterward, I crossed the Tesoro city limit and then veered north for a distance before slipping into the grapevines that bordered Dinkle's mansion on the east. By 7:45 p.m.—fifteen minutes before the scheduled dinner with Everson Dexter—I was successfully hidden in the last row of grapevines nearest the house, searching for a grim face in one of the dark windows across the lawn.

About two minutes before eight o'clock, the Duesenberg passed through the gated entry and cruised up the circular drive. Yurievsky was at the wheel with a silhouetted figure in the back seat—Everson Dexter, his solid chin, straight nose, and flop of perfectly tousled hair making him easily identifiable. The car swept around the first curve in the driveway and approached the house, disappearing after it cleared the edge of the mansion. This was my chance. I knew Dinkle would come outside to greet his guest the way he figured English dukes and

German barons and other fellows with oversized, under-populated houses did it. Yurievsky would then move the Duesenberg to the garage before re-entering the mansion. That left only the cook to worry about and I felt confident that her employer's exacting snobbery would keep her attention on her saucepans and roaster; hence, she'd be unlikely to see me when I emerged from the vineyard and dashed across the lawn. I heard the thud of the Duesenberg's door as it was closed and rose.

The next few seconds were thrilling as I raced across the lawn in full view of anyone looking out one of the east-facing windows. There was no shout of alarm, no sharp report from a well-aimed rifle. I reached the house and threw myself against the concrete foundation, pushing my back into it as if doing so might help me blend into its cool gray surface. I then had a few moments of near-hysterical regret. It had taken mere seconds to breach the distance between the safety of the vineyard and my unnervingly exposed position next to the house. I knew it would take only a few more to re-trace my steps, and I suddenly wanted to make for the vineyard, disappear within its leafy vines, and then hike back to the village. No one had to know I'd made it no further than the cold unforgiving wall at my back. No one had to know I'd lost my nerve.

Although I dropped out of college to enlist in 1942, intent on achieving glory, the U.S. Army thought it better to arm me with a pen rather than a rifle. I wrote for *Stars & Stripes* and never made it into combat. Alex was not so lucky. He became a Navy pilot and was killed in 1951, his jet shot down in Korea. I've since viewed war as a folly incited by fellows who have run out of ideas. However, I still harbor admiration and perverse envy for the boys who rise up and charge into the withering fire of enemy guns. Such men have a chance to show what they're made of. As a boy and a young man, I wondered if I could do what they did. I always wanted to believe I could, that I wouldn't turn tail and run. I wouldn't retreat now, of course, but at my age it's not hard to give up the rest of your life. Not so easy at nineteen or twenty. Or at ten years old. For what it's worth, even with nothing higher than a blade of grass to hide my position and my heart drumming in my ears, I didn't run away the night I snuck onto Dinkle's estate.

I took a minute to reclaim my momentarily dislodged gumption and then crept along the outer wall of the house, staying below the window sills. Halfway to the rear of the mansion was a set of French doors with panels of leaded glass. Just outside them was a small, unfenced flagstone patio with a table and one chair. I reached the doors and tested a handle. It turned and I slipped into the house.

Inside, I found a room brightly lit by a massive cut-glass chandelier. The place was otherwise a mismatched homage to wood: polished oak floors, cherry window-paning on the ceiling, a fireplace with a huge mahogany surround adorned with baroque carvings, a ponderous Brazilian rosewood dining table and chairs, a teak sideboard. Rather than a centerpiece, the table displayed a small sculpture of a naked, bearded man with impressive genitals. About twelve inches tall, the fellow held a cluster of grapes close to one ear. I noted two place settings at the table as voices sounded in the outer corridor.

Characters in books and moving pictures frequently hide behind drapes, eavesdropping as I intended to do, or leaping out to accuse a villain or save a damsel. Such a ploy had seemed entirely plausible to me until I tried it during one of our overnighters with Miss Lizzie. Alex and I had snuck from our beds and gone to the parlor where we hid behind the window drapes while Miss Lizzie listened to the New York Metropolitan Opera broadcast on her wireless. We thought ourselves great sneaks, but sibilant giggling and our toes beneath the lower hem of the curtains quickly gave us away. "I'm thinking about beating the dust out of those drapes with a broom handle. I sure hope no one is behind them," Miss Lizzie had called out, sending Alex and I scuttling back to bed. Afterward, I concluded that any success literature had attached to hiding behind window coverings was a contrivance of some writer's overactive imagination. Unfortunately, with the voices suddenly louder I realized that Cyrus Dinkle's dining room offered nothing I might hide in, under, or behind other than the heavy drapes framing the French doors.

The door leading to the dining room began to open inward and I was suddenly overwhelmed with images of a boy like me on a platter, seasoned with ginger and thyme, an apple jammed into my mouth. I wanted to abandon my mission, slip out the way I'd entered, and return to the village where I would lie to my friends about what really happened at Dinkle's estate. Then I thought about the advice given me by Mr. Judson. "Be a man people can count on," he'd told me.

I slipped behind one of the drapes.

The first hour of dinner conversation between Cyrus Dinkle and Everson Dexter was memorable for being completely unmemorable. From my hiding spot behind a drape made of thick velvet and smelling vaguely of mildew, I could only hear them but doubt I'd have learned much more had I been sitting in the middle of the table alongside the naked, bearded man. I expected Dexter to chatter like a sixteen-year-old girl, but he was a much better actor than I allowed and proved to be as boring as one would hope an analyst from the Allegheny Chemicals Corporation might be. Dinkle was no slouch when it came to being dull. He spoke not proverbially, but literally, about the price of tea in China—its impact on the Chinese economy and how it fit into the dispute between the Communists and some outfit called the Kuomintang, and how it didn't much matter anyway because war was coming given that the Japanese were already in Manchuria and all. As an adult I would have been impressed with Dinkle's worldliness and insight. However, at ten years old he nearly put me to sleep. Fortunately, the former gunrunner mercifully got to the point before I nodded off and spilled into the room.

"So, Mister Dexter, this analysis you're conducting," the old man began. "It's working out? The material is genuine?"

"Ninety percent pure," Dexter answered.

"And your company is paying almost three thousand per ounce?"

"That's the current bid."

"That's a hefty investment for a private company. They must be well capitalized."

"I'm a chemist, not an accountant," Dexter said. "I presume Mister Bell knows what he's doing."

I heard the sound of liquid being poured. Dinkle was filling their glasses with wine produced from his own grapes. He had spent a fortune cultivating the land, but the wine he bottled was much like him—sour and overbearing.

"We bottle this wine on the estate," Dinkle said. "I'm a bit of oenologist." He chuckled, although it sounded less like laughter than a mouse being swallowed alive. "I guess that makes me a chemist, too," he added.

This was a lie. Dinkle occasionally drew a glass from the barrel, but knew less about wine-making than Mr. Sprinkles.

"Perhaps you could share some details of your analysis with me?" Dinkle went on. "One chemist to another, don't you know."

It seemed an innocent request and yet filled me with dread. Had Dinkle nosed his way past Everson Dexter's false storefront? Could he see the vacant lot behind it? I recalled Mr. Judson's warning. *Dinkle might be too savvy to be taken in*, he'd said. *No matter how convincing the charlatan*. Now it seemed our town lawyer's concern was imminently in danger of being realized.

For a few moments, I seriously considered darting from behind the curtain, taking up one of the table knives, and driving it into Cyrus Dinkle's cold, black heart. Then, Dexter began to speak and I realized that my worry was misplaced. Dinkle was no chemist and Everson Dexter was intuitive enough to appreciate it. Moreover, I later learned that our imposter had many times appeared on stage with an ancient, once highly regarded thespian whose ability to learn his lines had given way to a combination of senility and pre-performance vodka. The dotty fellow was prone to long strings of ad-libbed verse as he struggled to make his way back to an actual script, forcing his cast-mates to extemporize. Among them, Dexter had become particularly adept at such improvisations and now put his experience to good use, filling the air with a mishmash of "covalent anions" and "double-bonded aromatic rings" and "phenols" and "phenolates" and "ethers" and "ethylenes" and "distillations" and "activated sludge processes" and "molarities" and "oxidations" and a nearly endless list of things that only came in moles or parts per million. It was a preposterous panoply of chemistry gobbledygook but proved effective. Dinkle was quickly bored, and after listening to Dexter's poppycock for only a few minutes, he launched into a soliloquy on the dismal state of affairs in Washington D Almighty C and how George Washington would have done better than President Roosevelt.

It was a nice segue-way into a discussion of rare documents—Dinkle's point, of course, being that he had a pair of them and Dexter didn't. Dinkle called for his man to retrieve the Washington letters from his study and afterward held the floor for thirty minutes before full bladders sent both men to separate lavatories. They returned a few minutes later and their exchange signaled an evening near its end.

"I've enjoyed our time together," Dexter said. "Especially the dinner. The cuisine in the village is rather unimaginative as I'm sure you know. Please extend my compliments to your chef."

When Dinkle answered his voice was gruff. He had yet to acquire the information that had prompted the dinner invitation and the effort to do so had stripped away whatever civility he was capable of mustering.

"I don't have a chef," he growled. "I have a cook. She receives adequate pay that I'm sure she finds preferable to compliments."

"No doubt," Dexter replied. He seemed unaffected by his host's curt manner and remained silent as if awaiting the cue for his next line. The moment of silence became several and I tipped my head forward far enough to catch a reflection of the two men in one of the dark glass panels of the door. As I watched, Dinkle filled his glass with wine and then held it up to the light as if inspecting the facets of a diamond.

"My man will drive you back to the village," he said without looking at his guest. "I'll expect a copy of your report by tomorrow noon."

This is when Everson Dexter proved to be worth whatever the Ambergrisians had agreed to pay him. Drawing back his shoulders, he cocked his head defiantly in the way of a browbeaten clerk who's suddenly come across a stiff backbone and a clear picture of what his son-of-a-bitch boss can do with his damned job. It was a posture both dismissive and surprisingly manly.

"Once again, thank you for your hospitality, Mister Dinkle," Dexter said, his voice unyielding. "However, as you are not a shareholder in the village enterprise I cannot provide you with the report without their permission. Perhaps you should ask them for it."

A well-circulated rumor around town claimed that many years earlier a man in the Indian Territories had attempted to face down Cyrus Dinkle, the dispute involving a promised case of whiskey for three dollars versus three dollars and fifty cents. Dinkle had allegedly shot and killed the man, afterward hanging the body from a tree in front of his trading post as a lesson to those who valued fifty cents more than their lives. It was

Trader Dinkle who now leveled rattlesnake eyes on Everson Dexter.

"I'm not making a request," he said. "You follow?"

Once again Dexter surprised me. With the viper about to strike, he didn't blink.

"When you threaten me, Mister Dinkle," Dexter said, his words issued with grave deliberation, "you threaten the Allegheny Chemicals Corporation and its president, Mister J. Piedmont Bell. Perhaps you've heard of him by his nickname… Bootleg Bell? He's rather well known in certain circles…colorful past and all that…Prohibition, don't you know…friends in places both high and low. You two would get along. He doesn't make requests either."

This time it was Dinkle who surprised me. The threat of J. Piedmont Bell was imaginary and three thousand miles away, yet the old man's discomfiture was apparent as he attempted to disguise squirming about in his chair as mere repositioning to give his figuratively squeezed testicles more air. It was a good lesson for me, one I carried with me throughout my life: Bullies like Dinkle need not be confronted by a bigger bully. They just have to be confronted.

Suddenly, Dinkle threw back the rest of his wine in a swallow, afterward refilling his glass. He drained it and then stood, glancing in my direction. I pulled back, praying he'd not seen my reflection in the glass.

"Good evening to you, Mister Dexter," I heard him say, followed by the sound of the old man's footsteps as he left the dining room, leaving Everson Dexter at the table and me still hiding behind the drape.

CHAPTER TWENTY-THREE

I steal a letter opener

Dexter remained in the dining room for nearly a full minute and I wondered if his host's abrupt exit from the dining room had put a crack in our actor's carefully crafted pretense. After all, despite his money and affectations Dinkle was a thug, his veneer of civility no thicker than his shaving balm, a dense layer of menace just beneath it. Given his profession, it's more likely that Dexter awaited the thunderous applause he believed was his after a masterful performance.

I heard Dexter sigh loudly, undoubtedly as much disappointed as relieved, followed by the abrasive protest of a chair sliding away from the dining table and then the click of footsteps, the sounds quickly fading into echoes and then silence. Next came the growl of an automobile engine and the crunch of tires against the driveway stones. I waited until the rumble of the Duesenberg's engine had faded to a hum before peeking out from behind the drape. The dining room remained lit but was deserted other than the statue of the naked, bearded man. Dishes remained on the table, waiting to be cleared. Dinkle's wine glass was empty, while Dexter's was nearly full.

It was time for me to make good my escape. My mission had been accomplished. I could report to the Ambergrisians that Dexter had not given us away. Further risk was foolhardy. Still, I hesitated. Somewhere in the cavernous mausoleum Dinkle called "home" were papers the Boops had collected. I was a child and won't pretend that I comprehended lines of credit or balances owed or foreclosures in the same way the adult Ambergrisians did. But I knew those papers were the trapdoors my friends and neighbors in Tesoro were about to fall through. I decided to steal them.

I padded softly across the dining room and then into the outer corridor. It was harshly lit, as turned out to be true for the entire house. As I noiselessly stole down the hallway, a series of rooms were revealed in which every light switch had been flipped on. Eventually I reached a grand circular foyer illuminated by a huge chandelier comprised of dozens of faux candles. It was suspended from four long gilded chains gloriously ascending through three open stories into a cupola whose underside boasted a reproduction of Michelangelo's *The Fall of Man*. On one side of the foyer a wide, majestic staircase swirled upward to a second-floor mezzanine that was the most blindingly lit of all. I paused beneath the chandelier and looked up, squinting against the brilliant glow, for a moment taken by the irony of so much effort to avoid the night. Despite Dinkle's intimidating demeanor and reputation, he was apparently afraid of the dark.

Several doors, all closed, marked rooms off the foyer and the sound of footsteps from the mezzanine sent me running for one of them. I reached it and slipped inside, discovering what looked to be a library with bookshelves lining three of the four walls from floor to ceiling. Like the other spaces I'd thus far seen, this one was well lit with six large glass-shaded pendants, a few wall sconces, and lamps on both the refectory table and a huge desk. The desk boasted a swivel chair with its high back given to the room's distinctive bay window, allowing Dinkle to simply rotate to look out. I recognized the window. Alex and I had once hidden just beneath it, plastered against the foundation of the house, secretly listening to Dinkle conduct business on the telephone just a few feet above our heads. I was now in the old man's study on the west side of the mansion, the lawn

I'd dashed across and the safety of the vineyard where I'd waited and watched just three hours earlier now on the opposite side of the house.

The footsteps I'd heard were Dinkle's and they grew louder as he descended the stairway to the foyer. Unlike the town meeting, when he'd glided to the podium, Dinkle, the homebody, walked on his heels, causing the entire house to shudder very slightly with each step. He reached the main floor and the sounds grew louder. Then the doorknob across the room turned and I ran for the desk, instinctively grabbing Dinkle's letter opener from a leather cup before diving into the chair opening.

I squeezed behind the swivel chair—an oak piece with a curved back, four wheels, and a sour smelling pad—careful to avoid moving it lest the casters squeak. From there I heard Dinkle cross the room, followed by the swish and thud of books moved about or knocked to the floor. The next sound was unmistakable—the whir and click of a combination lock being spun.

A hidden safe!

I cautiously peeked out and saw Dinkle from behind. He was on his knees in front of the nearest bookcase, wearing pajamas and a bathrobe, the safe blocked from view by his generous frame. The whir and click sounds stopped and then I saw the motion of his arm as he turned the safe's handle. Suddenly, he cocked his head as if listening, at the same time glancing over his shoulder. I ducked back under the desk. A second passed, then another and another. Now, the room was as silent as a held breath and I imagined the more graceful Dinkle from the town meeting, floating across the room to the recess where I now hid. I tightened my grip around the handle of the letter opener—a deadly looking thing six inches long with a pointed tip, its metal haft depicting a snake curled around a tree branch. More silence ensued. And then I heard a soft squeak as the safe door was opened, followed by the sound of papers being shuffled.

The contracts!

I chanced another look. Dinkle once again had his back to me. He held a sheaf of papers that were hurriedly perused and then set aside on the floor. He resumed rummaging about in the safe and extracted another set of papers. This time he stood to read them, the effort to regain his feet attended by tiny grunts and a bit of wheezing. For the next several minutes he walked about, whispering aloud as he reviewed the documents. When he moved behind his desk, I retreated as deeply into my mouse-hole as possible, eyeing the spot on his shin where I could bury the tip of the letter opener before making a run for it. He didn't sit, instead standing to read, his legs mere inches from my face. His robe was purple velvet, his pajamas silk, his slippers creased leather. I could smell him—old shoes, new farts.

After a few minutes the old man moved to the bay window and threw back the drapes, giving me a view that extended from heel to chin with only the back of his bald head blocked by the top edge of the desk. I burrowed more deeply into my hiding place, accidentally bumping the chair. It moved slightly, and yet as impossible as it might seem, Dinkle did not notice. He remained motionless and I imagined his round, porcine eyes searching the darkness outside his window. It was nearly eleven o'clock by then, the glow of twilight long past, the nearby ocean a sheet of black. Nevertheless, he peered into the night as if the pixie-like, phosphorescent sparkles on the water were overhead stars, remaining at his post for what seemed a very long time. Then, the slanted glare of a car's headlamps bathed the ground outside the window in white-yellow light and he stepped away.

The Duesenberg…Dinkle's man!

Dinkle left the drapes open and moved out of view. Once

again I heard the rustle of papers, a soft thud as the safe door was shut, a single buzzing whir as he spun the combination dial. He had nearly finished re-shelving the books that hid his safe when a knock on the door sounded.

"Enter," Dinkle called out. I heard the door open and then close, followed by a thickly accented voice.

"You are done with me for tonight, yes?" Dinkle's man asked.

"Yes," Dinkle answered. "No...wait. There is something. Did you use my letter opener? It's not on my desk."

Dinkle's man didn't answer.

"No...Of course, you didn't," Dinkle muttered. "God-damned housekeepers. They're a bunch of gypsies."

Suddenly, my head was flooded with images of the compost pile Tuck Garwood had described. In my mind it was just as Tuck claimed: a rotting mound filled with the body parts of boys—body parts that could well include mine before the end of the evening. I began to tremble, praying my shudders would not cause the desk chair to move and squeak, praying even harder for my crime to be pinned on the housekeepers. My prayer, as with most prayers, was self-serving. To save my own skin I was more than happy to throw his maids over the cliff. I understood what might happen. It would not go well for them. Dinkle was a harsh master. He would lay into the women for stealing his letter opener, maybe fire one of them. Maybe all of them. I didn't care. It was unfortunate, but their lives weren't at stake. Mine was. Then Dinkle's man spoke and the house-keepers were saved, just as surely and suddenly as my fate was sealed.

"You look under desk, yes?" Dinkle's man said.

"Why would it be...?" Dinkle growled, then, "Oh, what the hell."

I heard the old man's footsteps even though my ears were suddenly filled with a pounding sound. He drew closer and my skin began to tingle, the imagined heat and stench of his wolf's breath rendering me light-headed and dizzy. I now wonder if Alex felt such fear just before crashing into the China Sea. I hope not. I hope he enjoyed, in his last moments, the freedom of just not giving a damn. It's been suggested by poets that soldiers faced with the inevitability of death have such feelings and I suspect it may be true for others, as well, particularly a fellow at my advanced age. However, cowering under the desk with Death near enough to touch, it was not true for me.

And then it was. As amazing and unbelievable as it might sound, when Dinkle appeared in the chair opening—less than an arm's length from where I hid—my head suddenly cleared, my eyes sharpened, the wolf's breath grew distant, and my heart settled into a steady rhythm. I remember the frayed cuffs of his pajamas, the pale ankles above his slippers, the dangling tails of the belt on his bathrobe. He pulled back the chair and I more tightly gripped the letter opener. I was calm and no longer afraid. My mission had changed and I was ready to strike. There would be no need to steal the contracts in his safe, I told myself; instead, I would kill their author with his own letter opener. Then it would all be over. I would face the hangman's noose, but the town would be saved. Hip, hip, hooray.

Dinkle began to kneel and his chest appeared, followed by his soft neck. My heartbeat further slowed as his chin came into view, then his lower lip. I gripped the letter opener more tightly. I was ready, my body a coiled spring, the pointed letter opener as lethal as the artful snake curled around its handle. Suddenly, Dinkle straightened and stood as the unmistakable sound of a car horn pierced the night. It was loud and continuous.

"What the hell?" he snarled. I heard one of the desk drawers squawk in protest as it was jerked open, followed by a clatter as Dinkle rummaged about inside. He found whatever he was looking for and made for the study door, first ramming into the chair. It careened back into my hiding place beneath the desk, spinning on its column. One corner of the seat caught my cheek where it left a small bruise that I would later explain away to Ma as coming from a stray elbow Webb Garwood had thrown my way during a wrestling match. I remained motionless, listening first to the muffled, dissipating thud of footsteps in the foyer followed by a whoosh of air as I released the breath I'd held for nearly a minute.

I scrambled out from beneath the desk and made for the bay window where I fumbled open one of the casements and went through it. Seconds later, I had made my way to the other side of the mansion, breached the lawn, and slipped into the safety of the vineyard. I threw myself to the ground, then just as quickly leapt up, a tiny gasp of shock and fear exiting my lips. I was not alone. A figure crouched between the rows, someone small. A whisper followed.

"*Lái ba.*" The figure stood. "*Lái ba.*"

It was Mei Ling. She put a finger to her lips to keep me silent, then pivoted and disappeared into the wall of grapevines at her elbow. A moment later, her head reappeared among the leaves.

"*Lái ba,*" she whispered, "*Lái ba…*Come on."

We exchanged no more words, together stumbling between the rows of grapevines until we reached the open road. Once there, we ran all the way back to town. I left Mei Ling behind at Miss Lizzie's without breaking stride. There were no goodbyes and I didn't realize until long after climbing through the window of my bedroom that I had stolen Dinkle's letter opener. I still have it.

CHAPTER TWENTY-FOUR

The potato softens

Yurievsky's ability to follow orders and keep secrets had encouraged Grand Duke Pavlovich to snatch him from the ranks during the second Russo-Japanese War in 1904, using the Imperial Army sergeant as an aide, a courier, a bodyguard, and an assassin. The Duke quickly learned, also, to trust the tall soldier's native intuition. "The man is a veritable barometer for things suspicious," he boasted to his fellow officers, and it was true. In the years that followed—with the Duke's Tsarist political enemies far outnumbering his foreign military ones—Yurievsky more than once pointed the impulsive Pavlovich in a right direction when a wrong one might have proven fatal.

Now, the former aide's barometer was reading low—a storm was brewing—and this premonition kept him in the doorway after Dinkle bolted from the study, giving him a good look at me as I darted out from beneath the desk. He watched me escape and then moved to the window. *The boy from the town meeting*, he thought, as he watched me dash along the west side of the house, illuminated by gauzy moonlight. I didn't see him and had no idea I'd been spotted until much later. How did I find out? Be patient. I will explain in due time. For now, just accept that the spy had been espied.

As for Yurievsky, the tall Russian was accustomed to town boys sneaking onto the estate; indeed, he intentionally left windows unlocked in the guesthouse and servants' quarters to make their adventures more interesting. None had ever stolen inside the main house and another soft spot had now formed on the potato the villagers were harvesting.

Dinkle called out and Yurievsky tracked the old man's impatient snarl to the front entry of the mansion. The ex-gunrunner had made it only as far as the foyer and waited just inside the front door, unwilling to venture alone into the night despite the pistol he had retrieved from his desk drawer. The car horn continued to sound, a parrot's squawk intruding upon the distant sound of waves.

"Get out there," Dinkle growled.

He followed Yurievsky outside, but remained within the safe halo of light provided by the porch fixture, watching his tall manservant approach the garage. Inside, Yurievsky found a tire iron jammed between the seat and steering wheel of the Duesenberg. He removed it, replacing the harsh blare of the horn with the usual chirps and rustlings of the night. He then searched the garage for intruders. Dinkle would expect it done and would verify it had been accomplished with a slit-eyed interrogation. *The old man needn't worry*, his man thought. *I am a soldier. I follow orders, even the pointless ones.* At the end of the war, when mud and cold and the Bolsheviks had thrown the once grand Imperial Army into chaos, other soldiers had stopped following orders. Such men probably would ignore Dinkle now, Yurievsky mused; they'd lean against the painstakingly polished fender of the Duesenberg and enjoy a cigarette for a few minutes, assuming the prowlers were on their way to the village, the garage empty. Yurievsky would not succumb to such insubordination. He had never lied to Dinkle, to Grand Duke Pavlovich, or to any of the men who had engaged his services over the years. He had, on more than one occasion, omitted the truth. Omissions of truth were acceptable, he reasoned, if the truth had not been solicited. Lies, however, were the way of dishonorable men and Yurievsky saw himself as a man of honor, even though he knew most people, if apprised of the things he'd done at the behest of others, would see him as an amoral monster—an enforcer, a torturer, a murderer. He had been those things, but never a liar. When asked for the truth he had always provided it.

When asked.

Yurievsky thoroughly searched the garage even though he knew it was a waste of time. The person who had jerry-rigged the horn—likely the boy's brother—was by now halfway to the village along with his older sibling. Moreover, their intrusion on its own was of no interest to him—the two boys had snuck onto the estate several times in the past. However, neither had ever entered the main house. This was a bit of derring-do that would require further investigation. *Later,* Yurievsky thought. *Let the rabbits run for now. I know where the hutch is.*

Once his inspection was complete, he stepped back into the cool night air. Across the broad drive the porch was empty, the front door closed. Yurievsky smiled humorlessly. Despite the pistol and his bluster, Dinkle typically manifested courage in the form of foreclosures and leveraged buyouts. When younger, the old bounder had allegedly shot an unarmed man or two, but now assigned his fights to hirelings, mercenaries like Sergei Yurievsky.

The night was pleasant and Dinkle's man decided to put off his boss until morning, instead walking the grounds. Autumn loomed ahead with Labor Day behind them, adding a hint of fog to the salty air as he glided between the buildings and out to the sandy crest overlooking the ocean. Afterward, he made his way back to the garage, retrieved a flashlight, and then hiked to the vineyard on the east side of the estate. There, he found a set of small footprints and followed them until they were joined by a second set. Yurievsky crouched for a closer look at the faint depressions, his eyes narrowed. The smaller footprints were the boy's, but the others were larger. "*Ne mladsij brat,*" he said aloud in Russian. "*Strannyj.*" *Not little brother...Odd.*

Once satisfied the intruders had numbered only two, the former soldier returned to the main house. More than an hour had passed. Dinkle was now retired, but every light in the place remained on, the old bandit as fearful of the dark as a three-year-old child. Yurievsky climbed the steps to the mezzanine and went to his employer's bedroom door. He put his ear against the smooth surface. From inside came the sounds of snuffling and snorting—his boss didn't snore, rather he issued disgusting little noises as if blowing his nose into the pillow. Dinkle's man chuckled, pondering how easy it would be to assassinate his employer. *A man with so many enemies should not sleep this soundly*, he thought.

Yurievsky returned to his quarters, changed into bedclothes, and slipped under the covers. He could not sleep, the boy's intrusion on the same night Dinkle entertained the suspicious chemist too coincidental. Yurievsky did not believe in coincidences. Taken alone, the boy's appearance might have been a prank. He might have broken into the house on a dare from his friends. But the rest of it—the too-handsome chemist, the startled faces of the village leaders at the town meeting, the unease of the young woman Irina might have become when he picked up the old man's mail—these events were linked, Yurievsky thought, inextricably linked.

He had yet to share his misgivings with his employer. Dinkle would want proof and the former Russian soldier had none. He rose and relieved himself, then returned to bed and lay awake, staring at the dark ceiling. The villagers had put a guard at the marina to protect their treasure. But when he drove past the boathouse after dropping off the chemist at the Kittiwake Inn, their guard—the fidgety banker—was asleep.

One guard with millions at stake? Asleep?

It was another soft spot, the potato turning rotten before his eyes.

"The boathouse," Yurievsky said aloud.

181

He turned on the lamp next to his bed and began to read from a thumbworn book: Dostoevsky's *The Idiot*. The story of Myshkin—a man whose simplicity leads the book's worldlier characters to assume he lacks intelligence and insight—was his favorite, and after reading only a few pages, Sergei Yurievsky rose and climbed back into his clothes.

CHAPTER TWENTY-FIVE

Escape from Fort Buford

I awoke in a panic, my dreams populated by nightmares, each one the same. I was inside Dinkle's mansion, unable to escape—never discovered and yet always on the verge of discovery, the threat of horrific punishment ever-present. I was grateful when it was time to climb from my bed and head for the Sinclair station to pick up that morning's editions of the *Chronicle*. The damp, early morning air helped clear the dreams from my eyes, and by the time I reached Mr. Judson's, they had been replaced by grudging acceptance of my foolishness. Had Dexter been unmasked, the Ambergrisians would have known soon enough, I told myself. Moreover, despite my reckless escapade, the loan contracts remained inside Dinkle's safe and the idea that I could have murdered him was laughable. Thus, I had risked exposing the lot of us for no good reason. I had accomplished nothing.

I watched Mr. Judson as he flipped through his morning paper. Before I ran for my life across Dinkle's lawn and through his vineyard, I had figured a hero's welcome would be mine—the intrepid boy spy triumphantly returning with critical intelligence garnered from behind a drape in Cyrus Dinkle's dining room. I had imagined delivering my account of the mission with nonchalance, allowing the deed to stand tall on its own, the requisite awe and admiration on its tail in no need of coaxing. Instead, I had returned empty-handed and nearly empty-bladdered. It was a sobering comeuppance and I resolved to keep the entire misadventure to myself, praying for Mei Ling to keep it buttoned up, as well. Then I nearly broke my resolution immediately after making it.

"How did it go with Dexter last night?" I asked Mr. Judson as he scanned the newspaper headlines, my clumsy effort to seem casual putting a wrinkle of consternation between his brows. His eyes narrowed and I suddenly felt like a perjurer on the stand about to be skewered via cross-examination. He studied me for a few moments and then went back to his paper.

"It went okay," he answered. "Dexter did well." He didn't go on.

I finished my route and went to the mercantile. It was still early, but Mei Ling was there, sitting on the floor near the magazine rack, leafing through a movie rag with a picture of Jean Harlow on the front. The young Chinese girl had arrived in Tesoro dressed in a long patterned skirt, dark leggings, and a short quilted jacket—attire typical for girls in her region of China—but with Miss Lizzie's help and a couple of trips to San Francisco, she now looked like a typical American teenager. Her jeans were rolled up to her knees, her snazzy saddle shoes casually scuffed, and her collared white shirt a bit oversized and untucked. She looked up at me, then smiled as if to tell me the second secret we'd shared was as safe as the first.

"Hi, Treasure Boy," she said.

I needed to thank her after running off without a word the previous night. She had rescued me, propping a tire iron against the horn of the Duesenberg to create a diversion that masked my escape. Why had she followed me? How had she known I was in trouble, huddled under Dinkle's desk and mere seconds from discovery? I later learned that curiosity explained the former and intuition the latter.

"Mei Ling—" I began.

She stopped me with a finger to her lips.

"Shhhh," she whispered. "Shhhh, Treasure Boy."

I nodded. Yes, she had saved me—repaying my kindness at the gazebo—and years later we would share the story of our foray onto the Dinkle estate with Mr. Judson, Miss Lizzie, and the rest. But Mei Ling was right. For now, it had to remain our secret.

As for Everson Dexter, his part in our play was over and later that day Mr. and Mrs. C. Herbert Judson shuttled him back to San Francisco. I worried Fiona might go with him, but she didn't. "I was never in love with him, Connor," she told me once I'd stopped pouting over their affair. "He's an actor. He's already in love with himself. There's no room for anyone else."

It appeared Tesoro was starting to get over Everson Dexter and the Allegheny Chemicals Corporation, as well. The buying frenzy and constant effort to shop had both sated and exhausted most people in town. "I never understood why some rich folks commit suicide," Milton Garwood mused, "but I do now. They're tired." Of course, the fortune Milton and the rest thought firmly hooked on the end of their fishing line was about to reveal itself as seaweed, rather than sea bass, but they didn't know it and remained weighted down by the onerous responsibility impending wealth had dumped on them. The formerly ascetic Tesoroans had occupied much of the summer struggling to spend the ten thousand dollars provided by Dinkle's lines of credit, and with thousands more peeking over the fence, people frenetically leafed through the *Montgomery Ward* and *Sears, Roebuck and Company* catalogs; searched for places on shelves where they might wedge in more knick-knacks and doodads; and anguished over the inconveniences attending ocean cruises, European junkets, African safaris, and other trips rich folks had to make or risk coming off as country rubes to the city nabobs. Fortunately, a welcome distraction arose when Coach Wally forgot the combination for the vault doors on Fort Buford and was locked inside with his wife.

Even though *his* memory was the cause of their imprisonment, the coach blamed Judy. You see, as a security measure, he had refused to share the combination with her. "She can't keep her big yapper shut," he griped. "She'd give it to somebody and they'd blab it all over the place. Next thing you know our jeweled commode has somebody else's behind on it."

Of course, Coach Wally should have been more worried about his own yapper, given that he was by far the bigger gossip of the pair. Judy—who wasn't shy to remind folks that she'd been second runner-up to Miss Stinson Beach of 1899—could be a snark, but she confined herself to pissy observations about Fiona Littleleaf's preference for pants over dresses or Mrs. C. Herbert Judson's "uppity" haute couture. And insofar as other people's behinds were concerned, no one in Tesoro had indicated any interest in breaking into Fort Buford. There had been a couple of thwarted shop burglaries when the town was filled with prospectors, but the Ambergris Rush had ended by then, the Hoovervilles and outhouse squatters gone. Still, Coach Wally fretted that his jeweled commode was a target for kidnappers and had begun to lug it inside when he wasn't enthroned on the thing.

As for Judy, the allure of lording one's jeweled commode over people had faded for her, largely due to her husband's delight in breaking wind while perched on it. She wanted to give it away or move it from the front porch to the back where the morning and afternoon breezes from the west would carry her husband's discharges away from the house instead of into it. Coach Wally dug in his heels, and on the morning of the Fort Buford incident, decided to preside over his modest fiefdom from the living room inside the house rather than outside on the porch. Judy had imprudently prepared a dinner of franks and beans the previous evening and with the coach atop his now beloved commode, reading his paper, smoking a cigarette, and contentedly releasing toxic fallout, she pinched her nose shut and threatened to move her no-good, lazy bum of a brother in with them unless Coach Wally placed the toilet in the outhouse. This put the coach in a dither and he responded by leaping off the commode and into an argument with Judy, his side of it attended by a good deal of sputtering and arm-flinging. It was an impressive performance that eventually attracted the interest of a passer-by: Mr. Sprinkles.

The little monkey was puzzled at first but quickly figured out that the Bufords were having a dispute and slyly slipped through the wide-open vault door to take a bleacher seat on the jeweled commode. Succumbing to opportunity, he promptly defecated. Judy was an expert insofar as the aroma of her husband's emissions was concerned and immediately recognized an alien fragrance permeating the Buford atmosphere. She held up a hand to silence her husband, her nose wrinkling as she traced the smell to their jeweled commode. Suddenly, she screamed and pointed.

"What the goddamned hell?" Coach Wally shouted, afterward charging across the room with a lot of arm-waving and cursing that he figured would send the monkey on his way. However, Mr. Sprinkles was not at all put off by his behavior; indeed, he seemed to find it seductive.

It turned out that Milton Garwood was a decent blacksmith and welder but not much of a monkey gynecologist, as the creature he'd named Mr. Sprinkles was actually a Miss Sprinkles. She was also in heat and began to flirtatiously shriek and spit and flit about the room, eventually roosting on one of three chandeliers the Bufords had purchased and hung with the idea that one would eventually grow on them, the others to be given to their successful insurance agent son in San Rafael who inexplicably had two living rooms. Miss Sprinkles' obvious interest in mating with her husband unleashed an unexpected jealous streak in Judy and she retrieved a broom, using it to sweep the forsaken little thing off the chandelier and out the front entry. Coach Wally was right behind her and quickly slammed shut the heavy iron vault door. He levered the handle, spun the combination dial, and then ran to the rear door and did the same. About an hour later he felt an urge to use the outhouse and that's when he and Judy discovered they were locked inside Fort Buford.

Since the day several weeks past when the doors and window bars were installed by the boys from Alameda Safes & Security, and despite his obsessive fear of jeweled commode thieves, the coach had only once engaged the vault tumblers for either door. Instead, he and Judy left the doors open like everyone else in Tesoro during hot weather, allowing cool ocean air to flow through the house. Thus, when he tried to unlock the rear vault door Coach Wally was merely guessing at the combination. He would later find a piece of paper taped to the bottom of his underwear drawer revealing the number sequence to be the anniversary of the Buford nuptials—07-09-01—a date the coach had been unable to remember for years. Hence, his effort to recall the combination to the lock on the vault door was a bit like picking lottery numbers and had the usual success of such an effort, which was, of course, no success at all.

My brother Alex was the first to discover the Bufords' predicament. Riding past the house on his bicycle he heard the coach and his wife call out for help. He took a shot at freeing them, fiddling with the combination dial for a few minutes, then rode to Miss Lizzie's clinic and apothecary.

"Coach and his wife are locked inside their house," he told her.

"Good," Miss Lizzie said. "We should call a town meeting… Get some business done without an interruption."

I don't doubt Miss Lizzie would have been happy to leave Coach Wally locked up for a while, but her sense of duty and Alex's puzzled expression won out over poetic justice.

"Fine," she said. "Let's go free up the old poop."

Miss Lizzie hung a BACK IN AN HOUR sign on the door of her

pharmacy and they headed over to Fort Buford where they were met by a crowd nearly as large as the one gathered together earlier in the summer for the premiere appearance of the coach's jeweled commode. I was there with my friend Webb Garwood. People were tossing jokes at Coach Wally like peanuts thrown at a cage full of chimpanzees and the coach was not happy. Typically, he enjoyed a spotlight and was the last man in Tesoro inclined take a dim view of an audience. However, when folks started peering through the windows with their fingers wrapped around the iron bars, he took umbrage. He not only resented people taking advantage of the situation to view real, live Bufords in their natural habitat, but he also had a full bladder and the business part of the franks and beans poised in bomb's away position. He took a Mason jar into the bedroom closet to appease his angry bladder but had no answer for the distress provoked by the franks and beans other than to fill the air with flatulence that could have been used to execute condemned men at nearby San Quentin.

While Judy was less intestinally effusive, she was also about to have water spill over the dam when she decided to close the curtains and put a chamber pot in the jeweled commode. In a rare display of chivalry Coach Wally retired to the bedroom, allowing his wife to go first, a fortunate decision for her as the coach used his turn to noisily make an offering that threatened to rival the massive blob of ambergris I'd found on the beach more than three months earlier. I was outside one of the curtained windows when this happened. Webb and my friends and I howled with laughter, afterward sending forth a chorus of simulated fart sounds even the adults in the crowd found amusing. Meanwhile, Miss Lizzie sent for Milton Garwood who was not only the town misanthrope but also its only blacksmith and welder. Milton showed up with a torch and a small cylinder and that's when the negotiation began.

It seemed that Milton had had an eye on the Bufords' jeweled commode since it first arrived and saw their quandary as an opportunity to acquire it for the cost of a few cents worth of acetylene.

"This is extortion," Coach Wally bellowed from inside a front porch window when Milton offered to cut through one of the vault doors in exchange for the jeweled commode. "Tell him, Miss Lizzie."

"I'm no lawyer, Wally," Miss Lizzie said, winking at Alex and me. "I can give you something to tone down that gas, but you'll have to consult Herb Judson about legal matters."

"Never mind," Coach Wally snapped. "I already know the answer. You can't hold us in here for ransom, Milton. I don't need no lawyer to tell me that it's illegal, unconstitutional, and downright despicable."

"I ain't holding you in nowhere," Milton countered. "You locked your own selves in there. It ain't my responsibility to get you out for nothing."

"Just give him the commode, Wally," Judy pleaded.

"I'll be damned if I'll give in to that conniving son of a goat herder," Wally snapped. "I'll die in here first."

"We're dying in here now," Judy retorted. "Give him the commode."

"No!"

"Give it to him."

"No!"

"Wally, give him the commode."

"No!"

Judy Buford had been teaching fourth grade at Tesoro Elementary School for nearly thirty years. She was generally thought to possess the proper combination of primness and prudery expected of a schoolmarm and was a good teacher for the most part. As I have previously pointed out, she had some peculiar ideas about sex and pregnancy that resulted in considerable eye-opening once her former students were faced with the real things. However, she had never been less than lady-like nor indicated any potential to be profane or bellicose until that moment.

"WALLY, GIVE HIM THE GODDAMNED COM- MODE!" she shouted.

Things are different in the world now. I blame cable television where folks seem compelled to cuss like longshoremen. However, in 1934 Tesoro, California, no one had ever heard an elementary school teacher utter anything more wicked than "darn" or "heck." So, you can understand how a full-blown "goddamned" from Judy Buford quieted the Boys' Fart Chorus along with everyone else standing around outside Fort Buford. Even Miss Lizzie was shocked into silence as was Coach Wally. His mouth formed a perfect *O* and he ducked behind the curtain. The crowd had gone silent and now eavesdropped, scarcely breathing, as the coach and his wife flung whispers sharp as razor blades back and forth at each other from behind the window bars. After a minute or so the coach pulled aside the curtain and looked out. Milton Garwood waited on the porch, his welder's mask pushed back on his head, a smug grin on his face.

"Get us out of here, you son of a bitch," Coach Wally said.

Milton made such short work of the vault door one had to wonder if Alameda Safes & Security had sold the Bufords a lemon. He fired up his torch and cut the combination dial out of the thing in about ten minutes, exposing the interior tumblers. He then reached inside and manually pulled back the bolts, unlocking the door. It immediately began to swing open, allowing a blast of malodorous air to rush out of the house along with Judy Buford who shouldered past Milton and stumbled down the steps. Halfway up the front walk she stopped and bent over, hands on her knees, her chest heaving as she took one deep breath after another.

"The commode…" she called out to Milton. "Get the goddamned thing out of there. It's yours."

Coach Wally had joined her by then. He was far less olfactorily indisposed than his wife and started to make a pitch in favor of stiffing Milton on their agreement.

"Aw now, Judy," he began.

"Don't even start with me," she snapped. "I mean it, Wally. Don't even start."

Milton Garwood went inside and removed the chamber pot from the commode, chuckling when he saw Miss Sprinkles' contribution to the morning's festivities slowly drying at the bottom of the bowl. He still wore his welder's gloves and retrieved the dainty little pellets, adding them to the chamber pot before hauling the toilet out to his buckboard.

"Pleasure doing business with you, Wally," he called out once seated atop the wagon with his team's reins in his hands and Miss Sprinkles back on his head.

It was September 10, 1934. Three months and one week had elapsed since I discovered the ambergris on the beach. Summer vacation was over. Late that night the Bufords slept with the front door to their house pushed wide open while across town Milton Garwood snored peacefully, trusting Miss Sprinkles to guard his slightly used but mostly new jeweled commode. The rest of us slept, too. When midnight passed it would mark the end of ninety days since the Boops set up their folding tables in the assembly room of the town hall and put nearly the entire village in debt to Cyrus Dinkle. We would awaken to the ninety-first day, the trap the Ambergrisians had set for the ex-gunrunner already sprung.

CHAPTER TWENTY-SIX

A pheasant in the brush

On the same morning Coach Wally and wife Judy locked themselves inside Fort Buford, Dinkle's man walked from the estate to the mercantile and postal exchange. He could have driven but preferred the walk. Open air and a distant horizon had been his allies in Mother Russia, a place where Grand Duke Pavlovich and his ilk had for centuries skirted retribution for their acts by throwing peasants like Yurievsky into the pit. Fear of confinement was the vulture on his shoulder in those days, and as a soldier, he came to prefer a drafty tent to the stifling post barracks, an open sky to the ceiling of cracked plaster inside the St. Petersburg apartment he far too occasionally shared with Olga and Irina. Besides, during those few minutes spent on the road from the estate to the village he could pretend to be the old Sergei Yurievsky—husband to Olga, father of Irina—anything but Dinkle's man.

He reached the village and then the street leading to Fort Buford, glancing at the commotion less than a block away. A crowd was gathered around one of the houses. There was a good bit of laughter. The windows of the house had bars and the front door was made of iron with a combination lock. He hesitated. The affairs of the villagers were trivial—petty loyalties or squabbles, insignificant accords or disagreements. They were not his affairs. Still, he perceived comfort and predictability in their lives he might have thought enviable as a young man. They belonged to something, to each other. In Russia he, too, had belonged to something: the Imperial Army, Olga and his sweet *Myshka*. Their affairs had been his.

He did not further investigate the hubbub going on at the house with the iron door and the bars on its windows, instead continuing on to the mercantile. When he entered, Fiona Littleleaf was behind the counter.

"Good morning, Mister Yurievsky," she called out.

"Miss Littleleaf," he replied, offering the dignified nod learned from Grand Duke Pavlovich.

She turned to retrieve Dinkle's mail without being asked, afterward handing over three letters and a packet bound by string.

"Not much today," she said.

"Thank you," Yurievsky replied. He turned to go and then hesitated as if he were just another villager, someone taking a few minutes to talk with her about things of little significance, not because they mattered, but because they didn't; because simply sharing a few minutes distinguished a brief encounter from a relationship.

"Something else, Mister Yurievsky? We've some lovely apricot scones. Perhaps you've time for one?"

Yurievsky shook his head.

"That's a shame. They really are lovely scones."

Fiona smiled and then held up a hand.

"Wait," she said.

She retrieved a small paper sack and plucked two scones from the basket on her counter.

"Take them with you," she said, handing the sack to Yurievsky.

Dinkle's man began to reach for his wallet, but Fiona stopped him.

"No charge," she said. "They're on the house."

"Thank you," Yurievsky replied. He nodded again and then exited the mercantile.

On the way back to the Dinkle estate the tall Russian retrieved one of the scones from the bag and nibbled on it. He appreciated a kindness, few of them sent his way over the years. His *Myshka* had always been kind to him during his too seldom leaves from the Imperial Army. When he sat for too long, staring into the fireplace as if the heat and smoke coursing up the chimney could carry off harsh memories, she invariably crawled into his lap. "Don't be sad, Papa," she would say. "I love you ever so much."

He reached the street that led to Fort Buford. This time he stopped. A crowd continued to mill about the place. A buckboard attached to a team of horses had been added to the congregation. He swiveled his head to look in the opposite direction. The same street would take him to the water…to the marina and the boathouse.

The boathouse.

The former Russian soldier had been both a spy and an assassin—professions that required one to become a specter—and on the same night the too-handsome chemist had dined with the old man, Yurievsky had put aside his book, arisen from his bed, and made his way to Dinkle's own boathouse. There, he retrieved a kayak and put to sea. He'd had no difficulty breaching the laughable security put forth by the villagers. With dawn still three hours away and the now-awake banker fighting off sleep by pacing the walkway on the landward side, Yurievsky had silently paddled to within twenty meters of C. Herbert Judson's boathouse before slipping into the water and under the seaward door. Inside, he discovered why the village leaders had been so anxious at the town meeting. The boathouse was empty except for a terrible odor and an orange crate containing what appeared to be a huge egg.

Yurievsky resumed walking down the road toward the estate. He had not yet told Dinkle. It was unnecessary. The old man would eventually know, anyway, and the villagers knew it. It was information of no value. *No,* he thought, *it is not the empty*

boathouse they have concealed but their knowledge of it. That was the pheasant yet to be flushed. And he intended to flush it. "All secrets have reasons for being secret," Grand Duke Pavlovich always said. "Find the reason and you unearth the secret."

Yurievsky agreed. There were many pheasants concealed in the cornfield the villagers and Dinkle had together planted, many secrets. All were worthwhile to know. And, for now, he alone knew where all the pheasants were hiding.

CHAPTER TWENTY-SEVEN

The fourth town meeting

On September 11, 1934, the ninety-first day, the largest collection of certified mail in the history of Tesoro, California, was delivered. The content of each letter was filled with "pursuants" and "thereins" and "breach ofs," but the gist was that The Cyrus Dinkle Company, thereafter known as "Company," was laying claim to the ambergris shares used as collateral by the letter recipient, thereafter known as "Borrower," by "foreclosure pursuant to a failure to indicate in writing a desire to extend the line of credit agreement beyond ninety days, the aforementioned a breach of contract therein."

The certified letters began to arrive at 8:00 a.m. and the queue formed at C. Herbert Judson's office within minutes. Around twenty past eight, our town lawyer showed the first couple into his private chamber. For the next five minutes the only sound from behind the heavy oaken door was the low hum of Mr. Judson's voice. Then the wailing and table-pounding started. At eight-thirty, Mrs. C. Herbert Judson tentatively cracked the door and poked her head inside.

"Herb, there's a line all the way to the edge of town," she reported. "I think maybe you should get everyone together to talk about this."

Mr. Judson agreed, and at nine-thirty, the fourth town meeting was convened. Everyone was there save Cyrus Dinkle, his man, and Miss Sprinkles, a hastily put together sign posted outside the assembly room of the town hall barring all three.

197

NO MONKEYS OR DIRTY ROTTEN SKUNKS, it said.

For once Coach Wally Buford had no interest in the moderator's gavel; indeed, he was clearly reluctant to remind people about who had led the charge into what appeared to be a catastrophic mass default. Rather than sit on the stage with the rest of the town leaders, he took a seat next to wife Judy near the back, his round eyes ostensibly fascinated by the floorboards at his feet. I was up front alongside the Ambergrisians, our number increased by two: my mother and Mrs. C. Herbert Judson. Ma and James sat on either side of me, their eyes moving over the crowd as warily as Secret Service agents. With no argument from Coach Wally, Mr. Johns was nominated and elected moderator. He promptly turned the meeting over to Mr. Judson.

"I know you're all confused about the default notices and I will try to explain them to you," Mr. Judson began. "However, I need to start by asking each of you to take a moment to compare your letter with the person on either side. I suspect the language is the same, but should anyone have different wording, I'll have to break you up into groups or something." The delay seemed unnecessary to me as Mr. Judson had to know the letters were identical save the name following "Dear Mr. and/or Mrs." However, I could understand why he might want to put off the typhoon of anger and invective likely to follow his translation of the legalese into what plainspoken fellows around town liked to call "reg'lar 'merican."

The townsfolk took a few minutes to compare their letters with one another, noisily succumbing to the natural urge to liken Cyrus Dinkle, thereafter known as "Company," to a jackass, a sidewinder, and a lousy weasel, the sum of those appellations unanimously agreed upon by those in attendance to be henceforth known as "Conniving Bastard." Eventually, Mr. Judson borrowed Moderator Johns's gavel, nearly beating a hole in the podium before everyone finally settled down.

"Okay," he went on, "does anyone have a letter that differs from his or her neighbor? Hold up your hand if you do."

No hands went up.

"Good," Mr. Judson said, quickly adding, "I don't mean 'good' in that I'm pleased about your situations, just 'good' insofar as this meeting goes."

Mr. Judson went on, his voice indecisive, his entire manner uncharacteristically faint-hearted. I was surprised. The plan was going as we'd hoped. Dinkle had formally given notice of his intent to exchange the townspeople's debts for their ambergris shares. He would receive his fraction of the dinosaur egg in the boathouse and our friends and neighbors would be made whole. It was exactly what we wanted and yet Mr. Judson seemed reluctant to reveal that Dinkle's letters pulled everyone in the audience out of the holes they'd dug for themselves. Of course, he was simply acting, maintaining the ruse that he and Angus MacCallum and Mr. Johns and Miss Lizzie and Fiona and James and I were unaware of our empty boathouse. "Word will get back to Dinkle about this meeting," he later told the Ambergrisians. "He has to believe we were as upset as the rest of the town…that we never looked inside the boathouse."

As those in attendance listened, Mr. Judson interpreted the letters they'd received and the contracts those letters referenced. He further informed them that Cyrus Dinkle had hornswoggled them.

"I'm sorry to say that he legally owns your ambergris shares," he revealed. "The contract is ironclad. You all signed an agreement requiring a written request for extension by the ninetieth day. That was yesterday. None of you made the request. That allows Dinkle to confiscate what you put up as collateral…In this case, your shares."

He paused, then added, "Again…I'm sorry."

The Ambergrisians had many times discussed this moment, all of us anticipating a barrage of "This ain't right!" and "Not fair!" and "By God I'll sue!" Instead, there was not a sound— no loud angry voices, no fists slammed into palms, no chairs crashing against the wall, no boots stomped against the floor. Just silence.

"Perhaps I've not made myself clear," Mr. Judson interjected.

"We heard you," Milton Garwood growled. He stood off to the side, his mood already dark on account of the meeting's peremptory exclusion of monkeys. C. Herbert Judson's pronouncement had done nothing to brighten his disposition and Milton dispensed with "thereins" and "hereafters" to succinctly say what everyone now knew to be the main thrust of the certified letters. "Dinkle has cheated us," he said.

The silence in the room slowly began to give way to a low rumble—not the distant and oddly elegant thunder before a storm but the ominous and angry murmurs that predict a lynching. Mr. Judson held up both hands.

"Just a minute now," he said, "from a purely legal standpoint you've not been cheated. Dinkle has complied with the terms of the contracts."

"Ain't he supposed to give us notice or something before he forecloses?" someone called out.

"Ordinarily true," Mr. Judson said, "but you all waived that right. Look at page three, item seven, subheading eight." This was followed by the rustle and flap of 190 papers being handled. It was just as Mr. Judson told them:

3.7(8): BORROWER WAIVES RIGHT TO PRIOR NOTICE PRECEDING FORECLOSURE BY COMPANY.

There's nothing like the door to a legal loophole being slammed shut to turn the murmur and hiss of discontent into a furious outcry, With alarming suddenness, the assembly room was filled with shouting and fist-shaking. People shouted at C. Herbert Judson. They shouted at each other. They shouted at Coach Wally Buford for being the damned nincompoop who encouraged them to sign Dinkle's papers and Skitch Peterson who unfairly enticed them with a same day used car sale. Eventually they began to shout at the rest of us sitting at the front of the room: Mr. Johns, Miss Lizzie, Fiona, James. And me. I was just a kid, but they shouted at me, too, decrying the unsolicited streak of generosity I'd foisted on them, irrevocably shoving them into the promise of affluence against their wills.

People stood, filling the air with yelling and pointed fingers. A bit of pushing and shoving went on between a few of the young bucks, the entire affair edging closer and closer to a melee. Ma put a hand on mine, as if doing so might shield me while Mr. Judson stood at the front, trying to be heard, and Mr. Johns retrieved his gavel from the lawyer and banged it on the podium. Miss Lizzie could usually shut people up with a narrow eye, but even she was no match for the anger coursing through the room. A single voice from the back of the assembly put an end to it.

"CLAM UP!" Angus MacCallum bellowed. "PAT A CORK IN IT, ALL OF YE…JUS' PAT A DAMNED CORK IN IT!"

Angus slowly crab-walked his way up the center aisle, his crippled foot clip-clopping against the wooden floor like a horse's hoof, the wrinkles of his mastiff's face forming innumerable frowns. He reached the front and took the stage, standing between the crowd and the Ambergrisians. His voice had effectively silenced the mob as everyone figured Angus had pairs of socks older than most of them and had earned the right to speak his mind without being interrupted. More daunting, however, was the old Scot's disposition. Despite his age we all knew Angus MacCallum to be a wolverine—small and ferocious and utterly fearless. No one wanted to back him into a corner, the congregation remaining silent as the old lighthouse keeper glared at them for a few moments before speaking.

"I'd like to remind ye," he began, pointing a finger at Coach Wally Buford, "tha' only one person t'ought it a good idea to joomp aff'n a cliff and tha' fat fellow dinnae have the backbone to sit up here at the froont and take his loomps. Ye wannae yell at a body, yell at Mister Wally Buford, 'cuz I'm here to tell ya that noon o' these fine people behind me is e'en a wee bit to blame. Herbert offered to look o'er yer papers. Roger said his bank would make sure it was all on the oop and oop. Both of 'em advised ye to beg aff for a while…to t'ink t'ings o'er carefully before ye slapped yer John Hancocks on somethin' ye dinnae understand. And as fer James and Miss Lizzie and Fiona and young Connor, why they had noothin' to do wit' yer choices. Ye made your own beds and have only yerselves to blame if the pillas are mussed. Ye cannae blame these folks up here. It wisna' their doin'."

Angus dropped his shoulders and went on, his tone softened.

"Besides, if ye ask me yer're all better aff. Ye had yerselves a taste of the high life this summer, didn't ye noo, and it seem to me tha' most of ye got bloody tired of it. There're only so many t'ings ye can buy, are there nae? Did any of it make ye happier than ye already were? Any of it wort' more than wha' ye already had right here in Tesoro? I doobt it. So, stop your belly-achin'. Go home. T'ank the good Lord tha' ye have a roof o'er yer heeds when it rains and a breeze aff'n the sea when it's hot. That's more than a lot of folk have in these troubled times. Ye oughta be t'ankful for it, and those of ye who cannae see it need to clam the hell up!"

Angus was out of breath and stopped talking, allowing silence to hold the floor for the second time that morning. Everyone in town knew he wasn't shy with an opinion, but lengthy exposition was uncharacteristic for the old lighthouse keeper and no one was quite sure what to do. After Angus regained his breath, he rescued them.

"Herbert," he said, looking pointedly at Mr. Judson, "dinnae ye have more to tell these folk?"

Mr. Judson had been a formidable litigator during his time in San Francisco, blistering opposing counsels or charming juries with oratory some compared to the legendary Clarence Dar-row. However, Angus's unexpected eloquence had taken him off-script and he hesitated, searching to again find his place in our little drama. It gave Milton Garwood enough time to ask the question the town lawyer had wanted someone to pose before the entire room was looking for a short rope and a high tree branch.

"What about the stuff we bought?" Milton asked. "Do we have to pay Dinkle back?"

For the first time that morning C. Herbert Judson smiled.

"No, you don't," he said. "You put up your ambergris shares as security against ten thousand dollars, but nothing else was on the line. After foreclosure, the contracts make no provision for attaching other assets...your houses, businesses, and so forth. That's a critical point. Dinkle could have laid claim to those things *before* you defaulted but not *afterward*. He accepted your collateral. Now that he's foreclosed and confiscated it, his right to collect the money you borrowed has been abrogated."

Most in the room had hung in there with Mr. Judson until he dropped "abrogated" on them. Now, he looked out on a silent chorus of blank faces.

"Think of it this way," he explained. "Dinkle bought your shares for ten thousand dollars in a simple transaction. That means the collateral—your shares of the ambergris—is his. But it also means that the money, and whatever you purchased with it, is yours."

It took a few moments for this to sink in, but once it did, a peculiar thing happened. With the effect rippling across the room, the same folks who had shouted at C. Herbert Judson, the rest of the Ambergrisians, and each other now gazed about with the warm eyes and relaxed faces of those who have emerged from the confessional booth with unscalded skin and a fresh absolution slate to mark up. Amazingly, they seemed not disappointed but relieved.

The fourth town meeting was never adjourned. It simply came apart, folks wandering off or breaking up into small groups to discuss the weather or the upcoming first day of school or the fortunes of the Cal football team set to begin its season on Saturday. No one noticed or even questioned that the men guarding the ambergris for the last several weeks had all been present at the meeting, leaving the boathouse unattended. It would remain unattended until early afternoon when Angus MacCallum unlocked the seaward doors and threw them open, allowing Cyrus Dinkle to see what 190 foreclosed lines of credit and almost two million dollars had bought him.

CHAPTER TWENTY-EIGHT

Dinkle's comeuppance

Dinkle was furious when he discovered nothing more than our two-pound dinosaur egg in the boathouse, along with a stench equal to the odor of the bogus offer he'd foisted on the citizens of Tesoro. "The auld bastard damned near went aff his heed," Angus McCallum later told me, chuckling with delight. "E'en moreso when I tells 'im the Allegheny Chemicals Corporation went n' pulled their offer aff'n the table."

Dinkle immediately ordered his man to drive him into the village where he called upon C. Herbert Judson at the lawyer's office. Mr. Judson played his part well.

"Apparently, their research didn't stand up," Mr. Judson told the old man. "The stuff doesn't do what they originally thought it might. They're not perfumers and had no interest after that."

He denied prior knowledge of the amount of ambergris in his boathouse.

"All I know, Cyrus, is that there was a half-ton of something put in there. What happened afterward is as much a mystery to me as you."

Dinkle kept his anger at a simmer as he listened, determined to maintain his oft-pontificated assertion that business and personal matters slept in separate beds. Indeed, he seemed so cool and measured that Mr. Judson worried the old scoundrel might have caught enough of our lie's scent to have already dug it up. That's when our lawyer reminded the ex-gunrunner that he owned merely one-eighth of the egg in the boathouse given that he, Mr. Johns, Miss Lizzie, Fiona, Angus, and my mother had not signed the Boops' loan agreements and James's account had a zero balance. This raised the heat under Dinkle's pot.

"And what does one-eighth come to?" he demanded.

"Probably five or six thousand dollars," Mr. Judson answered. "More or less."

An estimated return of a few thousand dollars for the nearly two million doled out in unrecoverable loans turned Dinkle's face dusky purple and provoked a spittle-laced, highly profane outburst. Mr. Judson later reported that the fiery invective—the old man adding exclamation points by pounding the lawyer's desk until the diplomas on the wall threatened to rattle off—made him no longer doubt any of the homicidal rumors attached to the former Indian Territory trader's shadowy past. About the time Mr. Judson began to seriously consider retrieving the pistol he kept in his desk drawer, Dinkle abruptly put a lid on his pot and stomped out of the office.

The new owner of one-eighth of the town's entire ambergris holding returned to his estate and spent several hours on the telephone with his various lawyers, including the damned fool who had failed to include an independent verification of collateral as part of the line of credit contracts. Dinkle, an unapologetic anti-Semite, fired him along with his two best attorneys, both of whom were blameless but happened to be Jewish. He then wrote up a pair of flyers and sent Yurievsky to post one at the town hall and the other on the kiosk at Fremont Park:

EMERGENCY TOWN MEETING TONIGHT AT 7 P.M.
ATTENDANCE IS MANDATORY!

Yurievsky drove his employer into town for the meeting that evening and returned him to the estate after no one showed up. The next morning they went into San Francisco where Dinkle rehired the Jewish lawyers. The shameless bastard blamed them for their one-sided dust-up the previous day and then spent the next several hours in their office, freeing Yurievsky to visit City Hall. There, the ex-soldier pored over records in the thick logbooks, scribbling addresses onto a scrap of paper torn from one of the pages. That afternoon Yurievsky visited the sites, discovering either a warehouse or a vacant lot at all but one of the various locations, the last address on his list leading him to a house that rented rooms by the hour.

Around four o'clock Yurievsky drove the Duesenberg across town to retrieve Chirpy Boop from the apartment she shared with the Russian Boop. The old man was staying in the city with a plan for the young woman to meet him in a suite at the Fairmont where she would help salve a loss of nearly two million dollars to the great unwashed of Tesoro. Yurievsky chauffeured Chirpy Boop to the hotel and then returned to the Financial District where he waited for his boss to emerge from a tall building on Market. They then drove up the steep hill that was California Street, sharing their route with a cable car crammed with eyeballing tourists, the curious out-of-towners craning their necks for a better look at whatever tycoon or celebrity must certainly be occupying the back seat of such a magnificent machine. Dinkle ignored them, uttering not a word until the car rolled to a stop in front of the hotel.

"Nine in morning," he muttered before exiting the vehicle.

Yurievsky had the rest of the evening off and took dinner at his favorite restaurant in Russian Hill. He liked Russian Hill even though the area was not named for the heritage of its live inhabitants but its dead ones, a Russian cemetery inspiring the designation. The restaurant, too, was not Russian but Italian. Yurievsky had little use for Italians, whom he viewed as noisy people. However, he could not deny their gifts for cooking and making wine, and the former soldier feasted on *braciole alla barese* with an excellent Brunello before retiring to a modest hotel a few blocks from the Fairmont.

The next morning Yurievsky retrieved his boss and drove

him back to Tesoro. The old man's night had not gone well, his disposition more acerbic than usual. He repeatedly barked at Yurievsky during the trip, blaming him for traffic, potholes, and the annoying fly determined to homestead on the ex-gunrunner's nose. Upon arrival at his seaside estate, Dinkle retreated to the study and spent the next several days there, dining from the refectory table and sleeping on an overstuffed leather sofa.

While Dinkle brooded behind the closed door of his study, Yurievsky carried on. The Duesenberg was washed and polished, the grounds patrolled, the food trays set outside the door of the study and later retrieved, the sills and tabletops checked for dust the housekeepers had missed. Each day he walked to the village to retrieve Dinkle's mail. At the mercantile and postal exchange the young woman Irina might have become continued to greet him by name, but did not further engage him in conversation as had once been her habit. There was repentance in the way she kept her chin down and her voice falsely cheerful. She was ashamed and Yurievsky wanted to comfort her, to lift the burden of guilt from her shoulders. *You did what had to be done,* he wanted to say. *It was war and you were a soldier. You should be proud. You did what was necessary. I am a soldier as well. When the time comes I, too, will do what is necessary.*

Meanwhile, the servants' tongues waggled non-stop. "Dinkle was bamboozled," the cook and maids rehashed over and over, unable to mask the delight they felt at their boss's comeuppance. Yurievsky disdained their lack of restraint. "Mister Dinkle signs your paychecks," he reminded them, even though he understood their thirst for retribution. Dinkle treated the women as if they were insects with spatulas and dust mops. As the butler it was Yurievsky's job to keep the staff in line, but he did not again reproach them. *Let them cackle,* he thought. *Gossip is like smoke. It disappears on the wind. Only revenge is eternal.* And true revenge was not a whisper but a dagger.

CHAPTER TWENTY-NINE

It's alive

Following a summer of conspiracy and adventure, the time remaining before the first day of school was disappointingly commonplace. I awoke in the damp gossamer pink-gray of dawn, picked up my newspapers for delivery, sat with Mr. Judson on his porch swing for a few minutes, finished my route, and then stopped off at Fiona's mercantile for some warm milk with a little coffee in it. There were no more after-midnight meetings; indeed, the Ambergrisians disbanded without further mention of the affair that had preoccupied us for so many weeks. "It's best left behind us, Connor," Miss Lizzie instructed when I tried to talk about it. Although she had no love for Dinkle our town medical officer seemed embarrassed, as did Fiona and James and Mr. Judson and Mr. Johns. Only Angus MacCallum was unremorseful. "Dinkle's loaded the dice for more'n one game of craps," he asserted. "It's aboot time some'un rolled heavy sevens on 'im."

James bought Ma an engagement ring, picking one with a sapphire—her favorite stone—rather than a diamond. They set aside a date in October for the wedding. Ma had already accepted his proposal, but James repeated it after dinner one night, proposing to Alex and me, as well. "Will you boys be my sons?" he asked after getting down on one knee. Alex and I thought it was pretty funny.

Folks around town were in a bit of a daze. The road from middling to prosperity to ruin and back to middling had been a tumultuous one, much of it traversed in a single day that began with a passel of certified letters and ended with debt relief that rivaled any program President Roosevelt's vaunted New Deal could offer. People behaved as if just awakened from a bad dream, staring blearily at the various knick-knacks and doodads populating their homes as if all the stuff had been crafted by elves and left on their doorsteps during the night. Some folks didn't change much. Coach Wally recovered nicely from his brief flirtation with culpability and busied himself taking credit for hoodwinking Dinkle, while Milton Garwood was as misanthropic as ever, proving that some personalities are simply irreconcilable.

It wasn't long before people figured out what had happened along with a pretty strong suspicion that the Ambergrisians, and not Coach Wally Buford, had somehow made it happen. They must have been profoundly grateful, but no thanks were offered lest their gratitude be translated by Dinkle and his lawyers into evidence against the folks who had saved their bacon. Like Miss Lizzie, I think they wanted to leave the body buried rather than reinvigorate it with talk, only to have a Frankenstein monster then terrorizing the countryside. As it turned out, the body was neither buried nor dead. Far from it.

On the afternoon of the ninety-seventh day after Angus McCallum and I had raced for the ambergris on the beach, a grizzled private investigator with scuffed shoes and body odor attended a matinee at the Curran Theater on San Francisco's Geary Street. The play was *Ah, Wilderness* by Eugene O'Neill. He left at the end of Scene I, in which the character of "Richard Miller, an idealistic seventeen-year-old," was introduced. Inhabiting the role was an actor somewhat long in the tooth for a teenager. The next morning—the ninety-eighth day—Dinkle called for Yurievsky to join him in his study. The P.I. was there, too. The rumpled detective had showered for the meeting with his client and now reeked of fleabag hotel soap and cigarette smoke. Dinkle was still working on his breakfast.

"Have a seat," he said to Yurievsky as he slathered butter onto a wedge of toast. When his valet remained standing Dinkle stopped buttering.

"I said, 'Have a seat,'" he repeated, with a frown, the knife poised over his toast.

"I will stand."

Dinkle tolerated Yurievsky's occasional insubordination and even less occasional disdain because the tall Russian was dependably useful and as loyal as one criminal can be to another. But Dinkle was also afraid of his manservant and did not want anyone to know it. He glanced nervously at the private investigator. The fellow's eyes were directed at the floor, his face expressionless—fulfilling his duty to impassively deliver embarrassing news to people who detested being embarrassed. *He's good at it,* Yurievsky thought as Dinkle shifted his gaze back to his valet and chauffeur, fashioning the same expression a Roman emperor might offer a condemned gladiator. It was a look the old man frequently employed to figuratively remove a fellow's testicles during a negotiation and usually worked well. However, it had no effect on Yurievsky, the tall Russian's icy demeanor transiently evoking in Dinkle a feeling that the gladiator was about to climb the parapet, a sword in hand, his own thumb downturned. For a moment, the old man was clearly unsettled. The voices of the maids chattering in the foyer outside the study door rescued him, breaking the awkward silence.

Dinkle returned his attention to his toast, adding more butter and then jam. At the same time, he spoke to the P.I. without looking at him.

"You can go," he said.

After the rumpled detective was gone, Dinkle went on.

"I need you to deliver this to Judson," he said to Yurievsky, holding up an envelope. "I want it to go only to him and you must wait until he opens it. You follow?"

"Yes."

"I want you to pay attention to his pipe. He'll stick it in his mouth to read what I'm sending. After he's done reading, I want to know if he lights it."

"I understand."

"That's his tell," Dinkle added. "If he's part of this he won't light the pipe."

Yurievsky took the envelope. It was sealed, the address side blank.

"The pipe," Dinkle reminded him. "Don't forget."

"I understand."

Yurievsky exited the mansion, first retrieving a second blank envelope from the office supplies closet adjacent to the pantry. The day had begun overcast, but sun now threatened to dissolve the clouds and he removed his coat as he began the mile-long hike to the village. He walked quickly to the end of the circular drive, through the gated opening with its massive brick stanchions, and on to where Dinkle's grapevines began, their near-harvest green leaves gently undulating with the light breeze. Once blocked from the mansion's view by the vines, he stopped, opened the envelope, and examined its contents. Afterward, he placed the document inside the second envelope, sealed it, and went on, his pace perhaps less brisk than usual. There was no reason to hurry. The pheasants had been flushed. All the potato's soft spots were at last exposed.

Upon reaching the village, Yurievsky discovered dark windows and a CLOSED sign on the door of C. Herbert Judson's office. He went to the lawyer's residence next. Mrs. C. Herbert Judson answered the door and tried to accept the envelope.

"Only Mister Judson," Yurievsky insisted.

Mrs. Judson could ordinarily charm a man into pulling out his own teeth if she liked, but quickly sized up Dinkle's man as a nut no woman could crack. She left him on the front porch and went inside to retrieve her husband. A minute later Mr.

Judson emerged from inside the house, his pipe in one hand. He took the envelope and sat on the porch swing, the pipe between his teeth. He began to open the envelope, then hesitated, eyeing Yurievsky.

"Thanks, Mister Yurievsky, but you don't need to wait," he said.

"I have been instructed to wait for your response," Yurievsky replied.

A flash of uncertainty shadowed Mr. Judson's face. Then, he shrugged and broke the seal on the envelope. Inside, as Yurievsky already knew, was no letter. Instead, the lawyer pulled out a playbill for *Ah, Wilderness* by Eugene O'Neill. A cast member's picture had been circled. Printed below the photo was a name: LESLIE CARRINGTON. The face in the picture was Everson Dexter's. There was a handwritten note on the program:

My home at 7 p.m. Bring the rest—the boy, too.

Mr. Judson's pipe remained clenched in his teeth as he examined the playbill. Once finished he stuck his pipe into a pocket.

"Unlit," Yurievsky later reported to his employer.

"Prepare for after-dinner guests tonight," Dinkle instructed his man when apprised of the town lawyer's response. "I'll see them in my study. Set up chairs facing the desk."

Yurievsky knew the composition of the guest list without being told: the lawyer, the banker, the midwife, the barkeeper, the old man from the lighthouse, Miss Littleleaf, the boy. The village conspirators had been unmasked, just as Grand Duke Pavlovich and the rest had been found out after murdering the Mad Monk. *It's the way of world,* Yurievsky mused. Men in power nearly always prevailed over resistance fighters, because they relied on tactics rather than passions, on preparation rather than instinct. Yurievsky was an instinctive soldier but knew success in battle required more. *One must study until you know*

213

your enemy's weaknesses, he thought. He had studied, analyzed, planned. He was ready. *Are they?*

Yurievsky doubted it. The townspeople were not warriors, their armor stripped away as soon as the seaward doors to the boathouse were opened to reveal nothing more than a dinosaur egg and a greasy slick on the surface of the water. They were Christians to Dinkle's lion, lambs to his wolf.

And I am Dinkle's lion, Yurievsky thought. *I am his wolf.*

CHAPTER THIRTY

Our comeuppance

Dinkle's letter was received by C. Herbert Judson the Lawyer on the first day of the new term at Tesoro Elementary School. The first bell had already rung and I was in class when the rest of the Ambergrisians re-convened less than an hour after Yurievsky left the Judsons. Rather than the Last Resort, they met at the Mr. Judson's office.

"Why didn't he just call the sheriff?" Mr. Johns fretted after reviewing the ominous invitation to Dinkle's estate.

"Because he figgers to kill us, that's why," Angus growled. "He's gonna send tha' vampire of his o'er here to slash our throats and I say let's go after them first!"

"Mister Yurievsky won't do that," Fiona asserted. "He's not a murderer."

"Damned if he ain't," Angus retorted.

"Calm down, Angus," Miss Lizzie interjected. "Fiona's right. Dinkle isn't about to have anyone killed. He wants his money, that's all."

She glanced at Mr. Judson as if unconvinced by her own words, her face uncharacteristically drawn and narrow.

"As far as that goes, I don't think he expects to get it all. He probably just wants to put a scare into us."

"I ain't goin' to no damned meetin' up there," Angus announced. "He can coome for me if he like...or send his damned Russki. I'll give 'em bot' a taste of boockshot from me McNaughton, I will."

215

That afternoon Miss Lizzie and Mr. Judson waited on the broad walk outside the school, watching for me after last period as students poured into the sort of crisp, sunny day that makes September my favorite month. I was surprised to see them. Miss Lizzie waved and I went to her, trailed by Webb Garwood and the girl who would years later become my wife, Marjory.

"We need to talk with you, Connor," Miss Lizzie said, glancing at my friends. "...Privately."

"It's really important," Mr. Judson said. He glanced at Marjory. "It's about the newspaper. It's a paper route issue." I knew he was trying to puff me up in her eyes, but my future wife was no fool.

"You should take care of your *paper route issue*, Connor," she teased, rolling her eyes. "Webb can walk me home."

"Happy to," Webb added.

I frowned. Webb's interest in Marjory's affections matched my own, and even though he was my best friend, I didn't trust him.

"Sounds important, Con," he said with calculated earnestness. "You should take care of it."

I wanted to hit him. It would not be the last time Webb Garwood and I competed for the girl we both loved, but he'd just taken a battle in a war I had yet to win, and we both knew it. I sighed.

"I have to go with them," I said to Marjory without looking at her.

On the way to the cottage I shared with Ma and Alex, Miss Lizzie and Mr. Judson told me about the playbill and its ominous note. "What's going to happen?" I asked, hoping they could provide an answer that would reassure me.

"I don't know, Connor," Miss Lizzie answered. "We'll find out tonight."

"Does Ma know?"

"Not unless James told her."

We reached my home, but Miss Lizzie and Mr. Judson didn't come in, remaining on the road as I approached the door. I turned to them before entering. Miss Lizzie had pasted on a steadfastly encouraging look, but the angular darkness of Mr. Judson's face betrayed them. Both were accustomed to putting a veil on their worry, lest the already fretful folks who depended on them become even more rattled. I knew them well, particularly Miss Lizzie, and even a hint of anxiety on their part unnerved me, putting me back under Dinkle's desk with the old man about to find me—this time with no place to run, no snake-handled letter opener in my hand.

Inside, I claimed a spot at the kitchen table and immediately set about doing my homework. Across the room, Ma chopped tomatoes by the sink while Alex sat opposite me, working his way through a peanut butter sandwich. Like most boys I viewed my teacher's after-school assignments in the same way a tycoon views taxes, causing Alex to eye me with unveiled curiosity.

"What's the matter with you?" he asked.

When I didn't answer, Ma looked over. Alex had merely been curious, but launching into my homework without putting up a fight was apparently like smoke to a fireman for her. She set aside her knife and moved across the room.

"What's wrong?" she asked, after taking the seat next to me.

I didn't dare look at her face, as Ma had been working on her mom's look. She had yet to actually break me, but I wasn't sure how much pressure I could take without wilting.

"Connor, what's wrong?" she repeated.

"Nothing," I lied. "Just fifth grade, Ma. It's tougher. I don't want to get behind." I pressed my pencil harder into a paper fragrant with purple mimeograph ink, the sheet filled with arithmetic problems that I was ill-motivated to complete, since Cyrus Dinkle was about to send me to reform school or kill me outright

Ma put a hand on mine to stop the movement of my pencil. "Connor, did they tell you about Dinkle's letter?" she asked. When I looked at her with wide eyes, she went on. "I know about everything," she said. "James told me."

I would love to report that I took this news like one of those stalwart boys who live in the pages of a book, as undaunted as the Artful Dodger, as brave as Mowgli. I wish I could have mustered up a decent backbone, but I had simply run out of sand to bury my head in. All summer I had managed to ignore the consequences of what we had done to Dinkle, efficiently boxing up the unpleasant possibilities and then moving the box from one dark closet in my mind to another. Dinkle's letter and the foreboding expressions evinced by Miss Lizzie and Mr. Judson had cut the string on the box and thrown open the lid, releasing the prospect that I might soon exchange the mother I'd just regained and the father I was about to acquire for a term in reform school. It was more than I could bear. A knot formed in my throat along with a few tears, followed by a good many more. Before long I was sobbing.

Ma tried to comfort me and made a decent go of it, her hand gently patting my back as she pulled my head into her bosom and issued soft whispers, her lips touching the top of my head.

"There, there," she murmured, "...there, there."

I'm not sure how long I went on and don't enjoy thinking about it. Even then, I knew that the last thing Ma needed was a kid who couldn't face a little trouble without going to pieces. It was embarrassing, and at first, I thought Alex was embarrassed for me. His face dispassionate, he watched me fall apart for about thirty seconds before quietly slipping away. However, a few minutes later he returned, appearing in the kitchen doorway with a small duffel bag in each hand, his face that of the gritty Naval fighter pilot he would eventually become. He knew nothing about the letter or my part in scamming Dinkle. He simply knew that I was in trouble and was ready to stand with me. He was a good brother.

"Get your things together," he said. "We'll make a run for it." His face was as serious as an eviction notice, and whenever I now recall it, I'm amused. Ma must have been, too, but she didn't laugh.

"Alex," she began, reaching out to him. He shook his head, his lips forming a thin line.

"It's okay, Ma," he said, his dark eyes dry and somber. "We'll find someplace safe and then send for you and James."

Ma stood and crossed to the doorway. She took the duffels from Alex and set them on the floor, then wrapped him in her arms. I watched, vaguely aware that his words were familiar—undoubtedly taken from a book we'd both read—declarations of loyalty and self-sacrifice that suddenly filled me with false bravado as well. I wiped the tears from my cheeks.

"No, Alex," I said. "You're not leaving. I'll go alone."

This was bluster, although I utterly believed it at the time. That's the difference between boys and men. A boy can threaten to run away from home because he doesn't know what lies beyond the hills and there's someone to grab him by the seat of the pants before he finds out. "A man doesn't run," Mr. Judson had once told me as we raced before the wind on his *C. Breeze*. "The trouble just follows him." He was partly right. What I've since learned is that women are no different. A grown woman doesn't run either. Certainly, Ma wasn't about to run from anyone, especially Dinkle.

"That's enough," she said. Ma led Alex to the table, afterward taking a seat facing us. She leaned forward and rested a hand on each of our knees. "No one is running away," she said, her voice steady. "We're staying here in Tesoro…All of us. Together."

She cupped my chin in one hand. "I'm going with you and James tonight," she said.

"I'm going too," Alex blurted, adding, "...Where are we going?"

"It doesn't matter, Alex," I said. "I'll go alone. No one else needs to get in trouble."

Ma shook her head. "No, Connor, you're not going alone. We're all going...All four of us...James, you, Alex, me. We're a family now."

I continued to protest, but Ma was resolved. "That Cyrus Dinkle," she sniffed. "I've been watching that old scoundrel come to church for years, acting like he can do God's work on Sunday and the Devil's bidding the rest of the week."

She straightened slightly and pointed her chin, as if speaking directly to the former Indian Territories trader.

"Well, if he tries to harm anyone in my family," she promised, "I'm here to tell you that he won't be answering to God. He'll be answering to me!"

I stopped arguing. I loved my mother and admired her newly unearthed gumption, but I had been behind a drape in Cyrus Dinkle's dining room and knew she'd be no match for him.

"Okay, Ma," I said. "We'll all go."

"Where are we going?" Alex repeated.

We explained it to him. Afterward, there was no more talk of Cyrus Dinkle. James came over for dinner, as usual, and around six-thirty, Miss Lizzie knocked on our door. She had a story ready to reasonably free me up for Dinkle's meeting.

"The boys haven't spent a night at my place in weeks, Mary Rose," she began after Ma invited her in.

Ma interrupted her. "I know everything, Miss Lizzie," she said. "I'm going too."

Miss Lizzie frowned. "For crying out loud, Connor," she muttered, shooting a peeved look at me.

"I didn't tell her," I protested. "It was James."

Miss Lizzie then put James in her crosshairs and seemed about to give him the what-for when she hesitated, a flash of uncertainty clouding her features for the second time that day. She was the least uncertain person one could imagine and her unease filled me with dread, weighing me down as if the dinner I'd just eaten was comprised of raw bread dough and lard. Once again I relived those few endless minutes beneath Cyrus Dinkle's desk. Ma interrupted the nightmarish memory.

"I want to go, too, Miss Lizzie," she repeated. "I have to go."

Miss Lizzie studied my mother for a moment and then lowered her eyes, searching the floor. "You want to go," she echoed. She lifted her gaze, almost imperceptibly sighing. "Mary Rose, are you sure that's a good idea?"

"I'm pretty sure it's a bad idea," Ma responded, "but I'm still going. Alex too."

I expected Miss Lizzie to fire off a list of reasons for Ma and Alex to stay home. She didn't.

"All right," she said, afterward leading us out to her Model T where Fiona waited in the front seat. James, Ma, Alex, and I crowded into the back and we headed off, bouncing down the uneven road to the Dinkle estate.

As we passed Fremont Park, James took Ma's hand, then winked at me as if we were heading to the beach for a swim or a picnic.

"Everything will be fine," he said. He seemed to believe it, as did Ma. Even outside the safety of our kitchen her backbone remained stiff, her cheeks rosy. She was blissfully unafraid. Alex, too. Not me. I was scared, and for the first part of our trip, I thought Miss Lizzie and Fiona were scared as well. Usually talkative, they were silent, their faces as gloomy as undertakers. Now, these many years later, I am quite sure Dinkle did not frighten them. I think their silence and their sober aspects were provoked by the lie they'd been outrunning all summer, a lie that had finally caught them.

I don't recommend generalizing people into categories, especially men versus women. Folks can't be pigeon-holed that easily. However, after ninety-one years it seems to me that a lie at first blush might not weigh less on us men, but I think we move past it more quickly than women. We find an out-of-the-way place where we're not likely to accidentally stumble onto the thing, some crawlspace or root cellar in our minds where it remains hidden away, dark and dank and rotten. I think women never put a lie away. They circle it like a moon orbiting a planet, the lie always visible and bigger than themselves. I suspect Miss Lizzie and Fiona were orbiting the lie we'd told Dinkle because they knew, that however well-intentioned on our part or deserved on his, it was still a lie. It hung a shroud over them, an ash-gray thing like soot from a factory smokestack, a cloud that eventually drifted into the back seat of the Model T and hung over us, too.

By the time we reached the open iron gate of Dinkle's estate there was no more talking or winking. Miss Lizzie steered her Model T up the circular driveway to the main house. Outside the entry C. Herbert Judson's Chrysler Imperial was already parked and Miss Lizzie pulled in next to it. We climbed out and went to the door, but before anyone could knock, it opened to reveal Dinkle's man. I now realize that he was no taller than James, but as he stood in the doorway that night, I thought him between eight and nine feet in height with fangs instead of teeth and talons for fingernails.

"Please come in," he said.

CHAPTER THIRTY-ONE

We face the music

We followed Dinkle's man through the expansive foyer and crossed beneath the ponderous, overhanging chandelier to reach a door uncomfortably familiar to me. It opened into the old man's study and I suddenly wished I'd brought along the stolen letter opener to slip between his ribs. Dinkle's man held the door open and then followed us inside. Mr. Judson and Mr. Johns were already there. Mrs. Judson, too. Angus MacCallum was not, although we later learned that he heard everything from outside, tucked into the recess beneath the study's large bay window, his McNaughton shotgun at the ready.

Seven straight-back chairs had been moved into the study from the dining room, but no one sat. Dinkle stood by the bay window, looking out. On his desk was the small statue of the naked man with impressive genitals, the bacchanalian fellow's companionship apparently reassuring to the old man; perhaps, it was his Maltese Falcon, a solid gold statuette painted to look like clay, a masked treasure he could admire and touch when moved by a need to feel rich.

For nearly a minute Dinkle remained as silent and motionless as the statue on his desk. Then Mr. Judson nervously cleared his throat and the old bandit glanced at us before returning his gaze to the waves rolling onto the sand.

"Pretty smart bunch, aren't you?" Dinkle said. He moved to the wall where his authentic George Washington rare documents were displayed, peering at them as if searching for a code within the letters. "Well, I'm a pretty smart fellow myself," he said. He faced us. "Did you really think you could fool me?"

Dinkle's claim of shrewdness was a conceit. Despite his boast, he had been completely fooled until pulling open the boathouse doors. However, at that moment I did not appreciate his hubris; rather I saw the trader from the Indian Territories who had supposedly killed a man over fifty cents worth of whiskey, the elegant nonchalance and quietly sardonic voice mere disguises to mask a cold-blooded killer. He was terrifying, and I found myself trembling and on the verge of tears.

"That's enough, Cyrus," Miss Lizzie said, glancing at me. "You've made your point."

"I'll decide when enough is enough, Elizabeth," Dinkle hissed.

I felt my mother's hand on my shoulder. Like me, it trembled very slightly and I wondered if Miss Lizzie's green concoction would be up to the task of keeping Ma steady. Meanwhile, James, Mr. and Mrs. Judson, and Mr. Johns were calm but quiet, presumably sizing up their opponent. Fiona and Miss Lizzie were not so circumspect.

"Stop frightening these boys, Mister Dinkle," Fiona said.

"You want your money, Cyrus," Miss Lizzie added. "So, let's talk about that. There's no need to scare anyone."

"Ah, the money," Dinkle sneered. "You want to talk about the money, Elizabeth. That's good. It's a good start. It won't end there, but it's a good start."

His voice was thin, his face slightly red, his words leaving spittle on his lips. He was no longer the convivial Dinkle evidenced on the night of the second town meeting. He had shed that personality entirely, allowing us to see the rabid dog just beneath the surface. He was furious and had a right to be; yet I somehow knew it was not our fraud that had enraged him. He was a criminal. He understood crime, respected it. No, his anger was born of disgrace. We had embarrassed him and the taste of humiliation was far more sour than the wine bottled from his vineyard's grapes. Even at my tender age I knew that only a very large draught of revenge could wash it away, leaving him disinclined to lift his heel from our throats until we turned blue.

Despite Dinkle's malignant demeanor, I was oddly less fearful. Some men's egos are too fragile to allow reason to trump their lust for retribution. It is difficult to respect such men; indeed, one neither pities nor fears them. You simply face them and I was no longer afraid as Dinkle went on, pointing his finger first at Mr. Judson and then Miss Lizzie.

"Judson, you and Elizabeth will make me whole," he said. "You, too, Mister Johns. I believe a surtax is warranted. Let's say...fifty percent. That's a fair number I believe."

Dinkle's demand provoked gasps. "That's highway robbery," Miss Lizzie sputtered. "I'll not pay it."

"You *will* pay it, Elizabeth," Dinkle snapped, "unless prison appeals to you."

He curled his lips into something lizard-like and evil.

"Insofar as that goes I must insist that some of you go to jail. Frankly, you should be grateful. I have a number of business associates who would convict and sentence the lot of you to a cemetery. But I'm a forgiving man, so it's merely jail...I think for you, Miss Littleleaf. Perhaps you can learn to hold your tongue in there. Jail for you, too, bartender. You won't be missed."

Dinkle looked at me next and I felt as if his eyes had opened an artery in my wrist.

"Off to reform school, young O'Halloran. Both you and your brother. The pair of you are destined for prison anyway. Might as well get a head start."

"Now just ease up there a damned minute, Dinkle," James interrupted, taking a step closer to Alex and me. "You leave these boys out of it or I swear to God..."

James went on but I can't recall anything he said, his voice suddenly lost among other voices; indeed, while willing to swallow Dinkle's threats against themselves, James, Miss Lizzie, Fiona, Mr. and Mrs. Judson, and Mr. Johns weren't so circumspect with Alex and I in the old man's crosshairs. Only Ma remained silent, making for the desk where she grabbed the naked man statue. Holding it above her head with both hands she went after our host with murder in her eyes. It probably sounds funny—this small woman going after a thug like Dinkle—but the old man didn't laugh. Despite a pretense of amusement, he moved quickly to put his man squarely between he and Ma. Undeterred, she kept coming, but Dinkle's man easily thwarted the attack, pinning Ma against his chest with one arm, while disarming her with the other.

"You'll not do a thing to my boys," she shouted, struggling to escape the tall Russian manservant. "I'll kill you first."

After that, a good deal more shouting and threatening was pitched at Dinkle. The Ambergrisians' anger seemed to salve his own and the old man watched them in the same way a crooked boxing promoter views a fixed bout, a tiny smirk on his face betraying advance knowledge of the outcome. Alex and I stayed away from the fray, my brother observing Dinkle like an entomologist examining a beetle for the right place to insert a pin, while I simply didn't know what to do or say. After all, I was only ten years old.

The room was noisy for a time. Ma struggled to escape Dinkle's man, and for a few moments, it seemed that the ex-soldier and James might square off. Then, the tall Russian released my mother, offering James a slight bow as he turned her over to him. The exchange allowed Mr. Judson to get the horses back in the barn.

"All right, Cyrus, you've had your fun," he said, his voice loud enough to quiet the others. "Let's just be reasonable. There's a middle ground here. Let's bargain."

Dinkle erased his smirk, replacing it with an icy expression and a terrifyingly pithy observation. "I don't believe any of you are in a position to bargain," he said.

Dinkle was a canny fellow, a man who dealt in lies and shadows. Hence, he had a well-honed instinct that helped him hear the rattle of an enemy in the low grass or spot the glint of a badge in the high rocks. It was an instinct that was, for the first time in his life, about to fail him, offering nary a scent of the betrayal he was about to suffer—a bit of treachery mounted by the only person in the room whom Dinkle trusted, a man whose loyalty had been duly purchased, one who had always kept his opinions to himself.

"You are not in position to bargain, either," Sergei Yurievsky said to his boss.

Dinkle's head swiveled toward his valet-chauffeur, his face filled with both surprise and rage. He was met by Yurievsky's level gaze, an expression that silenced the old bandit. It was as if the ominous Russian's fierce eyes had peppered Dinkle with poison darts, rendering him as speechless and still as the statue of the naked man. I almost laughed. Even now, there is little I find funnier than a bully who suddenly realizes that he is a lamb trying to victimize a lion.

"Don't talk," Yurievsky said to his employer, afterward turning to us. His face had softened. "Please," he said, indicating the empty chairs with a sweep of his arm. His manner, menacing with Dinkle, was now courtly. Even so, we all remained standing. Fiona shook her head, her lips forming a tight line.

"Thank you, Mister Yurievsky," she said, "but you mustn't get into the middle of this. Things are bad enough. Don't lose your job over us."

Yurievsky smiled at her, a thing that seemed at first grateful and then somehow sad.

"I mean it, Mister Yurievsky. For your own good, stay out of it."

Fiona was a beautiful woman with both a voice and an expression in her toolbag that she used to get her way with men who were too damned obstinate to admit they were wrong. "I'm not proud of it," she once told me, "but this is the world the good old boys have created. It's their own damned fault if I use it against them." She'd never found it necessary to use her siren's voice or demeanor with Yurievsky and didn't now. Instead, her eyes seemed to plead with him to ignore her advice and save us.

"What the hell is going on?" Dinkle suddenly demanded, the prospect of his man trampling on his carefully orchestrated revenge stiffening his spine. "Now, listen here, Yurievsky—"

"Be quiet," Yurievsky said, holding up a hand for Dinkle to consider. The ex-soldier's eyes remained on Fiona, almost matching the desperation in hers; as if a great, internal struggle transpired behind his usually indecipherable aspect.

Dinkle's complexion reddened, the gash of a scowl cutting into his features.

"Who the hell do you think—?"

Yurievsky turned to his boss, dropping the hand. "Be quiet," he repeated and his tone—both lethal and dismissive—once again silenced the old man. The tall Russian turned back to Fiona, offering up a face I'd seen before—on that cold winter day when he drew a heart in the condensation on the mercantile's window.

"*Uspokoysya seychas*," he said, his words as soft and warm as old flannel. *Settle down now.*

A moment passed, and when Fiona didn't respond, he repeated the words. I looked at her. We all did. Her head was tipped to one side like an inquisitive puppy, her expression wrinkled as she peered at Dinkle's man as if trying to spot a distant lighthouse through thick fog.

"*Uspokoysya seychas, moya sladkaya myshka*," Yurievsky added, his voice quiet. *Settle down now, my sweet little mouse.*

I did not speak Russian and still don't. But the sadness within Yurievsky's words was unmistakable. Sadness and relief. He seemed strangely relieved.

"*Moya sladkaya myshka*," he repeated.

Suddenly, Fiona's lips parted. Her eyes widened and she blinked as if visualizing an apparition, one resurrected from long-buried memories and unanswered prayers. Her breathing grew uneven and she wobbled dangerously, trembling as if newly born. I thought she might faint and moved to help, but Yurievsky reached her first, supporting her with an arm around her waist.

"*Myshka?*" she repeated in a whisper, staring into his face. "*Myshka?*"

Dinkle's man helped Fiona to a chair. This time she did not protest.

"I don't understand," she stammered, even though it seemed as if she *did* understand; that lack of comprehension was perhaps less frightening to her than fear *of* it. Her eyes had filled with tears and she clutched Yurievsky's hand, her knuckles turning white.

"*Ne plach, Myshka*," Dinkle's man said. *Don't cry, little mouse.*

Fiona reached up to touch his cheek, moving her fingers across it like a blind woman seeking familiarity from darkness.

"*Moya myshka*," Yurievsky murmured. "*Moya sladkaya myshka.*"

Like most children, perhaps all, I did not easily fathom the notion of prior childhoods among the grown-ups in my life. My mother had been a child as had James and Mr. Judson and Angus and Miss Lizzie. And Fiona. Still, they seemed to me to have always been adults. Especially Fiona, whose adulthood put her outside my reach, whose effortless and very mature confidence was so mesmerizing to me. And yet, as Yurievsky whispered in her ear Fiona Littleleaf seemed tiny and vulnerable—as much a child as I, her face awash in memories of a past long forgotten. Of course, I did not understand what had changed her. None of us did. Only later would we learn about Yurievsky's wife and daughter and that Fiona was much more than the "young woman Irina might have become." She was, as it turned out, exactly the young woman Irina *had* become. The proprietor of our town mercantile and the Kittiwake Inn, the postmistress of Tesoro, California, and the person we'd all known as Fiona Littleleaf—adopted niece of Rosie and Roxy Littleleaf—had been christened in 1912 as Irina Yurievsky, the firstborn and only child of Sergei and Olga Yurievsky.

"Papa?" Fiona whispered to her father. "*Papa, eto ty?*" *Is it you?*

Yurievsky leaned over until his lips nearly touched her ear.

"*Prosto slushayte seychas, Myshka. Papa ispravit yego.*" *Just listen now, little mouse. Papa will fix it.*

Fiona nodded dully and her father straightened, releasing her hand.

"Mister Judson," he said quietly. "Forgive me. I am Russian and English sometime fail me." His words were directed at the lawyer, even though he kept dark eyes angled at his boss. "We have word in Russia when one person threaten another with secret," he went on. "Sometimes against men for money, sometimes against women for…the bedroom. Is word for this in English. You know it?"

Once again Dinkle interrupted, something I couldn't help admiring just a bit. Yurievsky was menacing enough to make Medusa look away, but the former Indian Territories trader had more courage in reserve than I'd appreciated. "That's enough of this damned nonsense," he barked.

Yurievsky then offered his employer a face I had never seen on anyone, his expression utterly emotionless, his eyes dead. It was a look of murder personified, the face of a man who had killed without feeling or regret and would do so again if necessary. Dinkle, too, had killed men, but it had been a product of impulsiveness and rage. The face of Sergei Yurievsky was not enraged, but the aspect of someone who had murdered without emotion, a man who took a life because it was his job and the next thing to do. It was far more terrifying than the killer's face I'd seen on Dinkle and the ex-gunrunner now seemed terrified as well. He stopped talking.

"This word, Mister Judson," Yurievsky reiterated, once certain his employer would not again interrupt, "You know it, yes?"

As a litigator C. Herbert Judson had been around his share of murderers and was not unnerved; indeed, he seemed almost pleased.

"'Extortion,'" he said. "The word you're looking for is 'extortion.'"

"Ah...'Extortion,'" Yurievsky replied as if testing the sound of it. He looked at Mr. Judson. "Is illegal, this 'extortion,' yes? Is against the law?"

"It is."

"A man go to prison for extortion, yes?"

"Yes."

"I see."

Yurievsky glanced at me and his murderer's eyes softened, replaced by something warmer and yet indisputably haunted. His lips began to curl upward, then flattened, his inner thoughts abruptly shielded as if lowering the visor on a helmet.

"So, two millions...and fifty percent. Very much money, I think," he continued. "And Dinkle use secret for this. Is extortion, yes?"

Before Mr. Judson could answer, Dinkle jumped in, the mention of money enough to replace his fear of Yurievsky with a trader's instincts.

"What do you want, Yurievsky? Is this a shakedown? If so, stop wasting time. Just name your damned price."

Yurievsky eyed his boss.

"No price," he said.

"Then stay out of it. This is none of your business."

Once again, Sergei Yurievsky offered the assassin's face to his boss.

"Is not business," the ex-soldier said. "...Is personal."

He went to Dinkle's liquor cabinet and poured a small amount of vodka into a glass, afterward downing it in a single swallow.

"You are not only one, Dinkle, who know extortion," he said. Yurievsky indicated the rest of us with a lift of his chin. "These people not only ones with secret. You have many secrets. I go to government hall...I find papers. You have warehouses with iceboxes and stoves, yes? I visit. No iceboxes, no stoves. Many guns and whiskey and cigarettes. But no iceboxes, no stoves. Can you explain? Maybe yes, maybe no. I find house where women see men for money. I find businesses that are not businesses."

He looked at Mr. Judson and shrugged as if to dispel doubt.

"Is true. I visit. Nothing there. Just address. They are...uh, shells. Is right word? Shells?"

"Shell companies," Mr. Judson replied. "But you're close enough."

Yurievsky returned his gaze to Dinkle.

"I also read papers you want delivered...and papers in your safe."

This was a revelation that might have raised Dinkle's eyebrows if he'd had any. Yurievsky chuckled at the shocked expression on his employer's face.

"Yes, your safe. I know how to open. I watch you open... many times. You are not careful."

He shook his head as if bemused.

"You have many papers for man with so much money to hide. Does American taxman know about hidden money? Again, I think maybe yes, maybe no. You have dangerous partners. They sentence enemies to cemeteries. This is what you say, yes? Do dangerous men know about safe? About hidden money? Do they? I think not. I think much those dangerous men do not know."

He eyed Dinkle, nodding grimly.

"But I know," he said.

Dinkle coolly appraised his employee. The terms of their relationship had been abruptly and unexpectedly re-defined; to his credit, the old scoundrel impressively transformed in response, his rage turning to reason as he weighed his options, mentally ticking them off until one emerged that provoked a sneer.

"You've got nothing," he snorted. "Papers! You think they'll prove anything? Papers disappear."

Yurievsky shrugged.

"Maybe," he said. "Such things can be like dead fish…float to surface even after you think them gone."

The tall Russian pursed his lips like a headmaster trying to decide what to do with an unruly student.

"Anyway, papers are matter for sheriff and judge. For lawyer like Mister Judson, or, perhaps, for your dangerous men. As for rest of it…?"

He nodded to indicate me and my co-conspirators.

"The boathouse empty. They hide it. A crime, yes, but how much crime? Not very much, I think. In Russia, put against wall and shoot, but this not Russia. You tell sheriff and judge, feathers ruffled…"

He looked at Fiona.

"Is right, *Myshka*? Feathers ruffled?"

She nodded. The color had returned to her face and she now stared at her father with a mixture of astonishment and pride.

"Yes, feathers ruffled, but not too much feathers, I think," Yurievsky went on. "No jail for my *Myshka*. No jail for Mister Judson, for Mister Johns, for Miss Fryberg. For any of them."

Yurievsky glanced at me and I am quite sure he winked.

"Boys stay with mother," he added. "No reform school."

Yurievsky poured more vodka but didn't drink, instead holding the glass to the light, peering through it as if it were a prism. I instinctively looked up, expecting to see kaleidoscopic colors cast against the ceiling. It was as blank as Dinkle's rapidly dissipating possibilities.

"Is not same for you, Dinkle," Yurievsky said without looking at his boss. "You have many crimes to answer for...Many rat holes, many rats. Can you hide them all?"

He shifted his gaze from the vodka to his employer.

"If the villagers' crime come out, I make your crimes come out, too."

Yurievsky drank the vodka, afterward offering his boss a stony smile.

"Things end more bad for you than them, I think."

I have never seen a wolverine in a trap, but suspect the snarl and futility on its face would mirror the expression Cyrus Dinkle exhibited as he considered what his man had said.

"You can't make any of it stick," he scowled. "Who will believe you? You're a foreigner...a damned Russian. You're nobody."

For a few moments it seemed quite certain that Yurievsky was about to strangle his boss. The threat was not attended by the crowing and indignation of a duelist, as I am quite sure Sergei Yurievsky cared nothing about Dinkle's opinion of him nor would he have found satisfaction in something as trivial as vengeance. No, had Yurievsky killed Dinkle, it would have represented a straight line—the shortest distance between two points—Dinkle's recalcitrance efficiently and permanently addressed by murdering him. Mr. Judson saved the old scoundrel's life.

"The sheriff may not believe Mister Yurievsky," he said to Dinkle, "but he'll believe me."

Mr. Judson went on to suggest that enough suspicious documents from Dinkle had been run through his office to put a

United States Attorney and the pencil-necked tightasses who made up the newly formed SEC in Washington D Almighty C in a considerable lather.

"What I know may not incur more than a fine, Cyrus, but it will be enough to get a search warrant for the rest of your records," Mr. Judson asserted. "That will open a big door. You won't be able to hide everything."

He offered Yurievsky a tight-lipped smile.

"And I disagree with you about Mister Yurievsky. I think a jury will find him to be a most compelling witness."

Dinkle listened to Mr. Judson with gritted teeth, his breathing coarse and angry. He was beaten, but like a junkyard dog on a chain, didn't yet know that he couldn't get loose.

"You can't use what you know, Judson," he barked. "I'm protected by attorney-client privilege."

This time it was Mr. Judson's turn to shrug.

"Attorney-client privilege isn't all it's cracked up to be, Cyrus," he said. "Neither is lawyering, for that matter. I'm prepared to give up both."

And that was that. Dinkle crumpled like a cardboard box in the rain, retiring from the battlefield to the safety of his liquor cabinet. He poured himself a finger of scotch followed by two more, afterward moving to the bay window.

"You're fired, Yurievsky," he said, his gaze merging with a sea turned ironically golden by the low-hanging sun.

We waited for a time, watching the old man, then showed ourselves out. Yurievsky came along, Fiona's arm linked in his. No one spoke at first. We stood in the driveway as the sun drifted toward the western horizon, splashing the sky in orange and rose. Inside Dinkle's study the air had seemed heavy and stifling, but a light ocean breeze now cooled and refreshed us. I felt reborn. We all did. We had overthrown the king, and even though his land was not ours, his pride was safely tucked into our pockets.

We lingered there on the circular drive with its white stones and grassy border, none of us indicating any desire to leave. Fiona remained uncharacteristically discomposed, appraising her father as if he were something near and yet something very far away, as if he were the chauffeur of a flying saucer rather than Cyrus Dinkle's Duesenberg. Suddenly, she stood on her toes, giving him a hug and then a kiss on the cheek, an overture that added unexpected color to his typically colorless complexion.

"Papa," she said. "Oh, Papa."

Yurievsky looked at her with the soft, haunted eyes I'd seen for the briefest moment inside Dinkle's study.

"You have room at Kittiwake for me, *Myshka*, yes?" he said.

"Of course, there's a room for you."

Yurievsky nodded.

"I must get my things. You can help?"

"Yes. I'll come with you."

Fiona and her father headed toward the apartment above the garage. A quiet man, he spoke loudly enough for me to hear as they walked away.

"I make more than two words at a time, yes *Myshka*?"

Fiona laughed. "Yes, you did," she said.

"So, you win bet with Miss Fryberg, yes?"

"Yes," Fiona answered, her eyes still soft with wonder, "I win."

CHAPTER THIRTY-TWO

It all ends

In 1917, running from the chaos of the Bolshevik Revolution, Irina Yurievsky survived the harrowing trek from St. Petersburg to Vladivostok with her mother, the pair of them traveling south and then east—always east, endlessly east—by train, car, wagon, and on foot, avoiding elements of the indiscriminately lethal Red and White Guards along the way. They arrived in Vladivostok without money, forcing Olga to temporarily join the world's oldest profession. Her plan was for them to sail to Shanghai where they would seek refuge with the large White Russian contingent settled there. By March of 1918, she'd saved enough money to book passage on a steamer, but continued to cough up blood from tuberculosis contracted during their trek across Siberia. Olga never saw Shanghai, the tuberculosis taking her during the voyage to the bustling Chinese port.

Upon arrival, the now-orphaned six-year-old Irina was turned over to British missionaries, who promptly added her to a group of children bound for America and adoption. Once again, the little girl went east, arriving in San Francisco where Rosie and Roxy Littleleaf plucked her from a holding facility. They re-christened her Fiona Littleleaf and fabricated the tragic backstory of a dead cousin and his Bulgarian wife to preempt the sniping and mean-spirited speculation sure to be attached to a refugee from newly menacing Bolshevik Russia. The two women brought Fiona home to Tesoro, attributing her accent to their cousin's fictitious wife. By then, the little girl had not seen her father since she was four years old and could no longer remember him.

It took years for Sergei Yurievsky to find his daughter. Following the lead obtained from the prostitute in Macao, he found his little *Myshka* in Tesoro. At first overjoyed, he then considered the life he'd led and the one she was leading. Fiona was happy and well. He was an enforcer and an assassin, someone she would find difficult to explain to her friends, to her adoptive aunts, or to a prospective husband. She was no longer Russian. She was an American without a hint of her native language in her speech. And she no longer knew or recognized the father who had been off soldiering for so much of their four short years together. And so Sergei Yurievsky remained anonymous to his daughter, taking a job with Cyrus Dinkle to be near her, satisfying himself with daily trips to the mercantile.

I got to know Yurievsky well in the years that followed. We became friends and he eventually told me about the rest: Grand Duke Pavlovich and the Mad Monk, the Chinese warlord and the Filipino strongman. He told me everything and this is why I have been able to share what he saw and heard and thought without actually being him. I promised to keep the darker parts of his story between he, Fiona, and I until after he was gone. I kept that promise. My daughter, Mary, had to wait until she was eleven years old to hear everything about the treasure of the Blue Whale. She was the first, but there have been many others since—my children, grandchildren, and great-grandchildren. It's grown into a big club. Mary, named after my mother, was one of the very few of its members to have known Yurievsky. She saw him as a child too often sees an old man—an oddity; the silent Russian who spent his days sitting in the parlor of the Kittiwake Inn or on its broad front porch. He was more than that. He was our savior.

Of course, Yurievsky never seriously considered betraying us. He sought only to protect his daughter once our ruse was unmasked, seeking answers that would allow him to lure Dinkle into a bigger trap than the one the ex-gunrunner had set for us. It was also an act of contrition. Yurievsky had committed heinous deeds at the behest of powerful men and believed the only way to atone was to bring one of them down—to send the wolf to the slaughter rather than the lambs. He carefully planned it all, yet never anticipated everything that might happen; he never realized until that last, fateful day in Dinkle's study that his atonement would providentially award him the right to reclaim the daughter he cherished. It was a row of dominoes that began to fall when I discovered the ambergris on the beach, and for that he remained forever grateful to me.

Sergei Yurievsky never returned to the Dinkle estate nor did he leave Tesoro, taking a permanent room at Fiona's Kittiwake Inn. He insisted on paying for it and seemed to have no shortage of funds as time went on, his knowledge of Dinkle's affairs undoubtedly meriting a severance package as generous as it was reluctantly given. Dinkle hired a new man. The poor fellow quit after a month, the next one lasting a bit longer. There were many Dinkle's men over the years that followed, none of Yurievsky's replacements as stalwart as the tall Russian.

We sold our dinosaur egg—the real ambergris—to the Jean Patou company for $750 per ounce, far below what was expected on the day Angus and I discovered the mysterious mass on the beach. The Ambergrisians and Dinkle netted just over $2500 each. Alex and I went to college on our share. I'm not sure what the others did, although James built a house for us after he and Ma were married. Things in Tesoro otherwise returned to normal fairly quickly. I had learned that money does indeed change people, and that taking it away has a good chance of changing them back. And so it was for us. The avaricious frenzy that overtook our little village was soon replaced by the blissful vicissitudes of life in a small place. We arose, went about our business, went to bed, and then did it all over again. In between we had our share of birthday parties, weddings, funerals, ball games, school dances, Fourth of July celebrations, Christmases. We knew nearly everything about our neighbors and weren't reluctant to share a rumor or two. We mostly liked each other.

The pressure to shop was gone, but rather than reclaim the usual inclination for those without money to covet things that require quite a bit of it, townsfolk were overwhelmed with guilt. Even though Dinkle richly deserved to be cheated, my neighbors were eventually ashamed to have been part of it, their remorse spilling over in the form of pies and cakes left on the flat-topped gate pillars outside Dinkle's estate. A few folks tried to get inside the walls for a face-to-face apology but were turned away; hence the avalanche of letters that began to fill up Dinkle's mailbox at the postal exchange. The written apologies were heartfelt and quite lengthy in some cases. A few included pictures of the old man obviously drawn by a child. Then items began to show up on his lawn.

The unsolicited offerings were small things at first—a faux-gilded picture frame, a set of oven cozies, a small toy tractor. Then the dam broke and each morning the old bandit awoke to a new collection of haphazardly distributed items: clothes, sofas, sideboards, dishware, radios, chandeliers, used automobiles, innumerable teak miniatures, about a hundred glass cats, a few doorstops shaped like whales, a broken, new-fangled electric toaster, a pair of genuinely fake rare documents, a coupon good for two vault doors with matching window bars, and a single, slightly used commode with a jeweled seat cover. It was the monkey named Miss Sprinkles leashed to the commode that finally did it for Dinkle. He placed the following notice in the *Tesoro Town Crier.*

TO WHOM IT MAY CONCERN:

Those who left their ill-gotten goods on my lawn with the idea that

I either desire such things or have any interest in paying to have them removed need to get it through their thick skulls that I have neither need of your deceit-coated spoils nor interest in spending my hard-earned money to have them hauled off. Therefore, please come get your blasted rubbish and be quick about it. God has lent a watchful eye and a long memory to the mischief that has transpired over the summer and will, on Judgment Day, provide the appropriate comeuppances you all richly deserve—Cyrus Dinkle

The full-page notice appeared in the paper the week before Thanksgiving, hitting doorsteps on a Thursday afternoon. By the following Monday, Dinkle's lawn was clear.

So many years have passed since Angus MacCallum had me believing I'd discovered a treasure on the beach. Yet, I confess more easily recalling that summer and those people than what I had for breakfast this morning. One might think the lost treasure haunts me. It doesn't. There were other treasures discovered in the sometimes languid, sometimes exciting days of that long-ago season. I was rich and then I wasn't. I shared in a great secret and a conspiracy. I learned how to sail a boat and about sex. I met a real actor. I snuck into Cyrus Dinkle's house and stole his letter opener. I almost went to jail. I loved Fiona Littleleaf. I found a father. And, best of all, Ma came back to Alex and me from whatever dark place had held her.

As a boy I had no understanding of death. As a young man I ignored it. The middle of life made me fearful of its end. But now, at ninety-one years old and the only one left from that time, I welcome death, not because of infirmity or lost will, but because it is possible that a reunion is waiting for me in the beyond. And if so—if I once again meet Miss Lizzie and Fiona and Angus MacCallum and Roger Johns the Banker and Mr. and Mrs. C. Herbert Judson and Mei Ling and James and Ma and Alex and Sergei Yurievsky—if I have a chance to rejoin my wife Marjory and those wonderful people, it will be fun to see everyone again. I have big plans should it happen.

We'll start the day early, riding bikes along my old paper route. We'll stop for a while to sit on Mr. and Mrs. C. Herbert Judson's porch swing and talk, then head off to Fiona's mercantile for a scone and a cup of warm milk with a little coffee in it, waving at Miss Lizzie and Mei Ling when we pass their house. Next, we'll beachcomb below the lighthouse in search of driftwood Angus can whittle into mermaids. In the afternoon we'll have a look at Fort Buford and then mosey over to Milton Garwood's to see if Miss Sprinkles has learned how to play the harmonica. Evening will bring a picnic in Fremont Park followed by a town meeting where, if we're lucky, Milton Garwood and Angus MacCallum will have a shouting match. When Mr. Johns finally gavels the meeting to a close we'll linger outside and walk home slowly, sitting on someone's porch to rehash all the things that might have been done better if we were in charge.

The night will lengthen, and eventually, we'll get around to telling old stories—the tales of that summer of 1934—and we'll talk about it over and over, remembering the treasure we found. We'll recall who found it and how it was found, how we strove to protect it and how it was lost, nevertheless. We'll marvel that a swindler like Dinkle could be swindled and wonder what became of Everson Dexter. And by the time we decide to call it a night we'll realize that the boathouse down at the marina is not empty; that it was never empty—that, inside, something of untold value still floats and bobs on the surface of the water. And if we listen closely we'll hear Angus MacCallum's voice calling out, too, his words filled with excitement and hope. "Cannae ye understand?" he'll say. "It's treasure, laddie…Treasure! Ye've foond a bloody treasure!"

ACKNOWLEDGMENTS

My thanks to the usual suspects: Leslie Gunnerson, Mike Christian, Chris Dempsey, and Barbara Herrick; to my dear friends B.Z. Petroff and Roy Kissin, who told me a story over dinner one night that became this book. Thanks also to Queen Bee Jennifer Bowen and the readers of her wonderful BookHive; to my agent, Jody Rein, whose pleas for "More" made this a better book than I could have accomplished on my own; to my keen-eyed editor, Jaynie Royal, and Regal House Publishing; and to my wife, Pam—first in my heart, first to read everything I write.